Large Print Wea
Weaver, Ingrid.
On the way to a wedding

On the Way to a Wedding...

INGRID WEAVER

First published in Great Britain 2001
Large Print edition 2003
Silhouette Books Limited,
Eton House, 18-24 Paradise Road,
Richmond, Surrey, TW9 1SR

© Ingrid Caris 1997

ISBN 0 373 04825 4

Set in Times Roman 16 on 17 pt.
34-1003-73870

Printed and bound in Great Britain
by Antony Rowe Ltd, Chippenham, Wiltshire

INGRID WEAVER

admits to being a compulsive reader who loves a book that can make her cry. A former teacher, now a full-time homemaker and mother, she considers herself lucky to have an understanding husband and three amazing children who have encouraged her to pursue her dream of writing. When she isn't trying to squeeze in time on her word processor, her favourite activities include watching old 'Star Trek' re-runs, and waking up early to canoe after camera-shy loons.

To Melissa Jeglinski,
my intrepid editor—
air travel really is safe.
Really.

Prologue

The jukebox was waging a losing battle against the escalating din from the patrons as the night wore on. Cigarette smoke hung in a stinging haze, mingling with the yeasty smell of spilled beer. Slouching against the bar, Nicholai Strada used his thumbnail to peel the label off a long-necked bottle as he scanned the room. It was July in New York, and the dripping air conditioner that wheezed over the barroom door was as hopelessly outmatched as the jukebox. But the sweat that gleamed from the forehead of the man who approached wasn't due merely to the heat.

"It's been a long time, Strada."

Nick shifted his gaze from the mirror behind the bar to the short, weasel-thin man who took the stool beside him. "Keeping yourself out of trouble, Bernie?"

"Sure, sure. You know me."

"That's the trouble. I do know you." Nick caught the bartender's eye and ordered a shot of tequila.

When the drink arrived, Bernie tapped his fingers against his glass for a moment before tipping it up and swallowing the liquor in one gulp. He coughed, then sucked in air through his teeth. A gold cap gleamed on his left incisor. "Yeah, we go back a ways, don't we?"

"Uh-huh," Nick drawled, propping his foot against the brass rail so it would be easier to reach his knife. "We're regular pals. How long have you been out, now?"

"Eleven months, nine days."

"I see you got the tooth fixed."

He grinned, a quick, nervous flicker. "Yeah. It was decent of you to get a real dentist to come to the prison infirmary."

"Hey, it was the least I could do, seeing as how I broke it in the first place."

The grin dissolved into a sneer. "That's what I like about you, Strada. You're a real prince."

"Golly, gee whiz, I'm touched."

A table tipped over in the corner to the sound of breaking bottles and loud, loose laughter.

Bernie jerked nervously, glancing over his shoulder like a man with a guilty conscience. He ordered a second drink, drained it faster than the first, then closed his fist over the empty glass. "Okay, let's cut the crap. I have a message for you."

"Since when did you start working for Western Union?"

"Shut up and listen. Whatever you're doing is really ticking someone off back in Chicago."

"That's his problem, Bernie."

"Yeah, well, now it's your problem, too. Word on the street is that you're worth five thousand dead."

"Only five thousand? I'm insulted."

"I'm trying to do you a favor here—"

"Bull. You don't do anything for free. If you really want to do me a favor, give me something on the man who's putting up the blood money."

"Can't. Don't know who it is. Honest."

Nick let his hand drop casually to his side. "Why don't I believe you?"

"I don't want any trouble. I don't work in your town anymore, remember?"

"So you waited until you heard I was coming here and arranged this little meeting out of the goodness of your heart? I'm deeply, truly touched."

The door swung open, swirling a blast of thick, humid air into the crowded room. Bernie glanced over his shoulder again and hunched closer to Nick as if trying to make himself invisible. "It's more, Strada. More than just you."

"What?"

"It's your mother. And your sisters. How many sisters you got? Three? Four?"

Nick's fingers brushed the side of his boot. "So?"

"So the word is, anyone named Strada's on the list. You better quit what you're messing with or—" His words cut off on a startled squeak. Eyes bulging, he looked down at his lap.

"Since you're into passing along messages, take note of this one." Nick moved the knife he held just enough for the tip to slice a fingernail-width tear in the denim between Bernie's legs. "Anyone who touches my family is a dead man, Bernie. Are you listening?"

"Dammit, Strada, get that blade away from me."

"Spread the word. They're citizens. They're not involved. If someone is stupid enough to lay a finger or anything else on them—" he twisted his wrist so that the dim light from behind the bar glinted off cold steel "—I'll personally remove it."

Sweat trickled down Bernie's forehead. Apart from blinking, he didn't move a muscle. "Geez, I'm trying to do you a favor, you crazy cossack. I'm not your enemy."

"Then prove it. Give me something on Duxbury."

"Who?"

"Adam Duxbury. Ring a bell?"

Bernie swallowed hard. "I can't help you. I swear to God, I can't. I'm just a messenger."

As smoothly as he'd brought the weapon out, Nick clicked the blade shut and slipped it back into his boot. It wasn't department issue, but at times it was more effective than the Smith & Wesson that nestled in his shoulder holster. Even in a place like this, a gunshot was bound to draw some attention.

Nick put his elbow on the bar and took a mouthful of too warm, too flat beer. "How much did Duxbury pay you to pass along this warning?"

"I got nothing more to say to you, Strada." Bernie slid from the stool and took a wary step backward. "Now I remember why I needed a change of scene when I got out. You're nuts, man."

Nick bared his teeth in an expression that no

one would mistake for a smile. "Thank you. I do my best."

Swearing under his breath, Bernie twisted away and angled a path toward the door.

For a moment Nick considered following him outside and persuading him to continue the conversation, but it wouldn't be any use. Duxbury had succeeded in covering his tracks so far, and he was smart enough to choose a messenger boy who'd have no credibility in court...if Nick ever managed to get him there.

"Damn," he muttered, tightening his hands into fists. During his past twelve years with the Chicago police department, Nick had dealt with the occasional death threat. It had never deterred him from finishing an investigation before. If anything, the adrenaline usually gave his reflexes an extra edge. It was all part of the job.

Yet nailing Duxbury went beyond the job. It was justice. The man was guilty of taking a life. Nick had seen him do it, had looked right into his flat, cold eyes through the windshield of the murder weapon. There was absolutely no doubt in his mind that Duxbury had been driving that car.

But it seemed as if money and influence could buy anything. It bought an alibi. It bought a one-way ticket to Buenos Aires for the witness Nick had tracked to New York.

It bought a contract on five completely innocent women.

Was it a bluff? If it had been his own life, Nick wouldn't have hesitated to take the gamble. But what choice did he have now? Drop the case? That's what his captain wanted. With no progress to date and dead ends everywhere he turned it was only a matter of time before Nick would be ordered to pursue something else.

But he couldn't give up. With the blood of cossacks and conquistadors mingling in his veins, Nick didn't know how to give up.

And when it came to the people he loved, Nicholai Strada was as primitively protective as any of his warrior ancestors.

Tossing some crumpled bills onto the bar to cover Bernie's drinks, Nick straightened to his full height. His lean muscles tightened with urgency and his pulse pounded a hard accompaniment to the music still blaring from the jukebox as he made his way to the phone in the back hallway. Gripping the receiver until his knuckles went white, Nick called the airport and arranged for a seat on the first flight back to Chicago.

Chapter 1

He was a difficult man to ignore. From the long, denim-clad legs that were braced too close to her silk skirt, to the broad shoulders that didn't fit against the back of the seat, his lean body exuded masculinity. There was a restlessness about him, a sense of leashed energy, an impression of predatory strength. He had the primitive, indisputable confidence of an alpha male. He would easily dominate any environment, whether it was a boardroom or a barroom. Here in the tight, forced intimacy of the airplane cabin, the very air around him seemed charged. Yes, he was difficult to ignore, but Lauren Abbot was doing her best.

Crossing her legs to give him more room, Lauren carefully smoothed her skirt to her knees and turned toward the window. The soap star she had met last year had been handsomer, and the linebacker had been larger, and the congressman she had just interviewed had been a heck of a lot better dressed, yet none of those men had come close to affecting her like...him. One glance and her breath had caught. One whiff of his cologne and her pulse had thudded. And she wasn't sure he was wearing cologne, not unless some lucky company somewhere had discovered how to bottle pure masculinity.

Out of the corner of her eye she saw him shift to claim the extra space she had given him. He stretched his left arm in front of him, twisting his wrist to check his watch, then dropped his hand to his thigh. Long, strong fingers tapped out an impatient rhythm against his knee.

Evidently, alpha male types didn't like to be kept waiting.

As if on cue, the pilot's voice crackled over the loudspeaker, announcing yet another ten-minute delay before takeoff.

Now the man's right foot took up the rhythm of his fingers as the toe of his scuffed cowboy boot whacked the metal supports of the seat in front of him. He twitched his shoulders, and the worn tan leather of his jacket creaked, whispering of energy that was no longer completely leashed.

Lauren bit down on the inside of her lip and focused on the lights at the edge of the runway. Unlike the man in the seat next to hers, she was in no hurry to reach Chicago. She had delayed her return as long as possible, and for a fleeting, guilty instant, she wished that the flight could be canceled altogether.

Her sister's wedding wouldn't take place for another two weeks, yet already Lauren could feel her stomach knotting at the prospect. She'd agreed to be Angela's maid of honor, and she'd been helping to organize all the peripheral details for months. She knew that she'd attend the ceremony no matter what, but she usually avoided weddings as determinedly as she avoided men like the one sitting beside her.

Then again, she'd never encountered a man quite like the one sitting beside her.

With a rumbling growl, the pitch of the engines changed. The plane eased forward to take its place among the others that waited for clearance. Somewhere toward the back of the cabin, a baby cried fitfully before lapsing into silence. A flight attendant hurried down the aisle, snapping closed the overhead compartments. She paused when she reached their row.

"Excuse me, sir?"

Lauren glanced toward her silent companion.

"Sir?" the young woman repeated. "Please fasten your seat belt. We're about to take off."

The man looked up quickly, flashing the flight attendant a tight, preoccupied smile. "Sure," he said. His voice was deep and rich, resonating with hints of the same suppressed power that surrounded the rest of him. "Thanks."

The smile the woman returned was much wider than the one she had received and no doubt a few degrees warmer than professionalism required. "You're very welcome. Do you need any assistance?"

He shook his head and reached for the ends of the belt. "No, thanks."

The sound of his voice brushed Lauren's skin like the charged breeze before a storm. Her gaze lingered on his profile. His forehead was broad, his nose long and narrow. His steel blue eyes, along with the dramatic angles of his high cheekbones and square jaw, evoked images of windswept steppes and endless horizons. His features were chiseled, honed and uncompromisingly male. And yet...

And yet there were lines at the corners of his firmly compressed lips that would probably deepen adorably if he ever indulged in a genuine smile. His hair was a gleaming, depthless brown, so dark it verged on black. Combed carelessly back from his face, it reached past his collar in soft waves that would slip sensuously through a woman's fingers. The steel blue of his eyes was tempered by long, sinfully lush lashes that made her wonder what would happen if his barely controlled energy turned to passion.

Lauren faced front and pressed her head against the back of the seat. This was ridiculous. Where was her customary objectivity? What had happened to her sense of detachment? Why should she speculate about this stranger's potential for passion?

She didn't want passion.

She didn't want to go to the wedding, either.

The plane quivered as the noise of the engines increased. The lights beside the runway became a blur, then a streak, then dropped away altogether. The pressure that had pushed Lauren into the seat eased and the plane leveled off. She unbuckled her seat belt, released the button on the front of her tailored jacket and leaned over to retrieve her briefcase. If she kept busy with her work, she wouldn't have time to think about this steely-eyed stranger. And if she concentrated very, very hard, she might be able to avoid thinking about what she would have to face when she got home.

For forty minutes it almost worked. With her briefcase open on her lap and her pen in her hand, she felt more at ease, drawing her professionalism around her like comfortable, well-worn armor. Lauren owed her career as a television journalist to her ability to distance herself from her subjects, to suppress her own emotions and her opinions and view each story with objectivity and logic. There were advantages to going through life as an observer rather than a participant. It was safer, smoother.

Less painful.

What kind of profession would suit the restless stranger beside her? Cowboy? Roving mercenary? With his striking features and his compelling voice, he would make a fortune if he ever decided to go into news broadcasting.

No, a man like him wouldn't be satisfied with a career in reporting or gathering the news. Everything about him indicated someone who would rather be a participant than an observer. He was the kind of man who would make the headlines, not read them.

He wasn't like her.

Was that why she found him so fascinating?

Was she a victim of the old cliché about opposites attracting?

There was no need to delve into psychological justifications to explain her reaction to this stranger. Considering the way he looked, and sounded, and smelled, any woman with a pulse would react. Whether she wanted to or not.

Lauren squared her shoulders as if settling her armor more securely. Resolutely, she reread the press release that was handed out at this afternoon's news conference and underlined a point she wanted to research further. She switched her attention to her notes, then frowned as the neat rows of her precise handwriting seemed to waver. The vibrations that rose through the floor of the plane were becoming rougher, causing the papers on her lap to shift sideways.

Anchoring her notes with her palm, she glanced out the window. A narrow sliver of moon shone weakly over cobblestone clouds that passed beneath the wing, but otherwise the sky appeared to be clear of the kind of weather that could cause turbulence. She leaned closer to the flattened oval of glass, listening to the steady drone of the engines for a moment. The vibrations continued, rattling the clasps of her briefcase.

"You feel it, too, don't you?"

The sound of the deep, rich voice so close to her ear made her jerk. She twisted around.

The man with the scuffed boots and impatient fingers was leaning across the armrest with total disregard for the concept of personal space. His knee pressed her thigh, a hard, insistent invasion of denim against silk. He reached in front of her to brace his arm beneath the window as he leaned even closer.

For a wild, irrational instant she thought he was about to embrace her. Paper crumpled beneath her fingers as she squeezed herself against the corner of the seat. "Feel what?"

"That rumble," he said, peering past her to look out the window.

"You mean the vibration?"

He nodded and narrowed his eyes as he studied the view beyond the wing. "Can't see anything."

"I'm sure it's nothing."

"Yeah."

Lauren took a shallow breath, aware of how his arm was mere inches from her breasts. "If you're worried, perhaps you could speak with one of the flight attendants."

"Right."

"In the meantime, would you mind straightening up?"

He glanced down quickly, as if only now realizing his position. Frowning, he turned his head toward her.

Lauren felt the shallow breath she'd just managed to take whoosh from her lungs. The brief glimpses she'd had of his profile could never have prepared her for the full impact of his face. Words flitted through her mind, adjectives like *handsome, rugged, virile,* but none of them were adequate. Her gaze touched the shadow of black whiskers that roughened the taut skin over his square jaw, the small scar that curved across his left temple, the tiny lines that fanned out from the corners of his eyes. And for the second time in less than an hour, she wondered about the passion that simmered behind his hard blue gaze.

"Sorry," he muttered. Immediately he withdrew his arm and leaned back to his own side of the seat, shifting his legs so that his knee no longer touched her thigh.

Beneath her skirt, Lauren's skin tingled. She clenched her jaw and smoothed out the papers that she had crumpled. Any woman with a pulse would react, she reminded herself. With the sides of her hands she shaped the pile of notes into a neat stack. "It's all right," she said tightly.

She had barely finished speaking when he rose to his feet and stepped into the aisle. He walked toward the front of the plane, pausing to talk to a pair of flight attendants. A few minutes later he returned, his frown deepening as he slid back into his seat.

Lauren stored her notes in her briefcase and snapped shut the clasps to keep them from rattling. The vibrations were getting worse.

"They assured me it was nothing," he said.

"It's starting to be a noisy nothing."

"Yeah." He drummed his fingers against his knee. "Sorry about startling you earlier."

"It's all right," she repeated.

He looked past her to glance out the window, then checked his watch. "Damn, I should have been there already."

She leaned over to slide her briefcase under the seat in front of her. "It shouldn't be much long—"

Her words cut off on a startled gasp as the floor suddenly tilted, knocking her off balance. She fell sideways, smacking her cheek against a hard, denim-covered thigh. Before she could react, the plane tilted the other way, tossing her against the side of the fuselage.

"They can't call this nothing," he said, wrapping his arm around her waist and pulling her back into her seat.

Her fingers sank into supple leather where his jacket covered his wrist. She hung on, struggling to regain her breath.

He muttered an oath and glanced around the cabin. His arm was still clamped across Lauren's body, keeping her firmly in place.

The plane leveled off. An agitated hum rose from the other passengers. Static crackled from the overhead speakers before the pilot's voice came through. In the steady, soothing tones of a radio announcer on a classical music program, he apologized for the inconvenience and assured the passengers the problem was minor. Unexpected turbulence, he said.

Flight attendants bustled past, reassuring smiles fixed on their faces as they did their best to spread calm. A chime sounded, and the seat belt light flashed on.

The man beside her loosened his hold, allowing Lauren to fasten her belt. He buckled his own, then turned back toward her. "Are you all right?" he asked.

Her heart was pounding. She wasn't a nervous flier, yet she was beginning to get nervous now. It was only turbulence, she told herself. Nothing to worry about.

"Miss?"

Pulling her anxiety back under control, Lauren forced herself to nod. "Yes, I'm fine. Thanks for the help."

He lifted his hand to her face, touching the side of her cheek with his fingertips. "You're hurt."

Although his touch was surprisingly gentle, her skin stung where her face had hit his jeans. She pulled back, breaking the contact. "There isn't any blood, is there?"

"No, but you might get a bruise."

She flexed her jaw experimentally. "It doesn't seem that bad."

He continued to study her, his gaze sharpening. "Channel Ten."

"Excuse me?"

"That's where I've seen you before. You do the news on that local station."

"Yes, I've been working there for nine years now."

"You're Lauren Abbot, right?"

She nodded. "That's right."

"I'm Nick Strada," he said, offering his hand.

Good manners dictated that he wait for her to offer her hand first, but Lauren suspected that this man didn't pay much attention to things as restrictive as manners. She put her hand in his. "How do you do?" she said politely.

His clasp was warm, firm and brief. "For a local station, you put on a balanced news program. It's pretty good."

"Thank you." Surreptitiously she flexed the fingers he had touched.

"Will it be a problem for you on camera?"

"Mmm?"

"The cheek."

"Makeup can do wonders. Besides, I'm off for the weekend." She glanced at his leg. "I apologize for falling against you like that, but—"

"It was an accident." The fine lines at the corners of his eyes deepened for a moment as a smile teased the edges of his lips. "Besides, I'm not complaining."

It wasn't a real smile, but it was enough to relax the taut planes of his cheeks and hint at a promise of dimples. And it was enough to give an extra kick to her already racing pulse. Lauren stiffened, fumbling to refasten the button on the front of her jacket. She wished she had a pen, or a notebook, or a microphone in her hand. Anything to attempt to reestablish the distance between her and this man. "I guess that vibration we felt was due to turbulence, after all."

"So they say."

"You don't sound as if you believe it."

His expression sobered. "I'm in a hurry to get back to Chicago, that's all."

"I noticed," she said dryly.

He glanced at his watch yet again. "Yeah, I guess anyone would, even if she wasn't a reporter. Were you in New York on a story?"

"Yes, I was attending a press conference put on by the congressional committee that's studying urban renewal. What about you? Business or pleasure?"

"What?"

"Your trip?"

His jaw tightened grimly. "Not pleasure."

Once more she got the impression of power that strained to be released. The toe of his boot tapped against her briefcase in an impatient motion that she suspected he wasn't even aware of. Obviously, he was too preoccupied to be interested in continuing this conversation. And why should they? As soon as the plane touched down, they would once more be complete strangers.

Nick Strada, she repeated to herself. The name suited him, a combination of strong consonants and lingering vowels. Strada sounded Hispanic. Had he inherited his dark hair from his father? What about his prominent bone structure and his blue eyes? And his passion?

Lauren suppressed a groan. That was three times.

Smoothing her skirt to her knees, Lauren clasped her hands in her lap and turned toward the window. She might not be in a hurry to return home, but there were beginning to be plenty of reasons why she would be glad to see this flight end.

She was doing her best to ignore him, Nick decided. The reddened patch of skin that marred her cheek must be stinging, but she was ignoring that, too. She had fallen face first into his lap, but that hadn't ruffled her silk-and-pearls composure, either. She was one cool lady, this Lauren Abbot. What would it take to stir her up?

And why the hell should he care?

She wasn't his type. He'd never been comfortable around reserved women. Her legs might be long and shapely, and the jacket of her tailored ivory suit might outline some interesting curves, but her body language telegraphed aloofness. The fine blond hair that she wore in a sleek twist didn't invite touching. With her slender hands and long manicured nails, she didn't look like the kind of woman who would enjoy touching back.

Yet her grip had been strong when she'd shaken his hand, and when she'd hung on to his wrist. And her body had felt softly feminine when he'd caught her around the waist and held her securely in her seat. And despite her efforts to put as much space as possible between them, she'd been intruding into his thoughts from the moment he'd boarded the plane.

It must be the adrenaline. Or his anxiety over the situation. Or all this frustrated, useless energy latching onto the first available target.

Raking his hands through his hair impatiently, Nick shifted his gaze to the blackness outside the window. There was no way to judge how fast they were moving, but at least they were on their way. Every minute that had passed while this plane had sat on the runway earlier had filled his mind with nightmare images of what might be happening back home.

God, they had to be all right. There was no evidence of Duxbury's threat against his mother and sisters, so there would be no official police protection. That's what the captain had said when Nick had called him from the phone in the bar. They'd send a unit through the neighborhood a few times a day, but anything more wouldn't be covered by the budget.

So it had been up to him to call his mother and ask her to stay out of sight until he finished the case he was working on. He decided not to give her any details about Duxbury—the less she knew, the less she'd argue—but he did tell her that someone was threatening their lives in order to force him to drop his investigation. As he had expected, she'd balked at the idea of running at first, but eventually she'd agreed to take the twins to her cousin's place in the morning. Convincing the two fifteen-year-olds to leave their friends wasn't going to be easy, but Natasha Strada could be as stubborn as her son when it came to protecting her family.

That still left two more. There had been no answer at Rose and Juanita's apartment, as usual. He'd left a message on their machine, telling them to call their mother, but instead of being sensible and disappearing for a few weeks, those two would probably insist on helping Nick solve the case. They wouldn't be able to walk away from a challenge any more than he could.

Gritting his teeth, he crossed his arms and leaned back in the seat. He had to get home. Only when he had assured himself of his family's safety would he be free to eliminate the source of the threat to them.

He was going to get Duxbury. Somehow, the man would pay for what he'd done.

Another rumble vibrated through the plane, harder and more ominous than the one he'd noticed before. More turbulence? Nick glanced toward the window. The woman beside him, Lauren the ice princess, was leaning close to the glass. She appeared as self-composed and as distant now as she did on the TV in his apartment.

It shouldn't bother him, but it did. Her composure only accentuated his restlessness. Her fastidious neatness made him feel like a slob. And there was something about her hands-off attitude that was almost like a challenge.

"How does it look out there?" he asked.

She hesitated, using her index finger to tuck a stray strand of hair neatly back into its twist before she replied. "The sky appears clear."

The rumbling continued as the plane banked in a wide, slow turn. The pilot announced they would be landing in five minutes. Nick checked his watch and drummed his fingers against his thigh.

"You might want to take a look at this, Mr. Strada," Lauren said suddenly.

He swiveled toward her. "What?"

She waved one of her delicate, perfectly man-icured hands at the darkness outside. "I don't think those flames are due to turbulence."

Chapter 2

At the first contact with the ground, the landing gear burrowed into the soft earth and snapped off, sending the plane tobogganing on its belly. It slid across a narrow road, metal screeching against asphalt in a shower of sparks. The burning engine dropped off seconds before the wing tip caught a light pole. A crack opened in the fuselage, splitting the metal skin apart. The tail section struck a tumbled heap of boulders near the edge of Lake Michigan and spun sideways, breaking the aircraft into ragged chunks of skidding debris.

The nose kept going, a maimed, manic white bird trailing spiraling clouds of oily smoke. It dove down the bank, its momentum propelling it across the surface of the water in a splintering, hissing, screaming rush. Blackness closed in as the lake gushed through the gaping wound in the back.

Lauren felt water swirl over her feet in a frigid wave. Her nostrils stung from the smoke, but cool, fresh air poured into her lungs.

Something was pinning her down, a heavy, warm body. The man who had been sitting beside her. He had sheltered her just before the impact. ''Mr. Strada?'' She tried to lift her head and his arm slid limply from her shoulder to dangle over her ribs. ''Nick?''

From the blackness around her came the sounds of a miracle. People crying, moaning, calling, people still alive.

She struggled to shift Nick's weight. ''It's over. We made it. We're all right.''

He didn't reply.

Metal creaked. It wasn't over. The nose of the plane tilted downwards with an ominous gurgling and the water rose to Lauren's ankles. She bent her arm awkwardly to reach the buckle of her seat belt. Fingers trembling, she unfastened the catch. ''Come on, Nick. Wake up.''

With a sizzling whoosh, the fuel that had spilled into the lake from the broken wing ignited. A carpet of flame unrolled beyond the window, painting the broken cabin in flickers of demonic orange.

Lauren tried not to hear the renewed hysteria around her. She dropped to her knees and twisted out from underneath Nick's limp weight. As soon as her support was withdrawn, he started to curl forward. Lauren braced her shoulder against his chest and pushed upward until he fell back into the seat.

She swallowed hard to tamp down the scream that rose in her throat. His face was something from a horror movie or a nightmare. Trails of dark red angled over his skin, seeming to pulse with a life of their own. On her knees in the rising water, she lifted her hand and pressed her fingertips against the gash at his hairline. Blood flowed over her skin and trickled down her arm in a hot stream. She fought down another scream. If he was bleeding, then he was still alive.

Water splashed over the seats as other survivors scrambled to escape the sinking wreckage. Lauren fumbled to undo Nick's seat belt. "Help!" she cried. "Somebody help me get this man out."

No one responded to her plea. There were so many others filling the night. A baby wailed, a woman sobbed brokenly. Lauren had a glimpse of a man cradling a shaking child in one arm, his other arm hanging crooked and useless. From the direction of the cockpit, an authoritative voice was shouting instructions. The emergency exits couldn't be opened or the broken fuselage would sink in seconds.

The aisle was filled with a sudden crush of people, most in far worse condition than Lauren. She felt the water at her hips. She knew she would never be able to carry someone Nick's size by herself, but she might be able to float him. Grasping him by the arms, she tugged him from his seat just as the floor tilted and dropped.

The woman with the baby lunged toward the back, half climbing, half swimming. Lauren maneuvered behind Nick and hooked her arm under his chin in a lifeguard headlock, then dragged him into the water.

Flaming patches of fuel and chunks of debris swirled across the lake's surface. A pillar of black smoke rose from a fire on the shore like a beacon, drawing the scattered survivors toward safety. Lauren kicked toward it, struggling to keep Nick's head above water.

Time seemed to suspend and compress as she angled toward the bank. Nick's limp body dragged at her arm until she felt as if her bones were being pulled from their sockets. It was impossible to swim straight, and she lost sight of the smoke beacon, her vision blurred by exhaustion. She didn't realize she had reached the shore until she felt her toes finally brush the bottom. She towed Nick into the shallows, straining muscles that already burned. Crawling, stumbling, she gripped him under the arms and inched him above the water before she allowed herself to collapse on the rock-strewn shore.

Lying on her back, her chest heaving, her throat squeezing shut, Lauren curled her fingers into the ground as if it might be snatched from beneath her at any moment. Each breath she drew was precious, each throb of her pulse a gift. Until now her actions had been ruled by instinct, by a primitive sense of survival. Only when her thoughts grew steadier did the enormity of what had just taken place begin to register.

Stifling a whimper, she rolled over and came to her knees. Half a mile away, the glow from burning debris lit up the sky, tinging the moonlight orange. She thought she recognized the tail section, its gleaming silhouette rising like a shark's fin. How far from the airport were they? How long would it take for help to arrive? She squinted through the spreading smoke but couldn't see any movement. Yet on the still night air she could hear noises. Oh, God, the noises. Crackling flames, broken sobs, cries, shouts, pleas. How many had managed to make it to shore? How many had survived the crash?

And how many hadn't?

She lifted her chin, her breath coming in short, sharp pants as she tried to maintain control. Calm. She had to stay calm. She was fine. She'd beaten the odds. She'd live to see another day, another story...her sister's wedding.

A bubble of hysterical laughter rose in her throat, frightening her into biting her lip. Well, she hadn't wanted to go home, and she'd almost gotten her wish. Once, during an argument with Angela, her sister had accused her of hiding behind her job as a way to avoid getting a real life. Ha. Not this time. No, this time there wasn't any handy microphone to clutch or Tele-PrompTer to follow. No chance for detachment or distance. For the first time in six years she had been wrenched away from her safe perch as an observer and...

And what on earth was she supposed to do now?

She twisted to look at Nick. He hadn't moved since she had hauled him onto the shore. Her gaze skimmed down his long legs to the waves that lapped the tips of his boots. He was a large man, solidly built, his body devoid of any fat that would have helped buoy him up in the cold water. How she'd managed to get him this far was beyond her.

Struggling to peel off her sodden jacket, she leaned over to look at his face. His steel blue eyes were closed, his chiseled features slack. Moisture gleamed from his high cheekbones and trickled down the edge of his strong jaw. Thankfully, the cold water had washed away most of the blood and seemed to have slowed the bleeding.

Something had struck him during the crash. Instead of protecting his head with his arms, he had wrapped himself around her and sheltered her with his body. Because of this stranger, she had escaped with nothing but bruises.

"Nick?" She coughed, shocked at the roughness of her voice. "Nick, can you hear me?"

He didn't respond.

She felt her body begin to shake with reaction. Had it been more than the cold water that had slowed the bleeding? Was he dying? Was he already dead?

Clamping down on another bubble of hysteria, she inched closer. She touched her fingertips to the side of his neck, but her hand was too unsteady to find a pulse. Swiftly she moved her hand to his chest, sighing in relief as she felt the shallow rise and fall of his breathing.

In the distance, over the sound of the flames and of human misery, another noise grew. Lauren lifted her head, holding her breath, not daring to hope that what she was hearing could actually be... Oh, God, yes. It was a siren. The warbling two-note shriek was still faint, but it was coming closer.

There was a faint rustle of movement by her knees. She glanced quickly back at Nick in time to see his eyelids flicker. She slid her hand to his cheek. "Mr. Strada?"

Beneath her palm his skin was cool and moist. The fine muscles under the surface tensed as he clenched his jaw.

"Nick?" she tried, louder this time.

The lines on his face deepened as his lips drew back in a tight grimace of pain.

She didn't know what to do. Stay here? Try to find help? If the siren meant that help was on the way, whoever it was wouldn't be able to see them here at the water's edge. They were too far down the shore from the crash site. She shifted her weight to her feet, preparing to stand up, when a large hand clamped around her wrist.

Nick held her in place, his grip amazingly solid. His eyes opened slowly, as if fighting against an invisible weight. He parted his lips, and the sound that he made was too rough to be called speech, too urgent to be called a groan. He swallowed hard, then tried again. "What...the...hell...happened?"

"We're safe, Nick. The plane's down. We survived."

His eyes narrowed. "Lauren?"

"Yes, yes. You sat beside me, remember? We saw the engine catch fire and—" She forced herself to slow down. "Something hit you in the head and knocked you out. I think that means you have a concussion. I don't know if you have any other injuries. How do you feel?"

He coughed, then inhaled sharply and muttered a short pungent oath. He released her wrist and raised his hand to his head. For a moment he warily probed the gash at his hairline. His fingers came away smeared with fresh blood.

"Maybe you shouldn't try to move," she said, watching a spasm of pain tighten his face. "I heard a siren, so help should be on the way."

"You okay?"

The muscles that she had overworked trying to get Nick to shore were cramping. Bruises that she hadn't wanted to catalog throbbed from every part of her body. Her stomach was rolling with a combination of nausea and panic. But just the fact that she was alive to feel it made all the discomfort insignificant. "Yes, I'm fine," she answered.

Nick hung on to the sound of her voice, trying to reorient himself. He seemed to be fading in and out, as if he'd been pulled backward through some crazy carnival ride. Cautiously, he flexed his arms and legs, checking out the rest of the damage. Apart from a stiffness in his left knee, everything seemed to be functioning.

He gritted his teeth and pulled himself into a sitting position, bracing an arm behind him as he was struck by a wave of dizziness. He breathed deeply, hoping the oxygen would help clear the ringing from his ears.

The plane had crashed. At least his brain had managed to absorb that much. He cautiously turned his head to survey their surroundings. "Where the hell *is* the plane?"

"Most of it's in the lake."

"How'd we end up here?"

"The fuselage was sinking. I pulled you to shore." She shuddered. "I've done stories on accidents and fires, but I've never done a plane crash. This will be my first."

That's right, he thought, pleased that the mist in his brain was starting to clear. Reporter

Channel Ten. Cool as chilled wine while she watched an engine flame out.

In the moonlight her face was as colorless as her pale blouse. The blond hair that had been so neatly confined was now straggling over her shoulders like wet seaweed. Yet she still kept her chin lifted and her gaze steady.

Either the woman had an astonishing reserve of inner calm, or she really did have nothing but ice water in her veins.

But what did it matter? They were alive. And he owed his life to her. "Thanks," he said, his voice rough. "For pulling me out, bringing me to shore. Thanks."

To his surprise, she raised her hand to his face, brushing her fingertips across his cheek. It was a gentle, feminine gesture, something he never would have expected from the unflappable Lauren Abbot he'd met on the plane. Her lips parted in a brief, unsteady smile. "If you hadn't sheltered me when we crashed, we both would have drowned with the wreckage."

A memory of the moment before the crash came back to him. Her green eyes had been widened in terror, her delicate hand had been gripping his knee. And her trembling body had felt warm and fragile and...good as he'd held her close.

She dropped her hand and twisted to look over her shoulder. The open collar of her blouse shifted, and moonlight whispered over the curve of a gently rounded breast.

His nostrils flared. Beneath the sour tang of the lake water and the bite of burning fuel, there was a hint of sweetness. Must be her. Nick's gaze flicked over the display that was mere inches from his nose. Those curves had been hidden by a stiffly tailored jacket before. He'd felt them, though, with his arm, when he'd pulled her back into her seat....

He looked away impatiently. They had just survived a plane crash, for God's sake. Why the hell was he thinking about her breasts?

He'd heard about this phenomenon. Heightened senses, physical awareness, it was all a type of primitive coping mechanism, something to do with adrenaline, or some kind of psychological reaction to escaping death.

He clenched his jaw and squinted toward the column of smoke farther up the shore. Flashing lights pulsed over what was left of the plane's tail section and strobed across the water. The ringing in his head coalesced into a siren, screeching closer, echoing from the darkness.

And all at once, the urgency that had made Nick board that plane in the first place resurfaced with a vengeance. He couldn't stay here. He'd lost too much time. He had to get home and find some way to protect his family....

"Nick?"

The last of the mist cleared and reality returned in a merciless burst. Duxbury. His family. No protection.

Nick slipped his hand beneath his jacket, checking for the hard weight that should have been there. His fingers probed the lose flap, the empty sling, and he cursed under his breath. The holster must have come unfastened when Lauren pulled him from that plane. His gun was either on the bottom of the lake or had fallen out when she'd dragged him out of the water.

Sweeping his hand across the ground, he searched the area around him, then looked at the black waves that lapped the shore. He hissed between his teeth. No gun. It didn't exactly make him defenseless, but it left him at a distinct disadvantage.

"What is it?"

He patted the side of his boot, grasped the heel with both hands and tugged until the sodden leather finally slid off his foot. Water splashed onto the muddy rocks in a sudden stream, followed by the reassuring clunk of his knife. He leaned over to pick it up, carefully testing the switch on the side of the handle. There was a click and a whisper, then moonlight glinted from the wet blade.

Gravel crunched as Lauren hurriedly moved back.

Nick fastened his free hand around her wrist to hold her in place. "Relax. I'm a cop."

With a sharp twist of her arm she broke free. Her eyes widened as she focused on the knife he still held. "What kind of cop carries a switchblade in his boot?"

"Lieutenant Nicholai Strada, Chicago police," he muttered. He shook the last of the water from his boot and put it back on, then closed the knife and slipped it back into its customary place beside his ankle. He emptied the water from his other boot, jammed his foot inside and braced his knuckles against the ground. Taking a deep breath, he shifted his weight and tried to stand up. The gravel shore rushed upward toward his face. With a frustrated grunt, he broke his fall with his hands.

"Wait here," Lauren said. "I can bring someone—"

"No." He crawled to where she had retreated and looped his arm over her shoulder. "No. I can make it if you help me get to my feet."

She hesitated, her gaze on his right boot.

Then she sighed, grasped his hand and braced herself against his side.

It took three attempts, but together they managed to get him upright. He took a wobbling step forward. Sharp shards of pain shot outward from his stiff left knee and his wet socks sloshed in his boots.

Lauren propped her shoulder under his arm and slipped her hand beneath his jacket to get a solid grip on the waistband of his jeans. Her head barely reached his chin, but there was a surprising strength in her slender form.

Stumbling, leaning into each other, they limped forward. As they wove an unsteady path toward the flashing lights, the ringing in Nick's head faded, but the anxiety that replaced it got worse.

His mother and the twins knew he was on this flight. Once the news about the crash broke, they probably wouldn't stay out of sight like they should. There was a good chance Duxbury would know he was coming home, too. But that man would have a very different reaction to news of this crash. He'd likely be ready to celebrate his good fortune, hoping not only to be rid of his adversary but to save the cost of a contract.

An odd thought blinked across Nick's mind.

Cost of the contract. Saved. If it hadn't been for Lauren, he would have drowned. If he'd died, there would be no more danger. His family would be safe. If he'd died...

The distinctive thumping noise of a helicopter intruded before he could finish the thought. Lights appeared, coming from over the water.

They were close enough to the wreckage to make out more details now. A tangled, burning trail of debris stretched to the water's edge. Heavy black smoke swirled around the broken fin that marked the tail section. The deep bellow of an air horn blended with more sirens as a pair of fire engines bumped over the gully the plane had carved into the ground. Help was arriving. People were swarming over the crash site, their urgent calls mingling with the confusion.

The throbbing beat of the helicopter grew loud enough to rattle Nick's teeth. A powerful spotlight shone a squashed circle on the ground as the helicopter reached the shore. More people were moving there, other survivors who had pulled themselves from the water. Some were in better shape than he and Lauren, some were worse.

Lauren's shoulders stiffened. "I bet that's Gord."

"What?"

"In the helicopter. Gord Skinner, one of the station's videographers."

Nick shielded his eyes and glanced upward. The Channel Ten logo was easily identifiable even through the pall of smoke. The light swept toward them. For a moment they were caught in the beam, but then it slid past.

"He's going to get some great footage," she said as they maneuvered around a piece of twisted metal. "He's probably drooling at the chance to beat me out of this story."

Nick bit back a groan as a stumble jarred his left knee. "You're one cool lady, Lauren Abbot. You almost died, and you're worried about getting your story."

She was silent for a while as they continued walking toward the light. "That's what I do best, Nick," she said finally.

He'd hit a nerve, he thought immediately. "Hey, Lauren, I didn't mean—"

"You handle things your way, Lieutenant Strada, and I'll handle them mine. I'd rather be an observer at a funeral than a participant."

More thoughts flickered in and out too quickly to grasp. Camera. Observer at a funeral.

Cost of the contract.

His family would be safe.

Nick looked at the string of vehicles that were

already clogging the narrow road on the far side of the wreckage, then swung his gaze back to the helicopter and the black emptiness of the lake.

And this time, when the outrageous thought blinked across his mind, his brain was quick enough to latch onto it.

Chapter 3

Lauren pulled Nick's leather jacket around her shoulders and made her way through the confusion in the crowded hospital corridor. The cloth slippers one of the nurses had given her loosened with each step, and the freshly cleaned cuts on the soles of her feet stung, but like the other survivors who lay on the gurneys that lined the walls, she had absolutely nothing to complain about.

The Miracle on Lake Michigan. That's what she would have called the story if she'd been the one to put it together. Out of the one-hundred and twenty-eight people who had been on that plane, it appeared that sixty-two of them had survived. That was the last official count

she'd heard. Forty-seven dead, nineteen missing, and sixty-two who were part of the miracle.

There were so many factors responsible, not
least of which was a skilled and resourceful pilot. Then there was the incredibly fast response
time, as the emergency crews and ambulances
converged on the crash site. And there were the
survivors themselves, who had found the
strength to help one another.

Lauren clutched the lapels of Nick's jacket
more tightly together as she headed toward the
admitting desk. She still had trouble believing
that she'd actually saved a man's life. How did
that saying go? If you save someone's life
you're responsible for that person from then on?

If that were the case, then Nick had just taken
on a load of responsibility tonight, too. He'd
been barely able to stand on his own, but when
the helicopter's spotlight had shone on those
people who were still in the water, he had tossed
Lauren his jacket, lunged toward the lake and
waded out to help them.

A young woman who had been struggling to
hang on to her crying baby had been the first
one he'd reached. After that, other rescuers had
arrived, along with paramedics and ambulance
attendants. In the confusion that had followed,
Lauren lost track of Nick. She'd been pressed

into service as well, passing out blankets, helping to record names, anything and everything until the station's helicopter had landed and she'd been cornered by Gord Skinner for an eyewitness account of the disaster.

Had she thought she'd feel better with a microphone clutched in her hand? Well, she hadn't.

She dodged a pair of doctors in surgical greens and stopped in front of the desk, trying to catch the attention of the harried nurse. "Excuse me?"

The nurse tucked a telephone receiver against her ear and held up her hand, signaling Lauren to wait. She spoke quickly, making notes on a list in front of her, then hung up the phone. "A doctor will see you as soon as possible," she said, glancing up. "Why don't you take a seat over—"

"No, I don't need a doctor," Lauren said. "I need information. I'm looking for Nick Strada. He was on the plane with me."

Rubbing her forehead tiredly, the nurse looked down at the list. "Strada?"

"That's right. Lieutenant Nick Strada. He's with the Chicago police."

"And he was on the plane?"

"Yes. We were separated, and I wanted to know which hospital he was taken to."

Her finger traced down the printed names. "No Strada here. Are you a relative?"

"Well, no, but—"

"Sorry. I can't release any more information until the next of kin has been notified."

"Next of kin?" Lauren rose up on her toes, ignoring the renewed stinging the action caused. Craning her neck, she looked at the list herself. "I know he's all right. We walked together to where the ambulances were pulling up, but then he went into the lake to help the other survivors. I just want to know where he is."

The nurse sighed. "I'm sorry, miss. There's no Strada at this hospital."

Frustrated, Lauren turned aside. He couldn't have just disappeared. That cut on his forehead would need to be disinfected and stitched. And he'd been limping heavily. He needed medical attention. Maybe he was at one of the other hospitals. Or maybe, from what she'd come to know of the impatient, unconventional Lieutenant Strada, he'd decided to walk away.

I'm in a hurry to get back to Chicago. That's what he'd told her. And his actions had proved it. Could he really have simply gone home?

"Lauren!"

She glanced around, suppressing a groan. It was Gord. He'd thrown on a suit jacket and a tie over his ripped jeans and sneakers, and instead of working the camera himself, he'd called in reinforcements. The rest of the crew that usually accompanied Lauren on location was setting up in the crowded waiting area.

Gord hurried forward. "Great news," he said, his usually mournful face stretched into a smile. "We've scooped the networks. There's a bidding war going on for the tape I shot from the chopper."

"How lucky for you."

"Yeah, talk about luck—" He broke off and took in her disheveled appearance. "Have you seen a doctor yet? They're not still making you wait, are they?"

"I've been taken care of," she said, gesturing to her feet. "The staff here is handling things as smoothly as can be expected."

"That's good. Hey, cool shoes."

"Thank you." Damp leather creaked as she raised a hand to rake her fingers through her hopelessly snarled hair. "What are you doing here? I thought you'd still be at the crash site."

"What am I doing here?" he repeated incredulously. "Tracking the survivors. Human interest. Drama and pathos are as good as hard news. Lauren, I envy you, being right on the scene like that.''

''I didn't have a chance to take any notes, Gord.''

''We'll put together a follow-up piece tomorrow, okay? Oh, I forgot. You're off this weekend.''

''Theoretically.''

''Bummer of a way to start it, huh?''

''Right. I'll come down to the station, anyway. I don't want to miss an opportunity like this.''

''No need, I'll handle things.'' He straightened his tie and glanced over his shoulder at the crew. ''Oh, your sister's been phoning the station, wanting to know if you were on that plane. You might want to let her know you're all right.''

Surprise and guilt shot through her. She hadn't given a thought to notifying her relatives, she'd been so caught up in the need to find out what happened to Nick. ''Do you have your phone?'' she asked quickly.

''Sure,'' he said, producing a small cell phone from the pocket of his jacket. ''Be my guest.'' He saluted sloppily and loped over to the rest of the crew. Lauren took the phone over to a relatively quiet corner and punched in her sister's number.

As soon as Angela heard Lauren's voice, she broke into noisy tears.

Lauren took a deep breath and waited for the sobbing to subside. ''I'm fine,'' she said firmly. ''Don't worry.''

''Where are you?'' Angela asked.

''I'm in the emergency ward of—''

''You're in a hospital? Oh, Lord, how badly were you hurt?''

''Just a few scrapes and bruises. Nothing serious, so they're letting me go.''

''All right, then we'll pick you up and bring you back here. You shouldn't be alone.''

The thought of having to put on a brave front for her sister and future brother-in-law made Lauren add an extra note of firmness to her tone. ''Thanks, but I really am fine. There's no need for you and Eddy to drive into town.''

''But you do need us. My God, Lauren, I could have lost you. When Eddy and I saw the news bulletin about that crash...'' Her words blended into the beginning of another sob.

The outpouring of emotion made Lauren uncomfortable. She shifted the phone to her other ear and leaned a shoulder against the wall.

"I can't talk right now, Angela. Gord has the news crew here."

There was a choking sound. "You're not considering working, are you? Lauren, for heaven's sake, that's carrying things too far."

"Sorry, I have to go. I'll call you tomorrow, okay?"

"Are you sure you're all right?"

It took another five minutes to calm her sister down. When Lauren finally said goodbye, she stayed where she was for a moment, leaning against the wall while the bustle of the hospital continued around her. Despite her sister's reaction to the idea, Lauren really should be working. This was a once-in-a-lifetime opportunity. She raked her hair off her forehead again, then pulled back her arm and stared at her hand in chagrin. Her fingers were shaking. She'd been fine until now, but one call to her sister and her control was slipping.

Angela would have Eddy there to comfort her. He'd probably held her in his arms from the time the news had first broken. The two of them were inseparable. So far. The way Angela depended on him was frightening. How could any rational woman throw away her independence like that?

And how on earth could a rational woman want to get married?

Pressing her lips together, Lauren leaned her head against the wall. Another one of those hysterical bubbles of laughter threatened to rise in her throat. What would it take to avoid thinking about the wedding? Even a plane crash wasn't proving to be enough of a distraction.

"Hey, Lauren."

She straightened and turned in the direction of Gord's voice. He was walking toward her quickly, eagerness evident in his bouncing strides. "What is it?" she asked when he reached her.

"I need to show you something." He grabbed her elbow and tugged her forward.

She fell into step beside him. To her surprise, they bypassed the crew in the waiting area and headed for the door. "Where are we going?"

"Come out to the truck. I was looking at the tape I shot from the chopper and I want you to tell me what you think."

"Why? What do you have?"

"If I got what I think I did, this story will be seen across the continent. Hell, maybe even the world. It's going to make my career."

"I already know what the story is, Gord. I was in the middle of it, remember?"

"That's not what I mean. It's more than that. I got some terrific footage of a big guy who was hauling people out of the lake."

"One of the rescue workers?"

"No, I think he was a cop or something. The camera picked up what looked like a harness. You know, the kind for those shoulder holsters. And whoever he was, he gave me some great material. Real heroic kind of stuff."

Her pulse sped up. From Gord's description, the man could have been Nick. Even if the tape didn't show where he went, it would be a starting point. Despite her stinging feet, she increased her pace.

Gord didn't say anything more until they reached the equipment truck. He yanked open the back door and climbed inside, squeezing past two technicians as he made his way toward one of the monitors. "Over here," he called, waving Lauren forward.

She followed and took a seat on the low stool in front of the glowing screen as Gord started the tape.

The events of mere hours ago replayed before her eyes. In the glare of the spotlight, people moved jerkily, their bodies flattened by the overhead angle. The camera zoomed in, and now the waves glittered against a mass of tangled debris on the shore. "It looks so much worse from the air," she said. "How could any of us have survived?"

Gord glanced at her quickly. "Hey, this isn't bothering you, is it?"

She lifted her chin. "Of course not."

"'Cause if you're not up to this..."

"I handled the interview at the crash site, didn't I?"

"Like a pro, Lauren. Okay, then. We're getting to the part I told you about."

More people thrashed in the black water of the lake. Lauren felt her palms grow damp as she remembered the ordeal of towing Nick to shore. "You're right," she said tightly. "You managed to get some outstanding footage."

"Here it is," he exclaimed, stabbing his finger toward the screen. "Watch this."

Lauren couldn't have looked away, even if she'd wanted to. The camera had caught the exact moment when Nick had waded into the lake. He was readily identifiable. As Gord had said, the straps of the shoulder holster showed up starkly against the pale shirt. So did his dark hair and broad shoulders. His actions dominated the screen as he clasped a woman and her baby in his arms and pulled them back to shore.

"Great stuff, huh?" Gord murmured.

Lauren swallowed. "Impressive."

"Wait. It gets better."

It couldn't have been better if it had been staged, Lauren thought, watching the way Nick continued to assist the survivors even after he was joined by the rescue team. At one point he tipped back his head, and his strong, distinctive features eliminated any question of his identity.

"This is too good to be true," Gord said excitedly. "The guy has a face that could go on a billboard. Look at that jaw. And those eyes."

His cut was bleeding again, she thought, focusing on the red streak that marred his forehead. She hoped he'd had it tended to—

She gasped. "Where did he go?"

"You missed it." Gord rewound the last few seconds and started the tape forward once more. "I did the first time, too. You have to watch carefully."

She braced her hands on her thighs and leaned closer to the monitor. She watched Nick hand a small boy to a fireman and then stagger back into the lake. His movements had been growing slower and clumsier, and she knew that he must have been in agony by that time, considering the shape he had been in to start with....

"Oh, my God," she said. "Rewind that again."

Gord complied in silence.

Lauren held her breath as the images played across the screen. Nick staggered. His right arm flailed weakly against the glittering water before he disappeared beneath the surface.

He didn't come back up.

"Oh, my God," Lauren said again, staring at the flickering picture. She didn't dare to blink, afraid that she would miss the moment when the dark head would reappear. But no matter how she concentrated, she didn't see Nick again.

"I've checked the rest of the footage," Gord said, stopping the tape. "He's gone. It looks as if he must have drowned. Wow, talk about drama and pathos."

"But he survived the crash," she said, stunned to feel the heat of tears in her eyes. "I pulled him to safety. He was okay."

"What?"

"He sat beside me on the plane."

Gord hesitated. "Do you mean that you know who this was?"

"He told me his name was Nick Strada. He's a lieutenant with the Chicago police. I've been looking all over for him, but they said they couldn't release any information until the next of kin..." She crossed her arms, holding Nick's jacket tightly against her chest. "No. He couldn't be dead."

Gord yanked a notebook from his pocket and clicked open his pen. ''Nick Strada? And he was a cop?''

''He didn't have to go back into the water,'' she said. ''There were other people already there to help. He could have stayed with me.''

''Geez, if he was one of the survivors, then he was a real hero. The genuine article.''

''I can't believe he's dead.''

He patted her shoulder in an awkward gesture of sympathy. ''I'm sorry, Lauren, but the tape is pretty conclusive.''

She wiped her eyes with the back of her hand, still trying to come to terms with the reality of what she'd seen. Nick? Dead? She'd never met a man who seemed more alive. Vital. Vibrant. The very air around him had crackled with energy. And passion.

Her teeth clamped down on the inside of her cheek. All the energy and passion that she'd tried so hard to ignore was gone. Snuffed out. The strength that she'd felt in his grip, the determination she'd seen in his eyes, the masculine power she'd sensed in his leanly muscled body... How could it be gone?

''What else can you tell me about him?'' Gord asked.

''What?''

"I'm sorry," he repeated, "but I'll need all the background information on your friend that you can give me."

She rubbed her face, trying to pull herself together. "I really didn't know him. We met on the plane. Why?"

"For the story, Lauren. This is the opportunity of a lifetime."

"A man is dead, Gord. A good man. How can you be so pleased about it?"

"This has nothing to do with him personally. You know that. This is news. It's our job."

Her job. Her defense against becoming involved with the world. Numbly she reached out to pick up the clipboard that was on the ledge beneath the monitor. She didn't even read what was written on the paper. It didn't matter. She pulled out the pen that had been stuck into the slot behind the clip and fitted it between her fingers, gripping it like a lifeline.

"You're shaking," Gord said. "Are you sure you're all right?"

She shook her head. "I think I'd better go home."

The images chased across the television screen in stark life-and-death shades. The moonlight, the harsh floodlight from the helicopter, the restless, menacing darkness of the lake all lent an otherwordliness to the slow-motion drama. Curling herself more tightly into a corner of her couch, Lauren cradled a mug of coffee in her hands as she watched Nick's final struggle.

He was officially listed as missing. Searchers had combed the crash site throughout the night, but no more survivors had been found. The death toll had risen to fifty-seven, and with dawn revealing the full extent of the tragedy, little hope was held out for finding anyone else alive. Especially Nick.

How would he have felt to know his last moments were being shown in millions of households on the top-rated network morning news program in the nation? And that his very public death was being used as a tool by an ambitious videographer?

Coffee spilled down the front of her robe, trailing a lukewarm path between her breasts. Not taking her eyes off the screen, she fumbled in her pocket for a tissue and wiped away the liquid. Her hands were still shaking. She didn't know if it was from delayed shock, or an attack of nerves or because of all the caffeine she'd had since she'd arrived home.

A doctor had given her a prescription for tranquilizers before she'd left the hospital, but she had no intention of taking any. She checked the grandfather clock in the corner of the living room. It had been less than four hours since she'd awakened the building superintendent and had him unlock her apartment door. She didn't think she had slept. She didn't really want to sleep.

The phone rang, startling her into spilling more of the coffee. She gulped down what was left and placed the cup safely on the shelf behind the couch, listening to her recorded voice go through its message. It was Gord again, asking her to call him back to set up a time for an interview.

Lauren sighed and leaned her head against the cushions. She didn't want to be part of Gord Skinner's climb to the top. His enthusiasm over Nick's demise bothered her. And she was honest enough to realize that what really bothered her was the fact that she would be doing exactly the same thing if she'd been in Gord's position. She would have been tracking down Nick's family and friends, his boss, his co-workers on the force, getting background interviews, putting together a heart-wrenching story about an honest-to-goodness dead hero—

Closing her eyes, she thought of the first time she'd looked into Nick's face. Lord, he'd been an impressive man. And it hadn't only been his looks, although his features could have sent half of Hollywood into fits of envy. No, the most impressive thing about Nick Strada had been the energy that had simmered beneath the surface.

He'd been in such a hurry.

And now he was dead.

The newscast ended and was replaced by the cloyingly perky jingle of a fast-food chain. Lauren reached for the remote on the cushion beside her and turned off the set.

This couldn't be normal. It must be the aftermath of her brush with death. What else could explain the way Nick was affecting her? She'd known him for less than an hour before that plane had hit the lake. Who was he really? What was he?

No, she already knew what he was. Or what he had been. A cop. One who carried a switchblade in his boot.

The phone rang again. After the beep, Angela's voice drifted from the speaker. "Lauren, if you're there, please pick up."

Lauren stayed where she was and stared at the ceiling.

"All right, I hope you're sleeping and not down at the station," Angela continued. "I don't know whether you'd be up to it or not, considering what you've been through, so I wanted to talk to you about the shower next week.''

The bridal shower. Of course. And she hadn't even bought a gift yet. Because of her travel schedule she'd already needed to postpone the shower three times. With only two weeks remaining until the wedding, there was no way to postpone it again. Lauren grimaced.

''I'd understand if you decide not to hold it,'' she said. ''Take all the time you need to recover. Did anyone talk to you about trauma counseling? Anyway, call me when you can.'' There was a click and a soft whir as the machine reset.

Counseling? Lauren thought. What good would that do? She was healthy, she was alive. And all the problems she'd had before the crash were still there. All except Nick. But he wasn't really a problem, there hadn't been time for him to become one. He'd been a distraction. A restless, alpha male who had sent her pulse racing with nothing more than the touch of his knee against her thigh.

Rising stiffly, Lauren wandered toward the window. The rain that had started at dawn pattered listlessly against the glass, casting a pall over the room. Maybe she did need to talk to a professional. It definitely wasn't like her to become fixated on a stranger. Yet he'd become much more than a stranger, hadn't he? She'd saved his life. He had become her responsibility—

And now he was dead. They still hadn't found his body, but it was only a matter of time. She had to accept it. After all, his death had been documented and broadcast into millions of homes this morning.

Lauren turned her back on the window and walked over to the closet by the front door. She hesitated, then lifted her hand and touched Nick's jacket. The leather still wasn't completely dry, and it probably would have a few new cracks in it, but judging by the weathered, scraped condition, it had been through worse.

What kind of life had he lived? She knew so little about him. Who had the authorities finally notified? Who was his next of kin? Was there a Mrs. Strada? No, that much Gord had already told her.

Knowing it was verging on maudlin, Lauren carried the jacket back to the couch and sat down with it across her lap. She looked at the pocket that was in the left front lining, hesitated only briefly, then opened the zipper that had held it securely closed until now. Trying to convince herself that her curiosity wasn't abnormal, she slid her fingers inside.

Her nose wrinkled as dampness surrounded her hand. She touched something hard and pulled out a set of keys. Her lips curved in a sad smile. It figured. She'd lost the keys to her apartment, but it looked as if she'd found Nick's.

She reached into the pocket again and retrieved a soggy chocolate bar. Her smile broadened. That figured, too. A man with Nick's energy would enjoy sweet high-calorie snacks.

There was still something left in the bottom of the pocket. She felt around until she grasped several small, flat squares. When she saw what she had found, she gasped and dropped the packets on her lap.

Condoms. Five of them.

"Five," she muttered, shaking her head. Evidently his energy extended to all kinds of activities—

She stood up abruptly, scattering keys and condoms on the floor. This was sick. Really sick. The man was dead. If she didn't find something else to focus on, she might need to call the hospital about counseling, after all.

One hour later, Lauren locked her car and hurried through the rain to the modest brick apartment building. A quick check of the number showed that it matched the address she'd copied down from the phone book. She still didn't know what had made her come here. After she'd showered and dressed and done her hair, she'd had every intention of going down to the station to talk to Gord, then hitting the stores for a gift for Angela's bridal shower. Life went on. At least for some people.

Firming her jaw, she shoved her keys into her purse and pulled out the set she'd found in Nick's jacket. All right, her behavior was skirting the edge of normal, but there might be a perfectly reasonable explanation for her refusal to let go of Nick Strada. Maybe she needed closure. He was still too alive for her. Chances were his body wouldn't be recovered for days, so she had to find some way to put her brief contact with him to rest.

Before she could delve too deeply into her reasons for being here, Lauren moved toward the front entrance. She paused to study the names on the mailboxes. An odd feeling whispered through her stomach when she found Nick's and saw the stack of envelopes that showed through the slot. She glanced at the keys in her hand, knowing one of them would unlock the mailbox. Someone would eventually have to clear up all these loose ends, tie up the threads of his life that he'd left dangling.

But it wouldn't be her. She did best as an observer, not a participant. Sorting through the keys, she found the one that opened the lobby door and stepped inside.

Nick's apartment was on the third floor. After she climbed the stairs, her hands started to shake again before she could fit the key into the lock. Taking a deep breath, Lauren finally managed to unlock the door. With the tentative caution of someone trespassing in a tomb, she stepped over the threshold and closed the door behind her.

Had this been a good idea? Probably not. Instead of allowing her to put his memory away, being here was only serving to strengthen her impression of him. She knew it could only be her imagination, but his presence seemed to vibrate in the air around her.

She moved forward, struck by how well the apartment reflected its tenant…no, its former tenant. There was nothing fashionable about the big, sloppy furniture, but a man like Nick wouldn't have cared about appearances. The chocolate brown corduroy sofa looked deep and comfortable, perfectly suited to a large man. So was the maroon leather recliner. An inexplicable lump came to her throat when she noticed how the coffee table was buried beneath layers of empty pizza boxes and newspapers. Evidence of hurried meals eaten alone.

There was a large television across from the couch, along with a sound system and a stack of CDs. Lauren moved nearer, not really surprised when she saw that the majority of the music was country. There had probably been a bit of cowboy in him, after all.

Her gaze slid to the photograph that had been placed on top of one of the speakers. It was of Nick, a smiling, carefree Nick surrounded by a bevy of beautiful women. Lauren looked more closely. Women? Two of them didn't look much older than fifteen, their dark hair pulled back into identical ponytails. Were they friends? Family? Whoever they were, would they miss him?

Of course they would miss him. Nick was—no, had been—the kind of man who would make an impact on anyone he knew.

Telling herself she would leave in another minute, she walked through the archway to the kitchen. An open box of breakfast cereal, the sugar-frosted kind, shared space on the counter with an empty carton of orange juice. There was a pile of dishes in the sink and more on top of the fridge. Shaking her head, she turned around, stepping carefully over a pair of basketball shoes and a scuffed cowboy boot....

She blinked. Cowboy boot? Frowning, she glanced at it over her shoulder, then backed up to study it more thoroughly.

Yes, it was Nick's boot, all right. It was certainly large and beat-up enough. And it appeared to be almost the same as the one he'd stuffed that lethal-looking knife into last night. As a matter of fact, the pattern of the scuffed leather looked practically identical.

The hair at the back of her neck started to prickle. No. It couldn't be the same one. It was probably her imagination again, a reaction to recent trauma, her mind skirting too close to the edge. She knew that Nick and everything he wore was on the bottom of the lake. She and a few million other people had watched him slip under.

She really shouldn't have fed her obsession with him by coming here.

She should leave.

Still, Lauren bent down to take a closer look at the boot. At the first touch of her fingers, she knew it wasn't only her imagination. This leather was still wet.

"Nick?" She grasped the wall to steady herself and slowly straightened up. "Oh, my God! Nick, you're al—"

Before she could say the word aloud, a large hand clamped over her mouth. She was spun around, her back pressed against the wall.

The first thing she saw was a chest. A bare chest, with whorls of black hair spreading across taut skin that was darkened with purple bruises. She looked higher and saw broad shoulders, then a strong neck and a stubborn chin covered with bristling black stubble. Then a firmly compressed mouth. And lines at the edge of his lips that would probably deepen into dimples if he ever indulged in a genuine smile....

Feeling as if reality were slowly tilting, she raised her gaze.

And she found herself staring straight into an emphatically alive and extremely familiar pair of steel blue eyes.

Chapter 4

Nick clenched his jaw against the pounding in his head and blinked to clear his vision. How long had he been out? It had been well after midnight by the time he'd climbed the fire escape and pried open the bedroom window. He'd meant to stay only long enough to get dry clothes and his spare gun. He'd meant to be out of here by dawn.

The last thing he remembered, he'd been reaching for a bottle of aspirin. The next thing he'd known, it was daylight, and there was someone moving around in the apartment.

Someone? It was her. Lauren. The ice princess from the plane. The woman who had saved his life. The journalist who kept her cool while...

The journalist.

Between the throbbing reminders of his injuries and the feel of Lauren's body so close to his, his brain was frustratingly slow to function. Only one thought kept overriding the rest.

She could ruin everything.

Her breath warmed his palm as she attempted to speak. Her words were muffled, but it was clear what she was trying to say. Without loosening the arm he held across the front of her shoulders, he lifted his hand from her mouth.

"Nick!" Her lips trembled into a smile. "Nick, you're alive."

"What the *hell* are you doing here?"

Her smile dimmed. "I could ask you the same thing. I thought you had drowned. Thank God you're all right."

A wave of dizziness made him sway. He flattened his palm against the wall beside her head and leaned closer.

"Where have you been?" she went on. "How did you get home? I looked all over for you last night."

"You shouldn't have come here, Lauren."

"I couldn't stay away. Nick, everyone believes you're dead. When Gord showed me that tape—"

"What tape?"

"The one he shot from the helicopter. It showed you going under. I saw it. Everyone saw it."

"What do you mean, everyone?"

"It was broadcast this morning." Her chin trembled. "You have to—"

Her next words were smothered by his palm as he moved his hand back to her mouth.

He had to think. The plan had been a long shot, conceived in a crazy instant, but it had worked. He'd done it. He was officially dead. And if the drowning he had staged for that news camera had been broadcast this morning...

Morning?

"Damn," he muttered. "What time is it?"

She grasped his wrist and jerked his hand away from her mouth. "What's the matter with you? I'm not about to start screaming. Let me go."

Let her go? How could he do that, when one word from her would make the hell he'd gone through last night worthless? Frustrated, he dropped the arm that had been pinning her in place.

She didn't move away. Instead, she continued to look at him, almost as if she really cared.

But he couldn't afford to think that way. Too

much depended on him pulling this off. "How did you get in, Lauren?"

"I found your—" Sudden color tinged her porcelain cheeks. She looked away. "I found your keys in the pocket of your jacket."

"Why did you come here?"

"I wanted…to see where you lived."

"For your story? Checking out the dead cop's apartment? Hoping to find some little tidbit to add to your newscast?"

"It wasn't like that."

"Right."

"I thought you were dead, that you hadn't made it. I thought you were on the bottom of the lake. Why did you leave like that?"

"I decided to come home."

She looked at his forehead. "You shouldn't have left. You should have gone to the hospital. That cut—"

"I'm fine."

"No, you're not." She raised her hand to his head, her fingers cool against his skin. "You need help. This should be disinfected."

"I cleaned it up already."

"It needs stitches. Let me take you to a doctor."

"No." He pushed away from the wall and moved across the living room, aiming for the hallway that led to his bedroom. He only made it as far as the nearest chair, grabbing onto the back to steady himself while he took several deep breaths.

"Your knee's worse, isn't it?" Lauren asked, coming to his side. She maneuvered her shoulder under his arm, lending him her strength the same way she had done the night before. "You should get it X-rayed. It could be broken."

That thought had already occurred to him and had been dismissed. The joint was merely sprained, or he wouldn't have had the mobility that he did. Besides, it was his head that was hurting more than his knee. "I walked on it fine last night. I've had sprains before. It'll get better in a few days."

"Nick, you're in worse shape now than you were then. I'm calling an ambulance."

He straightened his spine, pulling away from her support. "No."

"I don't understand."

"No doctor. No ambulance. Isn't that clear enough?"

"But you need—"

"I need you to forget you came here. Forget you saw me."

"What?"

"I'm dead."

"Nick, you're not making sense."

"Thanks to your friend in the helicopter, the world thinks I'm dead. I intend to stay that way."

"The blow to your head must have made you disoriented. You're not thinking clearly."

"I'm not crazy, Lauren, despite rumors to the contrary."

"No, of course not, but—"

"It's not your concern."

"Yes, it is," she insisted. She moved in front of him, placing her hand on his chest. "You saved my life, and I saved yours. I can't simply walk away and leave you like this. You need help."

The touch of her palm on his skin scattered his thoughts once more. He glanced down, wanting her to keep touching him, knowing he shouldn't want her anywhere near him. "No."

"But you..." Her words trailed off as she spread her fingers over his heart. She was silent for a moment before she slowly lifted her gaze to his. Whatever emotion he'd thought he'd glimpsed in her eyes had given way to cool logic. She withdrew her hand. "Nick, what's going on?"

"It's not your concern," he repeated.

"I think it is."

"Go home, Lauren."

"Not until you tell me what's going on." Her voice firmed. "Why would you say that you intend to stay dead?"

He swore under his breath as he caught sight of the glowing numbers on the VCR clock. "I don't have time to play twenty questions with the press."

"Why, Nick?"

Stepping out of her reach, he lurched as far as the bedroom. With one hand on the wall to steady himself, he managed to walk to the closet and pull out the box with his spare gun. He shoved the revolver into the waistband of his jeans, then grabbed a clean shirt and shrugged it on.

Lauren paused in the bedroom doorway while she watched him. "On the flight, you were so anxious to reach Chicago that you looked ready to jump out of the plane. Why, Nick? Has it got something to do with why you don't want anyone to know you're still alive?"

Tightening his jaw, he looked around the floor for his boots.

"And if you almost drowned, how did you manage to get out of the lake by yourself?" she persisted. "The place was crawling with rescue crews. They should have spotted you."

He saw his left boot beside the bed and leaned down to pick it up, but another wave of dizziness made him sit down heavily on the edge of the mattress.

Lauren crossed the room and picked up the boot. "They would have spotted you, Nick, wouldn't they? Unless..." She paused. "Unless you were *trying* not to be found."

"Leave it alone, Lauren. This isn't part of your story."

"You deliberately faked it, didn't you," she said in awed disbelief. "My God. You played to the camera all along. You knew they were filming, that they'd get your presumed drowning on tape."

Scowling, he raked his hair off his forehead. "Interesting speculation, Ms. Abbot, but you don't have any proof."

"I'm talking to the proof right now. What kind of trouble are you in, Nick?"

"What makes you think I'm in trouble?"

"Don't insult my intelligence."

He made a motion to reach for the boot she held. When she extended her arm toward him, he grasped her wrist instead. "You can't tell anyone. Not yet."

"Gord is busy making his career on the story of your heroic death. It would be completely unethical for me to let him continue with this farce now that I know you're alive.''

''No one can know.'' He pulled her closer. ''Lauren, no one can know,'' he repeated. ''The safety of my family depends on it.''

She hesitated. ''Your family?''

There was really no choice, no other option open to him. He had to trust her. At least with this. ''The suspect in the case I'm working on has put out a contract on me. Threats to me I can handle, but he's also after my mother and sisters unless I quit the investigation. I intend to stay dead until I nail this guy.''

''And you'd never consider simply giving up, would you.''

It had been a statement, not a question, so he didn't bother to answer. ''If you reveal the truth, if you broadcast the fact that I'm alive, you'll be endangering the lives of my family.''

''Why should I believe you?''

He took his boot from her grasp and tossed it to the bed behind him. Clasping both her hands in his, he pulled her closer still until her legs nudged the inside of his thighs. ''I don't have time to explain it any further. I hadn't meant to stay here this long in the first place. You're just going to have to trust me.''

''Why should I trust you?''

"It's the other way around. As I see it, I've got a hell of a lot more to lose than you."

She was still hesitating, her thoughts unreadable behind her cool green gaze. Her hair was once more styled in a neat twist, so different from the lank strands that had dripped onto her shoulders last night. There was a faint bruise on her cheek, but otherwise she was as distant and composed as her TV image.

Yet he could feel her pulse beating frantically beneath his fingers, and awareness of her proximity and her feminine warmth tingled through his aching body. He did his best to ignore it. This was just another natural reaction, the same thing that had happened last night when he'd looked at her breasts. It was a consequence of his anxiety, or his adrenaline, nothing more.

He wouldn't *let* it be anything more.

"All right," she said finally. "I'll keep the truth to myself on one condition."

"What is it?"

"That you give me an exclusive on the story once you finish your investigation."

He should have known there'd be a business angle, that a woman like Lauren wouldn't let sentiment or trust rule her actions. "It's a deal."

She pulled her hands from his and stepped

back. "Fine. I'm going to want some more details."

"Later. Right now we'd better get moving."

"What?"

"I intended to be out of here before it got
light." He glanced at the rain that smeared the
bedroom window. "At least with this weather
there won't be many people out on the street."

"You're in no shape to go anywhere. You
can't even walk on your own."

Taking a deep breath, he reached behind him
for his boot. Spots danced in front of his eyes,
but he managed to jam his foot inside and push
himself upright. He gathered the notes that he'd
left on the bedside table, stuffed them into a
large envelope and slipped it inside his shirt. "I
got what I came back for. And I'm not going to
wait around here to see who else decides to drop
in."

"But where will you go?"

Good question. He limped across the room,
pausing to pick up his wet clothes and roll them
into a tight bundle. He needed a place to stay,
to recover his strength and to let his knee have
a chance to heal. But the more people who knew
about his deception, the more risk there was that
word might get back to Duxbury. Bracing his

hand on the door frame for balance, he looked at Lauren.

The solution was obvious. She wanted his story, he wanted somewhere to hide out where no one would think to look for him.

"Nick?"

"Did you bring a car?"

"Yes. It's parked out front."

"Do you live alone?"

"Yes, but what does that have to do with—"

"Have you seen my other boot?"

"It's in the kitchen."

He set his jaw against the pain and walked through his apartment, carefully gathering up any traces of his recent presence. He pulled on his second boot and tucked his knife safely into place beside his ankle, then put on a hooded sweatshirt.

Lauren followed him. "Nick, what are you going to do?"

"Can you bring your car around to the back of the building?" he asked, adjusting the hood so that it covered his forehead. "There's a steel door at the bottom of the fire escape that can't be seen from the street."

"I take it this is your way of asking me to drive you somewhere," she said, picking up a bloodied tissue from the counter between her thumb and forefinger.

He took the tissue from her and stuffed it into his pocket. "Right."

"Where do you want to go?"

"Your place."

She raised her eyebrows. "You're not serious."

"Do you want my story or not?"

"Of course, but I report the news, Nick. I'm not going to get personally involved in—"

"Too late," he said, slinging his arm across her shoulders. Using her to help him balance, he guided them both toward the front door. "You got involved the minute you sat beside me on that plane."

Lauren had never thought of her apartment as being small. It had only one bedroom, but it was large, bright and more than adequate for her needs. The white-tiled kitchen was a model of efficient design and was fully equipped with every labor-saving appliance. The teak dining table and chairs that occupied the space between the kitchen and the balcony window looked clean and uncluttered. And the rest of the main room, from the long, low couch to the teak-and-glass entertainment center and the grandfather clock in the corner, had always given an impression of spaciousness.

Yet from the moment Nick limped through her door, the place seemed to shrink.

It was because of that energy he had around him, that overwhelming presence she'd noticed from the first. Despite his weakened state, and the pain he was so obviously fighting, his vitality stirred a response in her, crowding her into awareness.

Of course, his physical size alone was enough to crowd anyone. Even without his boots he was at least two inches over six feet. She'd already felt his weight, so she knew he had to be close to two hundred pounds of solid muscle. And it was solid, all right. She'd suspected as much last night, and she'd seen it and felt it for herself this morning.

Oh, yes, she'd felt it. Touching his chest had been like running her fingers over living steel. Only his skin had been warm, and the black hair that had tickled her fingertips had been a silky, tempting swath that narrowed to a provocative line that disappeared invitingly beneath his waistband. He'd been swaying on his feet, unable to support his weight, so how could she have been thinking about where that line of silky hair might lead?

This wasn't like her, to fantasize about touching anyone. She wasn't a person normally comfortable with touching. Her concept of personal space tended to encompass a zone around her that kept most people at a safe distance. She wasn't at ease with casual contact like a pat on the shoulder, or a touch on the arm, or a passing kiss on the cheek. Under normal circumstances, she avoided anything other than a handshake.

Of course, these circumstances weren't anywhere near normal. And Nick Strada wasn't only intruding into her personal space, he had barged into her life.

He looked so out of place here in her cool beige-and-ivory living room, with his blue jeans and chambray shirt and the rough black stubble on his taut, square jaw. Even though he had barely had enough strength to pull off his hooded sweatshirt, cross the room and stretch out on the couch, he somehow still managed to dominate this once-sedate, familiar environment. He was exhausted and half conscious, but the masculine aura that surrounded him hadn't dimmed.

If anything, it had grown more intense the longer he'd been with her.

"All done?"

She jerked her hand away, and the tape she

had been smoothing into place on Nick's forehead stuck to her thumb. "Sorry. I'll be through in a minute."

Nick shifted on the couch, leaning his head back against the pillows she had propped behind him. "Just slap a Band-Aid on and forget it."

Lauren pulled her chair closer. Carefully repositioning the makeshift suture, she squeezed together the edges of the gash. "It'll heal better if it's closed."

"I thought you said you don't know much about first aid."

"I don't. This is common sense." She rubbed the ends of the tape gently to anchor them in place. "Even with this tape, the wound will probably scar, you know."

He lifted one shoulder in a careless shrug. "It'll match the other one."

Her gaze moved to the small crescent of white beside his left eye. "How did you get that?"

"I stepped into the middle of a turf war."

"What was it? Drug dealers? Gang members?"

"My sisters."

"Excuse me?"

"Dispute over a tree house when they were kids. I fell out." The lines beside his mouth deepened as he tightened his jaw. "God, I hope they're all right."

She thought of the photograph with the bevy of smiling women, and the connection clicked in her brain. "How many sisters do you have, Nick?"

"Four."

There had been five women in the photo. The eldest must have been his mother. "Do they all live in Chicago?"

"Yeah. Rose and Juanita share an apartment, but Barb and Tina still live at home with our mother."

"And your father?"

"He died. Are you almost finished?"

She recognized the distant tone in his voice. It was the same one she used herself when she didn't want anyone to get too personal.

A lock of dark brown hair fell across the bandage she'd placed on his forehead. Lauren felt an urge to stroke it back, to learn its texture and warmth, to rub it between her fingers. She drew in a shaky breath and dipped the glass wand back into the bottle of disinfectant. "Better take off your shirt."

"What?"

"If you have any scratches, they should be

disinfected, too. The water you were supposedly drowning in last night isn't exactly sterile.''

''I'm all right.''

''Better let me take a look.''

''Now you're sounding like my mother.''

''I assure you, Nick, I don't have a maternal bone in my body.''

His gaze flicked down and then up. A distinctly male gleam came into his eyes for a moment, like the glimpse of sunrise through a tightly drawn curtain. But then he set his jaw, braced his elbows against the couch and levered himself into a sitting position. He blinked and breathed in deeply a few times before he was able to start unfastening the buttons of his shirt.

She itched to help him, to brush his hands aside and ease those buttons through the washed-soft chambray herself. Instead, she went on with her questioning, as if this were a normal interview, as if she always spoke calmly to men who were undressing on her couch. ''Are the police providing your mother and sisters with any protection?''

He grunted. ''Not really. I told my family to stay out of sight until I finish the case I'm working on, but they won't be hiding now that they think I'm dead.''

''Why not?''

"They don't know all the details, but they do know the purpose of the contract was to get me off the case. My death supposedly did that, so my family should be safe."

"What kind of case is it that you're working on, Nick?"

"Homicide," he said curtly. "Hit and run."

"And you think you know who did it?"

"Absolutely. I was there. I looked the bastard right in the eye as he drove past."

"Sounds as if the case is solved."

"He reported his car was stolen and arranged for an alibi. His lawyers claim I was too... distraught. Yeah, that's the word they used. Too distraught to see clearly."

"Why would they say that?"

"Because it was my partner that he ran down."

"Your partner?"

He peeled off his shirt and dropped it to the floor. He held himself stiffly, as if combating the pain of movement as much as the pain of memory. "His name was Joey McMillan. We'd worked together for almost three years. He was a good man, saved my butt more than once. After some of the situations we'd been in, I never thought he'd go that way, getting hit by some suit in an eighty-thousand-dollar car."

"I'm sorry, Nick."

"Yeah, well, I intend to get the bastard. I know Joey would have done the same for me."

She lowered her gaze, and her next question escaped her. She knew she should be focusing on his injuries, keeping her distance, treating him with professional indifference, but, God, his chest was magnificent. From his broad shoulders to his washboard stomach, he was all leanly sculpted muscle. Taut skin over living steel. A strip of tempting, silky black hair leading to...

Clearing her throat, she concentrated on the mottled purple swelling on the side of his ribs. A jagged red scrape mark oozed across the center. "This is going to sting," she warned.

He didn't flinch as she tended to him. "It was a silver Jag," he went on. "Ran a red light, swerved onto the sidewalk to miss a truck and knocked Joey through a plate-glass window."

"Who was driving the car, Nick?"

He lifted his head to look at her, his jaw working for a moment. "Adam Duxbury."

The name shocked her back to complete alertness. "Adam *Duxbury?* Of Duxbury Enterprises?"

"I see you've heard of him."

"Heard of him? I did an item on him two months ago when he donated that building to the city for a homeless shelter. My God, are you sure?''

''I'm sure.''

''But if the car was traveling fast and you'd just seen your partner—''

''I'm sure, Lauren. As sure as I can see that your eyes are green, and that your hair is starting to slide out of that clip it's twisted into, I saw Adam Duxbury kill my partner.''

''But...'' She sat back, struck by the complete certainty of Nick's expression. ''He's on half the boards of directors in this city. There's talk of him running for Congress.''

''Doesn't change the fact that he's guilty of murder.''

''That's...unbelievable.''

''That's what he's counting on.''

''But—''

''Duxbury arranged an alibi even before Joey got to the hospital. One of his vice presidents, some guy named Kohl, swore they were having a business meeting right up until the time they drove together to a charity fund-raiser.''

Frowning, she placed a folded strip of gauze over the wound beneath his ribs and taped it into place. ''It's your word against theirs.''

''It is now. I'd been putting pressure on Kohl, trying to shake his story, and it was starting to pay off. He was getting nervous, called me up, said he wanted to change his statement, but he never showed up for the meeting we arranged.''

''What happened to him?''

''I found out that Duxbury had sent him to some emergency meeting in New York, so I followed him there.''

''So that's why you were in New York,'' she said. ''What happened?''

''I was too late. Within hours, Duxbury gave him a promotion, made him president of one of his subsidiary companies and transferred him to Buenos Aires.''

''And I assume Kohl is no longer willing to testify?''

''Right. The promotion came with a sudden case of amnesia.''

''But what if you're wrong, if the man really had been confused and if he was about to be promoted, anyway? And how could someone as well-respected as Duxbury have the connections to...to put out a contract on you and your family?''

''I don't know yet, but I intend to find out.''

''It's simply...incredible. I didn't find even a hint of anything shady when I researched Duxbury's background.''

''Maybe you didn't dig deep enough.''

"I know my job, Nick."

"And I know mine. You don't have to believe me. All I really need from you is your
silence." He looked at her, his jaw flexing, his
gaze hard with determination. "I can find somewhere else to stay."

"No," she said quickly, reaching out to grasp
his hand. "Don't leave. I..." She hesitated, dis-
turbed by the strength of her desire to keep him
here. "I still want your story. Whether or not
you're right about Duxbury doesn't change that.
You're Gord's dead hero, and I want to be the
one to break the news about your return."

"And getting the story is all that matters,
right?"

"Yes. Just like bringing your partner's killer
to justice is all that matters to you."

Beneath her fingers, his hand hardened into a
fist. "That about sums it up, doesn't it?"

"We'll both get what we want more easily if
you stay here."

"For how long, Lauren?"

"Until you're ready to end the hoax."

"You didn't sound too pleased with the idea
an hour ago."

"I've had a chance to think since then. It
doesn't make any sense for you to risk—" She
broke off, looking over her shoulder.

There was a quiet knock on the front door.

Nick sat forward, his body tensing. "Are you expecting someone?" he whispered.

She opened her mouth to reply just as there was a second knock, this one followed by a soft voice calling her name. She tightened her grip on Nick's hand and rose to her feet. "It's my sister."

"Will she go away?"

"Probably not. She has a key."

"Aw, hell," he muttered, using the coffee table and Lauren's help to haul himself upright. "This is already complicated enough. I can't let her see me."

Pulling his arm over her shoulders, she fitted herself against his side in a way that was becoming oddly familiar. She staggered as he leaned into her. "Can you make it to the bedroom?"

He limped forward slowly, his face draining of color. "I'll make it. Just point me the right way."

"Lauren?" Angela's voice was louder, more urgent. She knocked harder. "Lauren, are you all right?"

"I'm coming," she called. She hooked her fingers into the waistband of Nick's jeans and kept moving. "Just a minute."

They reached the bedroom doorway and stumbled through. Nick started to pull away from her, but Lauren hung on until she'd guided him as far as the bed.

"My shirt," Nick said, glancing behind them. "I left it on the floor."

"I'll get it later."

He took another step forward, but his foot caught the edge of the bedspread. Off balance, he fell across the mattress. Unable to release her hold on him fast enough, Lauren was dragged along with him.

At the feel of his big body stretched full length against hers, Lauren's thoughts scattered. His arm was still around her shoulders, pressing her to his bare chest. Even through her blouse and loose sweater she could feel his heat. Somehow her skirt had become hiked up and his good knee was wedged between her legs, denim rubbing intimately across her sensitive skin.

The embrace was entirely accidental. Meaningless. But somehow their bodies had molded together as naturally as if they were longtime lovers.

Her gaze met his, their faces so close together she could feel his breath on her cheek. Instant awareness flashed in his eyes, intense and unmistakable.

With a muttered curse, Nick lifted his arm away from her and rolled to his back. "Sorry," he mumbled. "Lost my balance."

Her pulse pounding, her face flushed with feelings too tangled to analyze, she pushed to her knees and slid backward off the bed.

Neither of them acknowledged what had just happened between them. Neither of them could. In the next instant, a key scraped into the lock of the front door.

Chapter 5

Lauren pulled the bedroom door closed behind her and raced for the living room. She reached the couch, snatching Nick's shirt from the floor and stuffing it behind a cushion just as her sister stepped into the apartment.

Angela tucked her keys back into her purse, a wobbly smile spreading across her face. Her hair, several shades darker than Lauren's and damp from the rain, corkscrewed loosely around her head. "Lauren." She draped her yellow raincoat on the closet doorknob and walked toward her. "I've been so worried. I had to come and see you for myself."

"I'm fine," she said, inhaling deeply a few times to catch her breath. "Sorry I didn't return your call yet, but…"

"No, no, I understand." She opened her arms and enclosed Lauren in a warm hug. "I should have come last night. No matter what you said, you shouldn't have to go through this alone."

Alone? Even though Nick was safely out of sight, she still felt his presence. "Thanks, Angela, but I'm really okay."

"That's what you always say, keeping things inside, trying to make out that nothing bothers you." She pulled back to look at her, concern shining in her eyes. "You look tired. You should be in bed."

"I don't think that would be a good idea right now."

"You're not going to work, are you?"

"Not for a while."

Angela glanced past her shoulder and stifled a gasp. "Oh, Lord. What's all that for?"

Lauren turned to follow her gaze and saw the first aid supplies she'd left on the coffee table. She thought quickly, deciding to bend the truth only slightly. "I lost my shoes in the crash. The soles of my feet got scratched from walking barefoot. It's nothing serious."

"Why don't you sit down and let me fix you some tea?" she offered.

From the corner of her eye Lauren spotted the edge of a blue chambray cuff between two ivory cushions. She sat down, poking it back out of sight. "Thanks, Angela."

Her sister smiled and walked to the kitchen.

Lauren used the opportunity to do a more thorough check of the living room. She'd already put Nick's sweatshirt in her closet and his bundle of wet clothes in her laundry hamper, so apart from the envelope of notes that he'd dropped on the dining table, there wasn't anything in sight. She gathered up the bandages and disinfectant, storing everything neatly in a clear plastic box, then straightened the coffee table and returned to sit on the couch. She lifted her hand to smooth back the hair that had slipped out of its clip and realized with chagrin that her fingers were trembling.

This was crazy. How could she possibly think she could participate in Nick's deception? How was she supposed to sit here calmly and listen to her sister rattle teacups while a half-naked man was hiding in her bedroom?

Her pulse still hadn't returned to normal. And she knew her agitation was due as much to the situation as to the lingering feel of Nick's body against hers.

Not exactly her usual uninvolved, detached way of dealing with life, was it?

Unlike Lauren, Angela probably wouldn't

have any trouble dealing with a man like Nick. She wouldn't be awkward about putting on a bandage or helping him into bed. His vibrant male energy wouldn't send her scrambling for the safety of professional objectivity. And before she'd met Eddy, Angela certainly wouldn't be fighting the tug of Nick's pheromones.

Somehow, even though she and her sister had grown up in the same household, the bleak circumstances of their childhood had affected them in completely different ways. Lauren had been eight when their father had left, and she'd coped with the aftermath by withdrawing behind a defensive wall. Angela, three years younger, had done the opposite, becoming more outgoing and eager to please, constant-ly seeking the affection that was denied them.

By the time they were adults, the pattern had been firmly established. Lauren still preferred to distance herself from emotions and from the risk of involvement. Except for that one time, six years ago...

"Lauren, do you have company?"

At the sudden question, Lauren turned to look at her sister, forcing herself to resist the urge to glance toward the bedroom. "What makes you ask that?"

"I couldn't help noticing this. It isn't yours,

is it?'' she asked, Nick's leather jacket dangling from her hand.

''Oh.'' Lauren had left it draped over one of the kitchen chairs. She crossed the room and took it from Angela. ''No, it isn't mine. It belongs...'' She hesitated. ''It belonged to the man who sat beside me on the plane. He gave it to me to hold for him while he went back into the lake.''

''Oh, my Lord. Not that policeman who drowned trying to save those other people?''

''I take it you saw Gord's story?''

''At least half the country has by now. It's so tragic. That poor man must have been such a kind, noble person, to sacrifice his life that way.''

Her conscience stirred at the lie she was helping to perpetuate. Kind and noble? Nick? Unable to reply, she carried the jacket to the closet and hung it up. Her fingers brushed over the lining, and she remembered those small, square packages she'd found in the pocket that morning. With disbelief she felt another flush spread over her cheeks.

Ridiculous. She was thirty years old, well acquainted with the facts of life. Considering the story about Duxbury that Nick had just told her, she had far more important things to worry about than a handful of condoms.

Unwilling to let the conversation, or her thoughts, continue along this track, she joined her sister on the couch and deliberately changed the subject.

It wasn't much of an improvement. Now that she was reassured about Lauren's condition, it didn't take long for Angela to bring up the very subject her sister had been doing her best to avoid facing.

The wedding.

The bridal shower. The dress fitting. The hall, the caterers, the flowers.

Life went on. Even when she was sitting on a "dead" man's clothes, the ordinary details of life went on.

Lauren felt like tipping back her head, opening her mouth wide and letting loose with a good old-fashioned therapeutic scream. Instead, she lifted her cup and drank her herbal tea.

The feminine voices that drifted through the bedroom door were faint. Nick held himself motionless, straining to hear what Lauren was saying. He could distinguish no more than a word here and there, snatches of disconnected phrases, but so far the conversation seemed to be centering on someone's wedding.

Good. She wasn't panicking. From the sound of it, she was behaving normally. That was a far smarter way to handle things than trying to rush her sister out of here.

He felt his muscles cramping and flexed his leg. Pain stabbed outward from his knee, and he ground his teeth in frustration. It hadn't felt too bad while he'd been stretched out on Lauren's couch, but he knew from past experience with sprains that it would be several days before he could hope to move normally.

At least the headache had mellowed from a screeching ache to a rumbling throb. As long as he took things easy for a few more days...

Damn, he hated having to wait. All he'd done so far was to buy time. And it was rapidly being used up.

So far Lauren seemed to be cooperating with him, yet he wasn't completely comfortable about trusting her. He didn't know whether or not she believed him, but as she'd said, it didn't make any difference. She'd get her story, one way or another.

She could prove to be a valuable ally. She was one cool lady, keeping whatever thoughts she had safely concealed behind those gorgeous green eyes. There had been countless opportunities for her to give him away, yet she hadn't. Still, he'd hate to meet up with her in a poker game.

He wouldn't mind meeting up with her in a bed, though. Preferably when he was in better shape than this.

He scowled, but the memory of their awkward tumble across the mattress refused to go away. He might be officially dead, but he wasn't *that* dead.

Moving carefully so that the springs didn't creak, he rolled to his side. The bed had a brass frame, but instead of fussy scrolls and curlicues, the headboard was composed of two long, sedately curving rails. The bedspread he was lying on was green and slippery, smooth satin instead of ruffles or lace. It was elegant and sensual at the same time. Kind of like Lauren.

This place was nothing like his, he thought, letting his gaze roam over the shadowed room. Neatly framed prints of restful, civilized landscapes decorated the walls. A spotless ivory carpet stretched across the floor to the long, lacquered oak dresser. The top of the dresser was bare, except for a small jewelry box and a low dish that sprouted silk flowers.

There wasn't a dust ball or a stray sock in sight.

Nick smoothed his palm over the bedspread. His large, tanned hand looked rough, out of place. What would it look like smoothing over Lauren's thigh?

He curled his fingers into his palm and moved his gaze to the corner of the room. Beside the window there was an L-shaped desk. It was the same lacquered oak as the dresser, but it didn't hold any feminine touches like flowers or jewelry boxes. It held a computer.

What kind of woman kept a computer in her bedroom? Probably one who wouldn't want anyone like him feeling her satin bedspread or her thigh.

She could ruin everything.

He eased onto his back, and the rumbling throb in his head crested sharply, forcing him to close his eyes against the pain. Through the door the murmur of feminine voices seemed more distant.

Getting Duxbury. Getting justice. That's all he wanted. That's all he could allow himself to want.

Lauren nibbled at a wedge of cantaloupe as she spread out the Sunday paper. More than a day had passed, yet the front page was still filled with news of the crash and photos of mangled wreckage. Two of the survivors who had been listed as critical had died. More bodies had been recovered from the lake yesterday, bringing the number of missing down to twelve.

Chicago was in mourning. All the flags in the city had been flown at half-mast since yesterday and would remain that way until the memorial service that was scheduled for next week. It was still too early for anyone to know for certain what caused the crash, but most speculation pointed to mechanical failure. Aviation experts were arriving from all over the world, as much to find the cause of the tragedy as to explain why it had been possible for anyone to survive.

A sense of unreality stole over her as she read the headlines and scanned the photographs. Sitting at her dining room table, with her coffee cup by her elbow and the ordinary, Sunday sound of church bells in the distance, she almost might have been able to convince herself that she hadn't really been there.

But then she turned the page.

A face stared at her from the top left-hand corner. It was the same as the face on the man who was sitting on the other side of the table.

Well, not exactly the same. The picture must

be a few years old. It showed Nick in his uniform, clean shaven, with his hair short and neatly combed. Although he wasn't smiling, he didn't appear as hard or as…dangerous as he did now.

Biting off another chunk of cantaloupe, she looked up. Despite the fatigue that lingered in his eyes, he indeed looked dangerous. He wore his crumpled shirt open at the throat and rolled up at the sleeves, revealing the lean muscles of his forearms. The stubble that had prickled over his jaw had darkened, emphasizing the deep lines beside his mouth. He'd finger-combed his hair with casual indifference. One dark, sleep-tousled wave fell across the bandage on his forehead. On another man, that rebellious hair might have looked boyish. On him, it looked… tempting.

And Lauren couldn't stop thinking that he'd spent the night in her bed.

Not that she'd had much choice in the matter. By the time Angela had left, he was already asleep. Lauren had decided not to disturb him—considering the way he'd been pushing himself since the crash, she thought that he needed rest more than anything else. So she'd covered him with a blanket and done what she could to make sure he was comfortable.

Throughout the rest of the afternoon and evening she'd checked on him frequently, and to her relief he'd shown no signs of growing feverish and had seemed to be sleeping normally. He'd roused enough around midnight to drink some fruit juice, but he'd dozed off again almost immediately. She'd tucked an extra blanket around him, taken her clothes and spare bedding to the living room and had done her best to sleep on the couch.

Not that she'd been able to sleep.

She sipped her coffee and tapped her nail against the newsprint in front of her. "You made the paper, Nick."

He reached out to slide the paper toward him, taking a minute to scan the article. "Still missing and presumed dead," he said. "Good. Even if he never watches TV, Duxbury's bound to see this."

"Probably. It looks as if the papers were quick to pick up on Gord's story. Dead heroes make good copy."

"I'm no hero," he muttered.

She watched him read in silence for a while, wondering whether he was right. She now knew that the dramatic rescue work he'd done had been deliberately staged to draw attention to himself so the camera would capture his drowning. Not a very heroic kind of motivation.

And yet he could have staged his drowning earlier. He hadn't needed to keep helping until the rescuers had arrived. The longer he'd kept it up, the more chance there had been that the camera would move to some other scene.

And there were his reasons for putting himself through all this in the first place, for ignoring his injuries and driving himself to exhaustion. He was pursuing justice and protecting his family.

As motivations went, those were far nobler than her own.

Yes, well, some people were more suited to making the news, others preferred simply to report it.

"I'll be going down to the station later this morning," she said, "but only if you think you'll be all right here on your own."

He looked up quickly, then tightened his jaw and breathed hard through his nose.

After almost a day with him, she recognized the signs of pain. "How's your head?" she asked.

"Getting better, as long as I don't move too fast. Why are you going to work? On the plane you told me you had the weekend off."

"Gord wants to interview me."

"What are you going to tell him?"

"I won't lie. I just won't tell him the entire truth."

He grunted. "I bet you're good at poker."

"I prefer chess."

"Yeah. I should have guessed."

"Why?"

"You strike me as the type of person who would like a cool, sophisticated game. Something intellectual."

"And, of course, you'd prefer poker. Something fast-paced and risky."

"Depends on the stakes. Not much point gambling unless the stakes are worthwhile."

"I suppose one could say that about anything." She took the paper back from him and stacked the different sections into a neat pile. "While I'm at the station, I thought I'd pull all the background material I gathered for the Duxbury story. It might be useful to you."

"Does this mean that you believe what I told you about him?"

Did she? Part of her wanted very much to believe. Yet that part had very little to do with the logic she preferred to rely on. "Let's just say I'm keeping an open mind."

"Thanks, that's all I need." He lifted his

steaming mug from the table in front of him. "And thanks for the blanket last night. I didn't mean to take over your bed. I'll use the couch tonight."

"You're too tall for the couch."

"I'll manage, as long as you don't have any more surprise visitors who have their own keys." He swallowed a mouthful of coffee, propped his elbows on the table and gazed at her over the rim of the cup. "Anyone besides your sister who has keys?"

"No."

"What about a boyfriend?"

"No."

"You mean no boyfriend, or no boyfriend with keys?"

"What difference would it make?"

"I don't know how long I'm going to be staying here. I wouldn't want to cramp your love life."

What love life? she thought wryly. "That won't be a problem."

"So it wasn't your wedding you were discussing yesterday?"

She fiddled with the plate of cantaloupe, nudging the slices until they were all neatly aligned. "No, it was my sister's. I'd planned to hold a bridal shower for her here next Friday.

I'd hate to disappoint her by canceling altogether, so I'll try to find somewhere else—''

''No, don't change your plans. We'll work something out. Maybe I'll get lucky and this'll be over by then.''

''Yes, maybe.''

He drummed the fingers of one hand against his coffee cup. ''I noticed a computer in your bedroom. Do you subscribe to any of those information networks?''

''Several. Why? Did you want to use it?''

''Yeah. You mind?''

''Not at all. I often work at home and use my computer to do research.''

''I don't know if I'll be able to find anything useful, but I hate sitting around doing nothing. It's not my style.''

''From what I've seen of your style so far, I can believe that.''

One corner of his mouth lifted. ''Yeah. I've always been a hands-on kind of guy.''

She looked at his lips, intrigued by the way that tiny half smile softened his expression. ''Getting your death broadcast has its drawbacks, doesn't it? Now that your face has been so well publicized, you won't be able to show it.''

"That won't stop me. Once I can get around better, I'll come up with something."

"Mmm. I don't doubt it. I've noticed you have a flair for improvisation."

His smile spread to his eyes, crinkling the tiny lines at the corners. "Considering what we've gone through in the past two days, you're no slouch yourself."

Lauren shook her head. He was mistaken. She wasn't comfortable unless she had a script or a TelePrompTer to follow. "It's only been a day and a half. And I already told you, I merely report the news. I don't—"

"You don't get involved. Yeah, you keep telling me that, but so far you're in it up to your elegant little chin."

"These are exceptional circumstances." She pushed the plate of fruit across the table toward him. "Here, have some breakfast."

He moved his head back, his nostrils flaring. "No, thanks."

"If your headache is bad enough to make you nauseous—"

"It isn't," he said, eyeing the plate warily.

An image of his cluttered kitchen came back to her and her lips twitched. "Ah. It's not the headache, it's the menu."

"I don't want to seem ungrateful for everything you're doing, but..."

"Sorry, I don't have any Frosted Flakes or the kind of cereal that comes with prizes in the box."

"No jelly doughnuts?"

"I'm all out. How about a rice cake?"

"Only if it's got chocolate icing."

"The cantaloupe's better for you."

"Uh..."

"Yogurt?"

"Are you on a diet or something?"

"No. I just prefer light foods." She pushed her chair back and stood up. "How about some granola?"

"I'll get it myself," he said. He leaned over to grasp his left leg, which he'd propped on the chair beside him. "I don't expect you to wait on me."

"Stay there." She stopped beside him and put her hand on his shoulder. "The less you use that knee, the faster you'll recover."

He looked up, a touch of humor softening his gaze. "Having to go without jelly doughnuts is a great incentive to recovery, believe me."

"As much as it goes against my principles, I'll pick up a box on my way home from the station."

"Keep a list. When this is all over, I'll reimburse you."

"Don't bother. I'll claim it on my expense account."

He lifted his hand, his fingers grazing her cheek. "This is going to show up on camera."

"What?"

"You bruised your cheek when you fell against my leg before the crash. Does it still hurt?"

"Compared to the rest of my bruises, that's nothing."

"I never saw the rest of your bruises."

"They're not nearly as bad as yours." She felt the warmth of his shoulder through his shirt and slowly splayed her fingers. "Besides, they already took care of it at the hospital."

"You never know." He lowered his hand slowly, tracing a gentle path along her jaw to her throat. "Maybe you should take off your blouse and let me check you over."

It happened too fast, too unexpectedly. She didn't have a chance to control her reaction to his teasing suggestion. Her throat went dry as heat tingled across her skin. What would it be like, to stand here in the sober light of morning and unbutton her blouse in front of him? How would it feel, to part the silk over her breasts and feel his gaze on her body?

His head was tipped back, his face close enough for her to see awareness kindle in his eyes. It was the same as the day before, that timeless moment on her bed. He'd been the one to pull away then.

This time it was up to her. Crossing her arms in front of her, she stepped back. "That's not funny."

He dropped his hand to his side. The smile that had been playing at the corners of his lips disappeared. "Sorry. No offense meant. Must have been the blow to my head."

She took another step back, then stopped herself, annoyed with her urge to retreat. She was even more annoyed by her desire to return to his side and have him touch her once more. "I think we'd better get a few things straight, Nick. Despite the circumstances that have thrown us together, our relationship is basically a professional one."

"I already know that."

"Don't confuse my concern for your welfare with anything more personal."

"There's not much risk of that, Lauren. You've made yourself perfectly clear." He swung his leg to the floor, grasped the edge of the table and rose to his feet.

"You have to admit that our situation here could get awkward if we..."

He towered over her, his gaze hard and intense. "If we what? Were friendly to each other? Shared a laugh or two?"

"If you're saying I misunderstood your comment—"

"No, you didn't misunderstand me at all. I'm a normal man. And I'm not ashamed to admit I'd like to see what you look like underneath your clothes."

The room started to shrink again. She held up her hand. "Maybe we've said enough."

"Just because I've noticed you're a woman doesn't mean anything except that my senses are functioning as they're meant to."

"If that's supposed to be a compliment..."

"It's simply the truth. It's no big deal, no need to panic."

"I don't panic. You know that."

"Hell, Lauren, I've got a price on my head, a family to protect and a murderer to catch. Do you really think I don't have enough sense or self-control to remember that?" He took a step back. "I'm not about to screw up my only chance to get out of this by messing around with you.''

''That's putting it bluntly.''

''No one's ever accused me of being a diplomat.''

''No, I don't imagine they would.''

He raked his fingers through his hair in a quick, frustrated movement, then lurched sideways, catching on to the back of a chair to steady himself.

Remorse flooded over her as she watched him struggle to stay upright. She automatically took a step toward him, but he had already turned away. With one hand on the wall for balance, he limped toward the bedroom. A minute later, the soft hum and muted beeps from her computer drifted through the doorway.

Lauren had a sudden urge to go to him and say something, anything, that would ease the tension that had sprung up between them.

But this was for the best. If they were going to make this arrangement work, they had to get the ground rules straight early on. Despite his weakened condition, he was still the same alpha male she'd first tried to keep her distance from on the plane, still the same fascinating, compelling...

What a hypocrite she was becoming. It wasn't his suggestive remark that had sent her scurrying back behind her professional barricades, it was her own reaction to it.

Chapter 6

The set for the Channel 10 morning program was usually deserted on Sundays, so it hadn't been difficult for Gord to wheedle its use as a backdrop. Lauren settled on one of the chairs that had been placed in front of the mural of the Chicago skyline. Activity hummed around her as the crew checked the lighting and sound levels. She had watched these preparations countless times, knew the sequence of events and felt secure in the familiar environment. It felt good to be here—work was just what she needed.

"Are you ready?" Gord asked. In keeping with his rise in status, he wore a suit instead of his usual ripped jeans and sneakers. He straightened the knot of his tie as he took the chair across from her.

She glanced at the cameras that were moving into place. "Of course."

"Hey, I really appreciate your coming down here like this. I know this must be tough."

"Work is the best thing for me, Gord."

"I'm sorry about your friend."

"Mmm?"

"The cop, Lieutenant Strada."

"We barely knew each other," she said, dipping her head to adjust the microphone that was clipped to her lapel.

"You seemed pretty upset when you saw the tape."

"Naturally. It was a tragic story."

He leaned closer, his gaze keen. "You look like hell, Lauren. Haven't you slept since Friday?"

"Not much. And I look like this because someone told Chuck to go easy on the makeup so I didn't look too healthy. Know anything about that, Gord?"

He pushed at the knot of his tie again. "I thought it would add credibility to the interview, get the viewers to sympathize with you instead of seeing you as Lauren Abbot, newswoman." He said the last words in a deep, resonant voice, then grinned.

"Why don't we go over the questions while

we're waiting," she said, gesturing toward the papers on his lap.

"Don't worry about it. I'll be asking a lot of the same stuff I did after the crash, except I'll be using a different slant. You know, concentrating on how you sat beside Strada and all that."

"I understand."

"I'm not going to do much with the way you pulled our boy out of the lake after the impact, though. Too many dramatic rescue stories would divert attention from the hero."

"Oh, I understand that, too, Gord," she said, recognizing the calculating light in his eyes. Not only did he want to scoop her on the story, he wanted to make sure she didn't become too big a part of it.

If he'd tried that at any other time, she wouldn't let him get away with it. But staying in the background was to her advantage. The smaller the part she played in this now, the easier it was going to be when she revealed the truth.

She fought down a stab of conscience over what she was doing. Professional ethics weren't as important as the safety of Nick's family.

"I'm putting together a half-hour special," Gord said. "I'll be building it around the tape I shot from the chopper. They're giving me a time slot the evening of the memorial service. It's going to be great.''

''The service?''

''The time slot. Clips of the memorial service are bound to make the network news shows.'' He leaned forward, his face shining with enthusiasm. ''They'll probably pick up some of my special, too.''

''How nice.''

''And it's all because of our boy. He really was a hero, Lauren. All the cops who worked with him couldn't praise him enough. Tough, stubborn, completely devoted to the force. He had a reputation for being a loose cannon at times, but he got results.''

''So he was good at his job?''

''He was thirty-one and on his way to becoming a legend.''

''He sounds too good to be true, Gord. Are you sure you don't want to take a little more time with your research?''

''Oh, there's no lack of material about his exploits on the force. His personal life's still a bit sketchy. I haven't been able to contact the wife—''

''Wife? I thought you said he wasn't married.''

"Ex-wife, I mean. Been divorced for almost four years. The last anyone heard, she was re-married and living on the West Coast. From all accounts, he was too busy with his job to have any serious girlfriends. Too bad."

"Some people don't mind living alone, Gord."

"No, I mean it's too bad there's no grieving lover to interview. With the way he looked, I would have thought he'd have a whole string of women after him."

She wouldn't let herself think about his sex life. She wouldn't.

"I'm still trying to arrange a meeting with his family," he continued. "Never ran into such a stubborn bunch of women."

"Take it easy with them," she said. "They'll be going through a difficult enough time as it is, with his death being so public. You shouldn't intrude on their misery."

Gord shot her an incredulous look. "Hey, that's the nature of our job, remember? Chances like this don't last for long. It'll be over before I know it."

Yes, it would be over before he knew it, she thought, dodging yet another stab of conscience. For the most part, Gord was bringing this on himself by being so eager to cash in on someone's death. Still, Nick had better be right about the need for this hoax.

There was a flurry of movement on the edge of Lauren's vision. She turned her head in time to see Victoria Sandowsky, the station manager, walk into the studio. Victoria had met her when she'd first arrived, expressing her concern that Lauren might be returning to work too soon and suggesting she take a few days off.

Of course, Lauren had declined the offer. Even if she wasn't mixed up with Nick, she would be keeping herself busy with her job. She watched Victoria confer quietly with the news director before they were joined by a stocky, white-haired man.

It took a few seconds for his identity to register. When it did, a tight knot settled in her stomach. Her fingers curled around the arms of her chair. "Gord, what is Adam Duxbury doing here?"

He swiveled to look around. "He came? Terrific."

"Why is he here?"

"He's on the committee that's organizing the memorial service, so he's helping us coordinate the news coverage."

"Isn't that a little...odd? He's only a businessman."

Gord slid to the edge of his chair and leaned over to speak quietly into Lauren's ear. "If you ask me, he's using this for free publicity. There are rumors he wants to run for mayor."

"I heard it was Congress," she replied, the knot in her stomach tightening as she watched Duxbury's progress across the studio.

He was wearing a baby blue golf shirt underneath his navy blazer, the top button open at the base of his thick neck. He had the build of a bulldog and the face of a beardless Santa Claus. His smiles were appropriately solemn as he greeted the people who recognized him, yet his eyes were always busy assessing, weighing, observing, as if he were hiding something....

She folded her hands in her lap, forcing herself back into the role of objective observer. She was letting what Nick had told her influence her view of Duxbury. Although she hadn't particularly liked him when she'd met him two months ago, there was nothing overtly offensive about him. There was no crime in being a shrewd businessman, and no one could fault him for his willingness to do his civic duty.

The overhead lights came on with a hollow click, and the cameras started to roll. Gord conducted the interview according to a carefully charted agenda. As he'd said he would, he concentrated mostly on her brief contact with the doomed hero. Lauren held tightly to her composure as he asked his questions, all the time acutely conscious of Duxbury hovering in the shadows, listening to every word.

By the time it was over, she hadn't revealed anything that wasn't already common knowledge. Gord took off his microphone and thanked her heartily before he strode over to greet Duxbury. They spoke for a few minutes, then left the studio together.

It wasn't until an hour later that Lauren saw them again. She was on her way to her office and was passing by one of the editing bays when something made her glance inside.

There wasn't much visible on the small screen that was flickering in front of the desk, yet the scene was as readily identifiable as the two men who were watching it. For some reason, Gord was showing Duxbury the unedited tape that had been shot at the crash site.

There were a number of legitimate reasons for an ambitious businessman to get involved in planning the memorial service for the victims of the plane crash. But was it only coincidence that by making contact with the newsman who had recorded Nick's death, Adam Duxbury would be in an excellent position to verify it?

* * *

Nick scribbled a note on the back of another computer printout and dropped the page on top of the others that littered the floor around the coffee table. He'd been at this for three days now, and he was growing more impatient with every word he read.

There hadn't been any lack of material to start with, thanks to Lauren. She had brought home the files on Duxbury that she'd had in her office and had dug up a little more each day. Coupled with the notes he'd brought from his apartment and what he'd been able to obtain with some discreet hacking, they now had a dossier that any intelligence agency would be proud of.

Duxbury wasn't the man he tried so hard to appear to be. While there was no disputing his shrewdness when it came to finances, there were deals buried deep under the cover of subsidiary companies and corporate restructuring that skirted the edge of illegal. Bernie, the nervous messenger in New York, had held a job in a restaurant Duxbury once owned, an unprofitable restaurant that happened to burn down. There were whispers of other shady associations and back-alley connections, too, so Duxbury wouldn't have had much trouble arranging that contract on Nick and his family.

Yet for the past several years Duxbury's dealings had been above reproach, ever since his marriage to the only daughter of Theodore Van Ness.

It was because of his wife's family name—and old family money—that Duxbury first gained entry to the city's elite. He'd joined all the right clubs, given to all the right charities and had hired an image consultant in his campaign to reinvent himself.

Despite the mounting number of facts, there was still nothing that proved he was a killer, no scrap of information that could tie him to the place and time when Joey had been run down. So after three days of sitting around here and accumulating information, Nick still had nothing he could use.

He scowled, stretching his arms along the back of the couch as he turned his head to look at Lauren. She was sitting at the dining table on the other side of the room, an open notebook in front of her.

Ever since Sunday morning, they'd done their best to keep out of each other's way. She spent her days down at the TV station, and when she was here, most of their conversation was limited to topics like Duxbury or this charade they were carrying on. They were careful not to touch on anything too personal. As a matter of fact, they were careful not to touch at all. And that should have been fine with him. He had good reasons for keeping away from her—she still had the power to expose him at any time.

And yet more often than he'd like to admit, he found himself thinking about her.

She continued to be as politely aloof as ever, but yesterday she'd loosened up enough to buy doughnuts, the jelly-filled, rolled-in-sugar kind. She hadn't objected to his insistence on sharing the cooking, either. Instead, she'd drawn up a schedule to divide the duties fairly. Sure, she was a stickler for neatness, and a canary would have a hard time living on the kind of stuff she preferred to eat, but underneath the silk and pearls, she was a lot more human than she wanted to let on.

Lauren reached for a ruler and drew a line through something on the page in front of her, made a precise little check mark, then turned to the next page.

He glanced at his own crumpled papers and haphazard piles of notes and grimaced. "Find out anything new today?"

"Mmm?" she answered absently.

"I asked if you found anything new."

She capped her pen and set it down beside

the notebook before she looked up. "Nothing useful."

"Let me be the judge of that. What is it?"

"I was checking out the society pages and learned that the Duxburys always spend Sunday afternoons at the Van Ness estate."

"You're right. That's no use." He drummed his fingers against the cushions. "Damn, this is going too slow. We're getting buried in trivia."

"Maybe I could try contacting that man who went to South America. Kohl, wasn't it?"

"It wouldn't do any good. Besides, I don't want word getting back to Duxbury that you're snooping around."

"I prefer to call it background research."

"Whatever."

She shot a glance at the mound of crumpled printouts beside the couch, then returned her attention to her notebook, uncapping her pen again to print a neat little note in the margin. "It might help if you let me organize the information you have. It's probably difficult to keep track of things when they're spread over half the living room floor."

"No, thanks. I can keep track of things just fine," he said. Pulling his left leg off the coffee table, he pushed himself to his feet and hobbled across the room. He opened the glass door that enclosed her sound system and changed the radio to a country station.

Lauren shook her head without looking up and made another check mark. "I thought we agreed to take turns, Nick. It's your choice tomorrow."

Muttering an oath under his breath, he returned the tuner to where it had been. Their taste in food wasn't the only thing they differed on. Naturally, she had made up a schedule for this, too. As the refined sounds of a jazz quartet drifted from the speakers, he limped to the dining table and pulled out the chair across from Lauren.

This time she did look up. "Your mobility seems to be improving. How's the knee today?"

He reversed the chair so that he could straddle it as he sat down, stretching his bad leg out beneath the table. "Getting better. The swelling's finally starting to go down."

"That's good."

"Yeah," he said, tapping his fingers against the chair back. "Another day or two and I should be able to walk farther than across a room."

"Your headache hasn't come back, has it?"

"No."

She leaned forward, focusing on his forehead.

''That cut's healing well. There's no sign of infection.''

''Thanks to you.''

''I'd say it has more to do with your natural recuperative powers. You're really an exceptional man, Nick, considering the shape you were in a few days ago.'' She paused, then drew back and dropped her gaze to the table as if regretting the compliment.

Don't confuse my concern for your welfare.... Nick's frown deepened. Simply because she'd proven to be attuned to every spasm of pain and each small sign of recovery he'd experienced didn't mean anything. She was a professional observer, right?

''I know you must be losing patience with our lack of progress,'' Lauren said. ''Tomorrow I should have more information about Duxbury's real estate holdings. If wc could find something that might have brought him to the neighborhood where the accident happened, we'll have a point to work back from.''

''Good idea. I appreciate the help.''

She waved a hand in dismissal and underlined a word in her notebook. ''It's for my story.''

The music on the radio changed to a complicated piano solo, and Nick realized he was tapping his fingers in time to the rhythm. Was he

starting to get used to this stuff? "Mind if I ask
you a question, Lauren?"

"Mmm?"

"When did you start believing me?"

"What do you mean?"

"About Duxbury. You said it yourself. You'll
get your story whether I'm right or not, but
you've been knocking yourself out trying to
help me."

She paused. "I don't like basing my opinions
on a hunch, so I'm not counting the way Duxbury makes me uneasy. But the way he's been
ingratiating himself with Gord and taking such
an interest in your fate is definitely suspicious.
Now that I know more about the type of man
he really is, your story is more plausible."

"And that's it?"

"Well, I've heard you have a reputation for
integrity with your colleagues on the police
force."

"Those are all very logical reasons."

"I prefer chess to poker," she said, her lips
softening into the hint of a smile. "Besides, I'm
not really knocking myself out to help you. I'm
working the way I always do."

He gestured toward her open notebook. "Do
you always work in the evening?"

"This?" She shook her head. "This is my list

of wedding details. I was just crossing out what my sister and I have already done.''

''*Wedding* details?''

She flipped back a few pages and started to read off points. ''Choose bouquets and boutonnieres. Order flowers for the church. Check the menu with caterer. Change color scheme of decorations. Arrange limo—''

''Whoa. Enough. Why not throw some beers on ice and invite everyone for a barbecue?''

''Angela's a romantic. She wants the whole fairy tale.''

''You don't seem too enthusiastic about it.''

''I'm not particularly fond of weddings, but this is what she wants, so I'm doing it for her. She's been especially busy lately putting in extra hours at the accounting firm where she works so that she can take more time off for her honeymoon.''

He looked at the check marks and neatly underlined words. ''I've seen plans for international drug busts that seemed less complicated than that. How big is this going to be?''

''She's my only sister, but we have an aunt in Montreal, uncles in Cleveland and cousins all over the country. So far, everyone's planning to attend.''

''What about your parents?''

She hesitated. "Our mother died when Angela finished high school. Our father said he'd try to make it for the ceremony, but we can't be certain."

"Where's your father?"

"Somewhere in Russia, the last I heard."

"What's he doing there?"

"He's a foreign correspondent for Reuters. He's covering the civil unrest in the southern republics."

Nick whistled through his teeth. "Sounds like a dangerous job."

"It suits him. He likes to travel, and he's an astute observer."

"Is it because of your father that you chose a career in TV journalism?"

"I suppose it was. He'd always send Angela and me postcards from wherever he went. The things he described were fascinating, like flipping television channels. It struck me as a wonderful way to look at the world."

"That must have been rough, though, growing up with your father away so much."

She fiddled with her pen, flipping it over between her fingers a few times before she responded to his comment. "My parents divorced when I was eight."

He paused. "That must have been rough, too."

"It seems to be common enough, according to the statistics I've read. Marriages don't usually last."

"Yeah, I know what you mean."

"Oh, I'm sorry. Gord mentioned you were divorced."

"We all make mistakes. It's okay as long as we learn from them."

Lauren's expression grew distant. "After my father left, my mother went through two more weddings and two more divorces. She was on a cruise with the future number four when she died."

There was sadness in her tone, and a tinge of pity, but her voice was as matter-of-fact as if she were reporting a story, as if she were using the detachment she practiced as a journalist to protect herself from what had to be painful memories....

As Nick watched her efforts to maintain her poise, he felt a stirring of sympathy. "No wonder you don't like weddings," he said quietly.

"Yes, well, I probably take after my father in that, too."

A comment she had made after the crash came to his mind. He decided to paraphrase it.

"You'd rather be an observer at a wedding than a participant, right?"

"Well put," she said, closing her notebook and setting it aside, obviously doing the same for the subject.

The conversation turned back to Duxbury then, yet Nick found it difficult to concentrate. Instead, he found himself thinking about Lauren. Again. Yeah, under the silk and pearls she really was a lot more human than she liked to let on. Trouble was, once he started speculating about what she kept hidden underneath the silk...

Despite the differences in their personalities and their living habits, he still found her to be an extremely attractive woman. The more his body recovered, the more he was reminded of it. And that was yet another reason why his frustration over the lack of progress on the case— and this entire situation—continued to escalate.

The memorial service for the victims of the crash was held the next day. Lauren couldn't stomach the idea of joining Gord and the crew for the coverage, and she didn't want to risk displaying her feelings to a crowd of strangers, so she came home early to watch it on TV.

Nick was uncharacteristically subdued as he

cleared the stack of printouts off the living room chair for her. He settled on the couch, watching in silence as the camera panned over the crowd that had gathered to pay their respects to the dead.

Although Lauren had done her best to push the nightmare ordeal of the crash out of her thoughts, the memory of her terror was still vivid. She wiped her palms on her skirt, then clutched her hands in her lap, trying to keep them steady.

She and Nick had been so lucky. At times she almost felt guilty over her relief at surviving when so many others died. She looked at the way Nick was sitting forward, his fists braced on his thighs. It must be so much worse for him, not being able to let anyone know he was alive.

The coverage of the service blended smoothly into a number of interviews with people in the slowly dispersing crowd. There was a man with a cast on his arm, his other arm firmly around an energetically wiggling young boy. The child was the same one Nick had passed to a fireman just before he'd staged his disappearance. The boy's father blinked back tears as he related the rescue. Nick shifted on the couch and slumped back into the cushions.

"You really were a hero," Lauren murmured.

"The kid would have made it anyhow. Your pal Gord's just trying to milk his story."

Several other survivors gave their own accounts of escaping the burning plane and the long, disorienting struggle to reach the shore. Lauren curled her feet beneath her and clutched her hands more tightly in her lap.

"Did I ever thank you for saving my hide?" Nick asked.

"Yes, when you came to. I still don't know how I managed not to drown us both."

"Neither do I."

She glanced at him quickly, then sighed when she saw his wry smile. "This is hard to watch, isn't it."

"Yeah. Want to turn it off?"

"Maybe we should," she said, reaching for the remote. She had her finger poised over the off button when the camera panned to a group of uniformed police officers who were standing on the edge of the crowd. Gord moved up to the heavyset middle-aged man who was closest.

Nick hissed through his teeth. "I don't believe it."

"What?"

"That's Captain Gilmour. And the two guys on the right are Epstein and O'Hara. I haven't seen them that spiffed up since..." He paused. "Since Joey's funeral."

Gilmour said a few brief words of regret over the death of his fellow officer, then praised the selfless heroism that led to Nick's death. O'Hara went further, saying what a fine man Nick was, and how his loss would be keenly felt among all who worked with him.

Gord turned to a red-haired policewoman next, and the camera zoomed in on the tears that gleamed on her cheeks.

"Who's she?" Lauren asked.

"Ramona Brill."

"She looks really upset."

"Yeah. Poor kid. She's a friend of Rose's, was always hanging around the house when they were growing up, so she was like a member of the family."

Lauren listened to yet another testimonial of Nick's character and was struck by the sincerity of everything that was said. He was obviously a man who inspired deep respect among his colleagues, and judging by Ramona's grief, in her case he probably inspired something more. She was no "kid."

As the scene switched to another camera, Lauren muted the sound and looked at Nick.

X"Have you thought about contacting someone on the force and asking for help?"

He shook his head. "I wouldn't get any help if they found out what I'm doing. My captain was getting ready to pull me off the case."

"But they obviously think very highly of you."

"They're only saying that because I'm dead," he muttered.

"I don't think so."

"I'd rather give this plan a chance before I risk involving anyone else. They all have families, too. I wouldn't want to—" His words cut off as he sat forward once more, his body tensed.

Lauren looked at the screen. The camera was back on Gord. He was holding the microphone in front of a tall, vaguely familiar woman. "Isn't that your mother?" Lauren asked.

"Yeah."

Natasha Strada was almost as tall as Gord. She held herself with stiff dignity, her shoulders squared beneath the black dress that she wore. Her white hair was cut short, framing a feminine echo of the broad cheekbones and blue eyes that were evident in her son. Yet her cheeks looked hollow, and the skin around her eyes was bruised by dark circles of grief.

"She's been crying," Nick said, his tone grim. "Her eyelids get puffy like that when she cries. It happens whenever she peels onions or watches those sappy Christmas movies."

Lauren didn't know what to say. She hated seeing the woman's grief made public like this, but if she had been doing the coverage, she probably wouldn't have hesitated. That was her job, just as it was Gord's. "I'm sorry, Nick," she murmured. "I'll turn the set off."

"This whole crazy scheme was my idea. I might as well see what I've done."

Gord's conversation with Nick's mother was mercifully brief. A pair of dark-haired teenagers emerged from the crowd and moved to either side of her, slipping their arms around her waist as they drew her away from the camera.

"Barb and Tina," he said. "I've never seen them looking so quiet."

"They seem to be very protective."

"A Strada trait." He rubbed the back of his neck, not taking his gaze off the screen. "I always thought of them as the babies. They look so serious and grown-up."

The last two women Gord spoke with were Rose and Juanita, the remaining sisters. Rose's long hair was the same rich brown as Nick's and the twins', her eyes so dark they appeared black. Like her brother, energy seemed to pulse in the air around her, even when she wasn't moving. Juanita was closest in appearance to their mother, with her short blond hair and slender height. Yet like all the Strada women, their faces bore the same traces of grief.

"The last time I saw them was a month ago," Nick said. "Rose had trouble with her truck and we put in a new starter motor. One-up had just come back from another race."

"One-up?"

"That's what we call Juanita. She's kind of competitive."

"Another Strada trait?"

"You guessed it."

"What kind of races does she attend? Cars? Horses?"

"Marathons. And she doesn't attend them, she runs in them." His eyes clouded. "I've never seen her so still. Even Rose looks as if she's been crying. She never does, no matter what. Tough as nails, that's Rose."

The coverage of the memorial service finally wrapped up. Gord's special followed, opening with the tape of Nick's death that was by now famous nationwide.

Nick didn't watch. With one hand on the arm

of the couch, he levered himself to his feet. "I hate putting them through this."

"I'm sure they'll understand when you have the chance to explain."

"Right, but it doesn't help them now, does it."

She clicked off the TV. "I'm sorry, Nick."

He limped to the window and grabbed on to the edge of the frame. "Damn," he muttered. "It's Duxbury I'm after, but I'm making my entire family suffer in the meantime."

"You're doing this to protect them."

"The effect is the same. My death is the only thing that's phony here. Their feelings are real."

She couldn't argue with him there, she thought, remembering her own grief before she'd learned the truth. "Maybe you should tell them."

He looked through the sheer curtain to the street below, his jaw clenched so hard a muscle jumped in his cheek. "No," he said finally. "All it would take would be one slip and we'd be right back where we were before the crash. This is the only way. They might be miserable, but at least they're safe."

And what about you? she wondered, watching the tension vibrate through his body. He'd always been so strong and determined, so completely sure of himself. She'd never seen him like this before. The same misery she'd seen in the faces of his family was reflected in his own.

She uncurled from the chair and walked toward the window until she stood behind him. The urge to touch him was so strong, she lifted her hand. Her palm was a breath away from his back before she caught herself and moved to his side.

"I remember the way I felt when my father died," he said. "Mixed up with all the grief was a crazy kind of anger that he'd deserted us. My family's probably feeling something like that. And when they find out it's all a lie..."

"They'll forgive you."

"God, I hope so."

"How old were you when your father died?"

He hesitated. "Fifteen."

She thought of the twins, of how solemn they'd looked ten minutes ago. "But that means Barb and Tina..."

"They're exactly the same age I was when our father died. They never knew him, though. He was killed the week before Christmas. They were born the following March."

"Oh, Nick," she murmured. "How awful."

"Yeah. He was shot while he was chasing two punks who had robbed a liquor store. He was a cop, too." He crossed his arms and turned to look at her. "I'm putting them through it again, Lauren. Another funeral, another round of mourning. I should be the one protecting them, not causing them more pain."

"You've felt responsible for all of them since you were fifteen, haven't you?" she asked. "When your father died, you probably assumed his role as the man of the house, right?"

"I did as much as I could. I was only a kid, but I grew up fast. From the looks on their faces, that's what's happening to Barb and Tina. They're usually so easygoing. Now they're being forced to face..." He paused, then shook his head. "I was going to say they're forced to face reality. But this isn't reality. It's a hoax. A lie. They're crying for nothing."

"It'll be over soon."

"Not soon enough." He gestured toward the papers that he'd strewn around the couch. "This isn't my style. I need to go out. I need to talk to the kind of sources that wouldn't know the Web from a sewer grate."

Concern made her forget her own self-imposed limit, and she lifted her hand to grasp his arm. His skin was warm, stretched taut over hard muscle. It had been days since she'd touched him. She felt as if it had been too long. "But you can't go out yet. Your injuries—"

"Are practically healed."

"What if someone sees you?"

"I'll have to change my appearance, that's all." He looked down at where she clung to him, then covered her hand with his. He lifted his head, and the vulnerability that she'd glimpsed moments before was gone. Instead, his gaze gleamed with determination. And something more, something that sparked between them, warming the skin he touched, stirring awareness on a level that wasn't only physical.

She shouldn't be trying to stop him from going out. She should be eager to get him out of her home and out of her life. She hadn't wanted him here in the first place, had she? And the longer he stayed...

He moved his hand until their fingers aligned, then twined them together and pulled her nearer. "Tomorrow. That's when I'll go."

She was so close she needed to tip her head back to look into his face. She lifted her other hand and flattened it against his chest for balance. "Be careful."

"Are you worried, Lauren?"

"Of course."

"Because of your story?"

"Yes." She felt smooth, warm cotton slide under her palm as she moved her hand upward. A pulse throbbed hard in the side of his neck and she looked at it, fascinated by the sheer vitality he emanated. "Where will you go first?"

He didn't reply. He caught her other hand in his, lowered it to her side and stepped closer. She moved away when she felt his toes nudge hers, but for every step she took, he followed, guiding her backward until the wall stopped her retreat.

Neither of them spoke. The slow ticking of the grandfather clock in the corner, the soft whir of the air conditioner and the sound of her own heartbeat filled her ears. Tension hummed, growing with each motionless second. Lauren felt the heat from his body and the whisper of his breath on her cheek and then gradually, finally, there was more.

It started as a light pressure, no more than a hint of contact, but at the first brush of his chest across her breasts, Lauren gasped.

Nick eased their joined hands against the wall on either side of her and leaned closer, fitting his body to hers in a wordless, full-length…kiss.

Lauren looked at his mouth, feeling her lips tingle with the need to touch him there, to make the kiss a real one. Her pulse quickening, she lifted her gaze to his.

A quiver coiled through his tightly flexed body. He held her gaze as boldly as his weight pinned her in place.

Oh, God. What were they doing? This was madness. She shouldn't kiss him. She shouldn't touch him, either. This wasn't the way she handled her emotions. She didn't *want* to need him. She didn't want to need anyone.

She twisted her wrists, trying to loosen his grip on her hands. "Nick, no," she murmured. "Please. We can't."

"No?"

"This isn't what we agreed on."

Gradually the glaze of passion faded from his eyes. In its place was a dawning realization of what they had almost done. He blew out an unsteady breath, then released her hands and pushed himself away from the wall. "Sorry," he muttered. "I guess I lost my balance again."

Chapter 7

Brushing her palms nervously over her skirt, Lauren surveyed her apartment, trying to make sure that there were no more traces of Nick's presence. The stack of spare bedding was gone. So were his disorganized, overflowing piles of notes. There were no stray boots or crumpled shirts or doughnut crumbs. To a visitor, her home would seem exactly the same tidy, serene, neutrally decorated place it had always been.

Neat. Clean. Sterile. Empty.

She couldn't possibly be missing him, could she? This was the first time he'd gone out since she'd brought him here, and she had to admit she was concerned about him. At least he'd agreed to use the items she'd brought home from the station, and he'd borrowed her car, so as long as he was cautious...

Nick? Cautious? She chewed the inside of her lip, trying to get her anxiety under control. Worrying was pointless. If anyone knew how to take care of himself, it was Nick. She knew he'd be back. Still, it seemed as if his absence was as tangible to her as his presence had always been.

She glanced at the flowers she'd placed on the dining table. Neatly aligned wineglasses sparkled on the linen cloth, along with the silver trays that would hold the food she had picked up on her way home from the station. A pair of crepe paper wedding bells hung from the light fixture, and another pair decorated the table that would hold Angela's gifts.

Maybe it was just as well that Nick had gone out tonight. This bridal shower was going to be difficult enough to get through without worrying about hiding a man in her bedroom.

Smoothing her hand over her hair, she found her gaze straying toward the corner by the window. Instantly she remembered the feel of Nick's hands holding hers, and the weight of his body and the smoldering intensity of his blue eyes....

''No,'' she said. There was no one to hear it but herself, but perhaps she needed to hear it more than he did. After all, she had been the one who had touched him first. And she had been a willing participant in what had followed. Even now, the memory of his body pressing against hers...

"Enough," she muttered. All right, so her body responded to his. Considering the circumstances—and the blatant sex appeal of the man—that was understandable. But she'd built her life on her ability to control her emotions, and she wasn't about to change.

The soft knock on the door made her jump. She glanced at her watch, then smoothed her palms over her skirt again and went to answer it.

It was Angela, and she was early. She grinned and held up a bottle of wine in each hand. "Estelle and Salimah said they'd come, so I thought I'd better bring some more supplies."

"You're the guest of honor, Angela," Lauren said as her sister swept into the apartment. "You didn't need to do that."

"No, I didn't *need* to, but I wanted to." She paused to brush her cheek against Lauren's, then went to the kitchen and stored the bottles in the fridge with the others. "Can I help?"

Following her, Lauren shook her head. "Everything's under control."

"I really appreciate your doing all this. Especially considering what's been going on with you."

She started. "What do you mean?"

Angela turned around, her smile quizzical. "The plane crash. You're handling things remarkably well."

"Oh. Thank you."

"Are your feet better now?"

"Yes, they're fine, but don't worry about me."

"There you go again." She slipped her arm around Lauren's waist as they walked back to the living room. "I know there's more going on than the plane crash, you know. That's another reason I wanted to help."

Her gaze darted around the room, in case she had overlooked something of Nick's. There was nothing in sight, so she forced herself to relax. "Really?"

"It's the whole wedding thing."

"We've talked about this before, Angela. Believe me, I'm over what happened. It's ancient history."

"You always say it doesn't bother you, but I realize how you feel about marriage in general."

She gave her sister a quick hug of reassurance

before she pulled away. "It's no secret that I feel marriage isn't for me. But it's what you want, and it's obvious Eddy makes you happy. I do want you to be happy, Angela."

"Oh, I am."

It was true, Lauren thought as she listened to her sister go on about what a wonderful man she was marrying. Angela positively glowed with happiness. Maybe marriage really would suit her, maybe the love she felt for Eddy would overcome the odds as well as their family history.

Resolutely she stopped herself from dwelling on her aversion to matrimony. She wasn't throwing this party in order to cast a pall of gloom over Angela's good spirits. She loved her, despite the differences in their personalities and their ways of dealing with the world. And by concentrating on making sure Angela had a good time, maybe she'd be able to forget about her own problems for a while. After the tension she'd been living with lately, it would do her good to have a break.

Over the next few hours, Lauren did exactly that. Everyone she had invited came, and soon the apartment was filled with almost two dozen of Angela's friends and coworkers. Not everyone was happily married, of course. Salimah was in the middle of her second divorce, and kept one of Angela's extra bottles beside her elbow for most of the evening. One of the secretaries from the accounting firm had just separated from her husband of twenty years, and kept jumping up to phone home to check on her children. Yet the general mood soon settled into that special, festive intimacy, the kind that was unique to a gathering of women.

When the time came for Angela to open her gifts, the conversation tapered off. Those who couldn't find seats on the furniture kicked off their shoes and sat on the carpet. Lauren perched on the arm of the couch and handed her sister the brightly wrapped box on the top of the pile.

"I am not wearing a hat made out of the bows," Angela said immediately. "So put away the camera, Estelle."

There was a chorus of laughter and a few boos. Estelle, a former neighbor of Angela's who looked like a white-haired pixie, shook her head. "Oh, no. I intend to get a picture of your face when you open that one. It's from me."

Angela checked the tag. "And so it is. Thanks, Estelle," she said, ripping into the paper. She tipped the package and peeked inside, then grinned. "Just what I've always wanted," she declared, pulling out what appeared to be a knot of red-and-black lace.

Lauren leaned to the side to get a better look. It was a fire-engine red garter belt trimmed with black bows. Angela pulled two black lace stockings out of the package and held them up just as the flash went off.

The next gift was more traditional, an embroidered tablecloth, but the one after that was a set of satin sheets. Lauren took a sip of her wine, imagining how it would feel to sleep on sheets like that, or to lie naked on them with someone like Nick....

She tightened her grip on her wineglass and reached for the next gift, which happened to be hers. The cut of the nightgown she'd finally decided on was modest at first glance, but the sheer silk would flow over the wearer's skin like water. While her sister stroked the fabric appreciatively, Lauren had a sudden image of wearing that nightgown herself...and having a large, masculine hand mold that silk against her body, and watching a pair of steel blue eyes spark with passion.

Clearing her throat, she passed Angela another gaily wrapped package. Inside was a can of whipped topping and a bottle of maraschino cherries.

There was a moment's silence, then a general burst of laughter, as well as several explicit suggestions on the best places to use the topping. Lauren fanned her face with her hand before passing her sister a heavy, rectangular package. At first glance it appeared to be a recipe book, but one look at the illustrated instructions and it was clear that the book would seldom be used in the kitchen.

By the time all the gifts had been opened, the women were down to the last of the wine and had dissolved into giggles. Naturally, the conversation turned from weddings to the wedding night and the best things to look for in a man.

"Good looks and height," Estelle said.

"So he can sweep you off your feet and carry you up a staircase," someone added. "Like Rhett carrying Scarlett."

"In that case he'd better be strong, too."

"Of course, it's how tall he is when he's lying down that really matters, if you know what I mean."

Angela clapped her hand over her mouth, her eyes dancing. "Shame on you, Estelle," she gasped.

"He'll need stamina, too. And a good appetite, if he's going to do justice to all that whipped cream."

Lauren thought of Nick's love of sweet food, and the healthy appetite he'd shown when it had been his turn to fix dinner. He was a tall man, too, and judging by what she had felt when he'd held her against the wall with his body—

She choked on her wine, coughing as she put down her glass. She'd hoped this party would take her mind off her situation with Nick, not make it worse.

"But if the man is all that wonderful, how will you ever keep him at home?" someone asked.

Angela picked up the garter belt and let it dangle from her finger. "I thought that's what this was for."

"Only if you tie him up with it," Salimah grumbled.

"Hey, there's a thought."

"Or better yet, lock him in the bedroom. Keep him all to yourself."

"Oooh, I like that idea. Imagine coming home to some tall, good-looking—"

"Strong, energetic—"

"Hungry hunk of a lover you keep hidden in your bedroom."

Yes, she could all too easily imagine it, Lauren decided, rising to her feet. Keeping her gaze firmly away from her own bedroom, and the closet where Nick's things were hidden, she went to the kitchen. Bracing her hands against the counter for a minute, she took a few deep breaths before she set about making coffee.

Feminine voices and laughter reached her from the living room, and she knew the conversation was yet again turning to sex. Normally it wouldn't bother her. Even though in her opinion sex was highly overrated, there was no denying it was a part of life. Just because it wasn't a part of *her* life didn't mean she couldn't enjoy some lighthearted banter about it.

She set down the cream and sugar containers with a clatter. It had been six years since she'd been to bed with a man. She remembered the occasion clearly. Harper hadn't even tried to hide his dissatisfaction that time. She'd attributed it to prewedding nerves. She hadn't known then that it was because he'd just spent the afternoon with another woman.

Time had dulled the pain she'd felt. The humiliation had lasted longer. The worst of it was, she should have known better. She never should have made herself vulnerable in the first place. She'd been getting along just fine on her own, keeping her emotional barriers strong, holding herself aloof from the chance of involvement with anyone. That's the way she'd always been, until Harper had started to work at Channel Ten.

He'd been a smooth operator. He'd have to have been, in order to talk his way past the barriers that had served as her defense since the time she was eight. Still, she hadn't let her defenses down entirely. No, he'd touched her hopes but he'd never touched her heart. That had been one of their problems. He'd claimed that she was too cold, that she couldn't let herself love anyone, that it was her fault he'd sought another woman to make up for what Lauren lacked.

There was no denying that Harper had been a rat, but he'd been right to put some of the blame on her. She didn't do well with emotional intimacy. She knew it, she'd always known it. That's simply the way she was. Marriage might be fine for people like Angela, but Lauren had long ago come to grips with her own inadequacies. She'd turned them around and had made her desire to distance herself an asset. She had a successful career and a promising future. She didn't need marriage or a man to make her life complete, did she? It was possible to live without sex, wasn't it?

A muffled giggle filtered through the swinging door. Lauren stacked coffee cups on a tray and paused to listen to an off-color joke that made her cheeks burn.

Sure, it was possible to have a happy and fulfilling life without sex.

And once this hoax was over and she was no longer hiding a tall, good-looking hunk in her apartment, maybe she wouldn't be thinking about it every other minute.

The cane Lauren had found for him was a nice touch, Nick decided, hooking it over his arm as he unlocked the door to Lauren's car. So was the gray beard and the baggy overcoat. If only the beard didn't itch so much, he thought, raising his hand to scratch carefully at the angle of his jaw.

But he wasn't complaining. Oh, no. After what had almost happened last night, he was damn lucky she was still cooperating. Instead of tossing him out on his ear, she had made it possible for him to move around the city more easily than he could have hoped.

He slid behind the wheel and caught a glimpse of his reflection in the rearview mirror. The disguise Lauren had helped him create was exactly what he'd needed, allowing him to blend in with the derelicts and winos he'd been questioning. Tonight he'd been wandering around the small park and loitering in the alleys near the intersection where Joey had died, hoping to find a witness his initial investigation had overlooked.

No one had seen Duxbury, but someone had remembered seeing his car.

He allowed himself a smile as he backed Lauren's white compact out from its concealed spot behind a darkened grocery store. Duxbury's arrogance might be his undoing. That silver Jag of his was too unique to go unnoticed forever. And one just like it had pulled into a parking garage in this area only three days ago.

What was the man doing? Returning to the scene of the crime? Nick knew in his gut it was more than that. No, whatever had brought Duxbury here the day Joey died had brought him here again.

So all he needed to do was to find out what it was and work backward from there. Lauren had said she'd work on the real estate angle....

Lauren again. For someone who didn't want to get involved, she was becoming a vital part of his investigation. A week ago, if someone had told him he'd not only be working with her but living with her, he would have told them they were crazy. Yet here he was, driving her car, wearing the clothes she'd found for him and eagerly wanting to tell her about his progress when he got home.

His smile disappeared and he deliberately eased back on the accelerator. He was doing it again, feeling just a little too pleased about the prospect of seeing her, spending too much of his time thinking about her. He had other priorities here, and so did she.

Yeah, right. Maybe if he told himself that enough times, he'd eventually listen.

It was past two in the morning when he let himself into Lauren's apartment. A single lamp had been left burning, its soft glow giving the plain furniture a warm, rosy hue. Nick paused, holding his breath to listen carefully, but obviously Lauren's guests were long gone.

He shrugged out of his overcoat and hung it from the closet doorknob, then scratched his cheek and headed for the bathroom where he peeled off the beard. Ten minutes later, yawning as he unbuttoned his shirt, he walked back to the living room.

It was just like Lauren to leave a light on for him. That was another one of the things he found so intriguing about her. She was so cool and businesslike on the surface, but now and then she slipped up and let him see the sym-

pathetic, compassionate woman beneath the facade.

Then again, it wasn't her personality alone
that he found himself dwelling on. No, it wasn't
her sympathy he wanted to run his hands over,
and it wasn't her compassion he wanted to see
naked—

He froze in midyawn, his eyes widening
when he rounded the corner of the couch. He'd
been wrong. Lauren hadn't merely left a light
on for him, she had waited up. Or at least, she
had tried to.

His jaw snapped shut as he looked at the
woman snuggled sound asleep against the cushions. Her legs were curled up underneath her
long flowered skirt, one bare foot peeking out
from beneath the hem. She was still wearing the
same pale cotton sweater she'd had on when
he'd left, yet now the wide neckline had
drooped, revealing a creamy shoulder and a thin,
ivory-colored bra strap. Long, blond softly curling strands of hair that had escaped from the
twist at the back of her head lay gently across
her throat. Her lips were parted, her cheeks
faintly flushed.

And she was undoubtedly the most tempting
sight he had seen in years.

He should either wake her up now or put the

beard back on and leave. Instead, he moved to the chair across from her and sat down. Propping his left leg on the coffee table to ease his aching knee, he laced his fingers together and rested his chin on his hands. For a few short, stolen minutes, he decided to indulge himself and watch her sleep.

She sighed, flexing her hand against the cushion in a vague stroking gesture. What was she dreaming about? he wondered as he saw her eyes move beneath her lids. Another story? Another job? Her lips moved into a sleepy pout— or could it be a pucker? He lowered his gaze to her breasts, noting the increasingly rapid rhythm of her breathing. If he didn't know better, he'd have to guess that her dream involved something far more interesting than her job.

It was two in the morning, and he was alone with a beautiful, barefoot woman. If their situation had been different, if she was someone else, he knew what he would be doing. He'd be waking her up. Slowly. Quietly. He'd ease that sweater farther down, run his fingers over the skin of her shoulder, brush back those silky blond strands and...

What would she do if he took up the invitation of those moist, parted lips, if he pressed his mouth to hers while she was still sleep-warm and vulnerable? Would she taste as good as she looked?

And what would he see in her eyes when those long, lush lashes swept upward? Would there be an answering glow, a spark of the same mindless pull that he felt?

Or would she stiffen the way she had last night?

Nick shifted, the chair springs whispering a mocking echo. This was stupid, sitting here and fantasizing about Lauren the ice princess. It was only going to make things worse. Tipping back his head, he exhaled harshly. It was a good thing he'd found a lead tonight. He didn't know how much more of this he could take. He pulled his leg off the table and rocked forward.

With a murmured sigh, Lauren opened her eyes. She blinked once, then focused on his face. "Nick?"

Her voice was low and raspy, not quite aware. And it was sexy as hell. What *had* she been dreaming about? Nick curled his fingers into his palms. "Sorry. I didn't mean to wake you."

She pushed herself up. Her nostrils flared delicately as she suppressed a yawn. "No, it's okay. I didn't mean to fall asleep. What time is it?"

"After two."

"That late?"

"And getting later by the minute," he muttered, feeling his self-control slip a notch.

"Are you all right? Did anyone recognize you?"

She'd been worried about him. Or had she been worried about her link to the story? "Everything's fine. No problems."

Her gaze roamed over him, lingering on his open shirt. "Did you learn anything useful?"

He looked at her bare shoulder, noticing the shadows at the edge of her neckline, trying not to imagine where the shadows led. "Could be. How did the party go?"

"Fine. Angela liked her, uh..." She hesitated, curling her legs beneath her as she tucked her skirt over her bare feet. "She liked her gifts."

Nick knew he should move away. Considering the hour, and the intimate mood the hushed shadows were creating, he'd be crazy to prolong this conversation. He was only asking for trouble.

But since when did he ever like to play things safe? Rounding the table, he sat on the couch beside her. "What kind of gifts? You mean dish towels and things like that?"

"Not exactly."

He stretched his arm along the back of the couch, his fingers inches from the lock of hair that teased her nape. "What's that mean?"

"Angela's friends are a lively bunch."

Was that a blush on her cheeks? he wondered. "What did they do? Hire a male stripper?"

Beneath her sweater, her breasts rose and fell in a rhythm almost identical to the one of her dream. "Of course not. They gave her some off-beat things, that's all."

He watched her blush deepen, and understanding came quickly. "Ah. I think they're called marital aids."

"It was all in good fun."

"Any honey or chocolate sauce?"

She hesitated. "Honey?"

"Maybe you should do a story on it sometime."

"Maybe." Her gaze darted toward his open shirt again, lingering for a long, delicious moment. "Let's talk about what you learned tonight."

"I learned you don't snore."

"I'm referring to your case. Duxbury. Did you make any progress?"

Nick felt her gaze on his body like a physical touch. Her words might be all business, but that wasn't the message in her eyes. "It's not much, but it's a starting point. Duxbury's been back to the area several times. I have an address of a parking garage he uses.''

"That sounds promising," she said, her voice dropping.

"Uh-huh. Things are definitely looking up."

"I'll check the parking garage against our files."

"I figured you would."

"Yes. First thing in the morning."

"Sounds good."

"Then we might as well say good-night."

"Lauren?"

"Mmm?"

"Why are you staring at my chest?"

"I—" She raised her eyes to his face. "I'm not."

He lifted his hand, stroking the ends of her hair. "Go ahead. I'll take my shirt off if you like."

"Nick, I..." She sighed, tilting her head as his fingers reached her neck. "I don't think this is a good idea."

"Your pulse is racing," he murmured, pressing a fingertip to the delicate skin beneath her ear. "You can't expect me to believe it's because we're making progress with the case."

"It's late, that's all. And you startled me when I woke up."

He moved closer until he could feel the warmth of her body soak through their clothes like sunshine. Awareness surged over him. He shouldn't be torturing himself like this. He shouldn't forget the frustration he'd felt the last time.

That was the problem. He *couldn't* forget the last time. Yet she still had the power to ruin everything...

But she wouldn't, would she?

The realization made him inhale sharply. When had he started to trust her?

Probably about the same time she'd started to believe him.

"Don't you think we'd better admit what's going on here, Lauren?" he said, dropping his hand to her shoulder. He slid his palm over her bare skin, and a delicate tremor followed his touch.

She glanced down at his hand, her breathing growing more rapid. "I'm not naive, Nick. This is only a natural reaction. Perfectly understandable."

"You've got that right. Not many things more natural than this," he said, hooking his thumb into the edge of her sweater's drooping neckline.

"We're both adults. Considering the forced intimacy of our circumstances, there's bound to be a certain amount of awareness...."

"Oh, there's that, all right." With the back of his fingers, he rubbed the shadowed dip between her breasts.

"We both know it would be best if we don't—"

"I'm not so sure about that anymore, Lauren."

"What..." Her breath hitched. "What do you mean?"

"Why don't I show you?"

"Nick, what are you doing?"

"When I figure it out, I'll let you know," he said, lowering his head.

Chapter 8

At the first touch of his lips on hers, Lauren sighed with pleasure. At last. At long last. Who cared if it was wrong, or reckless, or doomed to end? This had been building for days, and it was a relief to finally let go.

He kissed the same way he did everything else. Boldly, decisively, with an impatient energy that defied convention. He nibbled, tasted, then angled his head so that his mouth fit perfectly over hers. Lauren didn't even consider resisting. She could no more stop this than she could have stopped the plane from crashing.

It was the wine, that's all. She'd had only three glasses, but it must have gone straight to her head. And then there were those gifts, and the ribald conversation. That could have affected anyone. She hadn't meant to fall asleep waiting for Nick. And was it any wonder that when she'd awakened from that hazily erotic dream and had looked straight into his face that she would be a little...aroused?

Nick lifted his head, a slow smile spreading over his face. ''Not ice water,'' he murmured. ''Definitely not.''

She didn't even bother trying to make sense out of what he said. Her brain didn't seem to be functioning. ''They do go into dimples.''

''What?''

''Those lines beside your mouth.'' She blinked, struggling to focus. ''Nick, don't do that.''

He pressed his thumb to her bottom lip, rubbing lightly across the moisture he'd left. ''Do what?''

Tingles chased along her nerves at his gentle touch and her thoughts scattered.

''Don't do what?'' he repeated, trailing the tip of his index finger along her jaw. He touched her earlobe, then traced around the pearl earring in the center. His smile grew, transforming his face from rugged to...irresistible.

She closed her eyes, but she could still feel the power—and the passion—in his gaze. ''Please, don't smile.''

''Yeah. I can think of better things to do with my mouth.'' He lifted his other hand from the neckline of her sweater and framed her face between his palms. ''Much better.''

She drew in an unsteady breath, hoping to find some scrap of her disappearing control. Instead, she inhaled the scent she'd been trying to ignore for seven days. That musky tang. That essence of the man who kept a knife in his boot and who grieved for his family's tears. And instead of slipping out of his gentle hold, she swayed toward him.

He kissed her again, but this time he used more than his lips. His hands slid across her cheeks, the friction of his callused palms against her smooth skin making her gloriously aware of the differences between them. He brushed the tips of his fingers over her closed eyelids in a touch that hummed with restraint, wooing her with strength held in check.

She could still break away. One of them should call a halt to this insanity. But then the tip of his tongue brushed her tingling lips, and she responded instinctively, crumpling the front of his shirt to pull him closer.

A low groan rumbled from his throat as he deepened the kiss, submerging her reason along with it. She parted her lips, and the taste of him flooded her senses. Fresh. Wild. Blatantly sensual.

Her fingers slipped inside his shirt to splay across his chest. Sensations burst over her as she felt the masculine textures, the crisp hair and the taut skin. She moved her hand, and his reaction rippled under her fingertips.

It was a heady feeling, to know she could affect him with her touch. She skimmed her palms upward, tracing his collarbones, spreading her fingers greedily across his shoulders.

He moved quickly, shrugging out of his shirt and tossing it to the floor behind him. Without breaking off the kiss, he fastened his hands on either side of her waist and leaned back against the corner of the couch, bringing her down on top of him.

She had been pressed against his naked chest once before, she thought dimly. But that brief, accidental embrace on her bed had been nothing like this. Murmuring her approval, she wriggled closer.

His hands released her waist and slipped under the hem of her sweater, burning a path upward to the hook fastening at the back of her bra. He opened it deftly and brushed the ends aside, then swept his fingers downward to caress the sides of her breasts.

The boldness of his touch stole her breath. She raised her head, gulping air as she blinked open her eyes.

His smile was sensual, as straightforward as his touch. Holding her gaze, he slipped his thumbs inside the cups of her loosened bra.

"Nick!" she gasped.

"Sh. Fair is fair."

"What?"

"Where are your hands, Lauren?"

She glanced down at where she had flattened her hands against his chest. Her own thumbs were scant inches away from the flat, brown circles of his nipples. She flexed her fingers, and a jolt of pleasure shot through her. "That's different."

"Yeah." He moved his thumbs another inch. "You still have too many clothes in the way."

"This…we can't…it's…"

His hands stilled. "It's what?"

She inhaled shakily. "Too fast. We have to think about this."

A flare of heat gleamed in his eyes. "Believe me, I've been thinking about this since the first time I saw you."

"But…" She moved her hand, hearing the hushed rasp of his chest hair under her palm.

Oh, God. What was it she wanted to say? "But we have to work together."

"So?"

"But this...changes everything."

The dimples beside his mouth deepened. "Damn right it does."

She wished he wouldn't smile like that. "Then you know this is impossible."

"Not anymore," he said, hooking his good leg over hers. "We've worked together just fine for a week, and we'll keep on working together. The only thing that's going to change is what we do in our time off."

There were arguments, so many of them, but pressed so closely to his body like this, breathing his scent, feeling his warmth and his strength, she couldn't make her brain latch on to a single one.

She pulled her lower lip between her teeth, feeling the swollen flesh tingle. A sudden spark came into his gaze as he focused on her gesture. She swallowed hard and looked away.

"Was it that bad?" he asked.

At the plain question, she shook her head. Her hair tumbled out of what was left of its twist to fall around her face. "You know it wasn't."

He pulled his hands from beneath her sweater and gently pushed his fingers into her hair.

Gathering a handful together, he stroked the ends across her cheek until she returned her gaze to his. "What are you afraid of, Lauren?"

"I'm not..." She couldn't complete the lie. Yes, she was afraid. She'd known from the first moment she'd seen him that Nick was the kind of man to threaten any woman's attempt at detachment. But she needed her distance. She didn't want to be vulnerable, to risk being rejected and hurt again.

Silence spun out between them as he continued to look at her, his gaze intense, as if he were trying to probe past the barriers she was scrambling to reerect. "Is it me? Or is it men in general?" he asked finally.

It was both, she thought, bracing her hands on his chest. Setting her jaw against the temptation to caress him one last time, she pushed herself upright and straightened her clothes. "It's late," she said. "We both have work to do tomorrow."

Nick stayed where he was, his broad shoulders propped against the corner of the couch. He drew his right leg up, resting his arm on his bent knee. He watched her with the simmering restraint of a lounging predator. "It's still our time off, Lauren."

She clenched her hand in her lap. "We made

a mistake here tonight, but that's no reason why we should let it interfere with—''

''The only mistake we made was thinking we could keep ignoring what's going on between us. I don't believe that's possible anymore.''

Lauren looked at the way his bare skin gleamed in the lamplight, and how his dark hair curled at the base of his neck. Passion barely leashed glowed in the depths of his eyes, and his lips still bore a sheen of moisture from their kiss.

No, it wasn't going to be possible to ignore a man like that. ''Nick, six years ago I promised myself that I wasn't going to get involved with anyone again. Although I admit I'm attracted to you, I meant it when I said I'd prefer to keep our relationship strictly professional.''

''Too late for that. What happened six years ago?''

She realized he wasn't going to give up on this unless she explained everything. Well, why not? It wasn't exactly a secret, was it? ''I was engaged to be married.''

He lifted his eyebrows. ''You?''

''Yes, me. Despite what I'd learned about the risks of marriage, I was foolish enough to give it a try.''

''Who was he?''

"His name was Harper Beauchamp. He was an assistant producer at the station. We began dating about three months after he started working there and became engaged a year later. We'd planned a June wedding with all the trimmings. He didn't show up, so—"

"Wait a minute," Nick said. The muscles on his abdomen rippled as he slowly sat up. "Do you mean he didn't show up for the wedding?"

"That's right. He changed his mind on our wedding day. Unfortunately, he didn't see fit to notify me until I had been waiting in the church for almost an hour."

Nick leaned forward and covered her hands with his. "What did you do?"

"I told everyone to go home."

"Then what?"

"I changed into my suit, stuffed my wedding dress into a used clothing drop box and went to my office."

He moved his thumbs over her whitened knuckles, stroking gently. "And you tried to pretend what had happened to you was nothing but a picture on a postcard."

She blinked hard, shocked at the sudden moisture in her eyes. "Yes. I tried."

"But it didn't work, did it?"

"Not right away. There were so many things

that needed to be canceled and people who needed to be notified. I had to do it from my office, because I'd already moved out of my apartment. I stayed with Angela for a few weeks until I found this place. It was very awkward seeing Harper at the station afterward, but he moved to Des Moines a few months later, so things eventually improved.''

Nick was quiet for a while, his gaze focused on their joined hands. When he finally looked up, his eyes were filled with sympathy. ''I'm sorry, Lauren. He must have hurt you deeply.''

''It was a cowardly, hateful way to break an engagement, but it was probably for the best. Being jilted on my wedding day was a good reminder that some people simply aren't suited to relationships. In a way, Harper did us both a favor.''

Nick shook his head. ''No. However you look at it, he still hurt you. But I'm not sorry you didn't marry him.''

''As it turned out, neither am I. I've been just fine on my own. I've learned from my mistake.''

''You must love your sister very much.''

His sudden change of topic puzzled her. ''Why would you say that?'' she asked.

''All the help you're giving her with her wedding must be a constant reminder of what you went through.''

''I'm all right.''

''You're all right as long as you have a pen in your hand and you're making check marks on one of your lists. That's how you cope, isn't it? You bury your feelings and get on with the job.''

Her throat felt thick with all the feelings she wished *were* buried. She'd held things inside for years, but it had seemed so easy to tell Nick. There was something about his blunt honesty that cut right through the layers that kept everyone else away. And somehow telling him about it had been more like draining a wound than opening one.

''Considering what happened with your parents, it must have taken a lot of courage to risk marriage yourself,'' he said. ''I understand that you don't want to be hurt like that again.''

''That's right.''

''After my divorce, I swore I wouldn't try again, either.''

''So you *do* understand.''

''Yeah. But Lauren?''

''What?''

''There are lots of different kinds of relationships.''

"I know, Nick. I told you, I'm not that naive."

"And there's a big difference between marriage and two adults enjoying each other." He slid his hand up her arm, drawing her forward. "You know that, too, don't you?"

"Yes, I know that."

"Have I done anything tonight that you didn't want me to?"

She parted her lips to reply, but the answer she wanted to give wouldn't come. There was that bluntness again. She couldn't pretend that she hadn't wanted his kiss. She sighed. "No."

He cupped the back of her head and fitted his mouth to hers. His kiss was deep and thorough, sweeping away the echoes of her remembered pain. He drew back slowly, his gaze holding her steady. "That wasn't a proposal or a commitment, Lauren. That was simply a kiss. Think about it, okay?"

It sounded so easy, the way he put it. "It's late," she said. "We're both tired and not thinking straight. Let's talk about this in the morning, all right?"

"You can bet on it." He kissed her again, then leaned back, stretching his arms out on either side of him. Lamplight gleamed softly on his hardened muscles, making him look lean and dangerous. And incredibly...male. "Until the next time, Lauren."

The next time. From anyone else, the comment would have been the height of arrogance and conceit. From Nick, it was more like a promise. She stood up and moved away. She'd almost reached the hall that led to her bedroom before she heard his voice once more.

"And Lauren?"

She paused, glancing behind her. "Yes?"

He smiled. "Pleasant dreams."

After almost a week of overcast skies and drizzle, the sun streamed through the bedroom window the next morning with the earnest exuberance of a reformed sinner. Lauren groaned and pulled the pillow over her head. As hangovers went, this one wasn't bad. The queasiness she felt was probably due more to lack of sleep than the moderate amount of wine she'd had. She never overindulged. No, she was always under control, right?

To say that she regretted what had happened last night was the ultimate understatement. Now that she'd tasted Nick's passion, it was going to be more difficult than ever to keep this...thing between them from flaring again.

This thing? she thought ruefully. He'd already

made it clear it wasn't a proposal or a commitment. Might as well be honest and call it what it was. Sex. Despite what she'd tried to tell herself during Angela's shower, she wasn't as immune as she'd wanted to believe.

Yet just because the sexual attraction that had been building between them was finally out in the open, that didn't mean they wouldn't continue to work together. Nick had said the same thing himself, hadn't he? So she should be concentrating on their investigation. They had a starting point now. At least, that's what they'd been talking about before they'd been distracted by that kiss.

God, the man could kiss. In those delightful, endless minutes, he'd given her more pleasure with his lips and his tongue than she'd thought possible. And the way he'd swept his hands over her back and around her ribs and had brought his thumbs so achingly close to...

Muffling another groan, she kicked off the tangled sheet. He was doing it again, distracting her, and he wasn't even in the room.

She dressed carefully. She wouldn't be needing to go in to work this weekend, so she didn't have any excuse to armor herself with one of her tailored suits. Instead, she chose a pair of loose-fitting pants and a blue silk blouse, taking care to tuck the blouse securely into her waistband and topping it with a stiff tapestry vest. Nothing suggestive, nothing a man could get his hand up. Buckling on a thin leather belt, she finally forced herself to cross her bedroom and open the door.

Music came from the living room. It wasn't anything she recognized, but it had a simple, catchy tune. The whine of a steel guitar warbled over the twang of the singer, and she realized Nick must have already tuned the radio to a country station—it was his turn to choose the music today.

Of course, he would be up by now. It had been a vain hope to be able to delay what was likely going to be an awkward confrontation. She knew he was an early riser. Something to do with all his energy.

Well, she might as well set the proper tone right off, she decided, turning around to go to her closet. She leaned over to pull out the briefcase she'd brought from work with her latest notes on Duxbury.

"Good morning."

At the sound of the low voice she whirled around, her pulse tripping.

Nick stood in her doorway, his arms crossed, his shoulder propped negligently against the door frame. He wore his faded jeans and a plain white T-shirt that molded to his body like a lover's touch.

Pleasant dreams, he'd said. Lauren tried not to stare. How could he look that good in a T-shirt and old jeans? She tightened her grip on the briefcase. "Good morning."

He watched her in silence for a minute. "I've spread out a map on the dining table. We'll need those notes about Duxbury's real estate holdings."

Relief washed over her. He was going to be sensible about what happened between them, after all. "I've got them right here," she said, crossing the room.

He didn't move out of her way immediately when she reached him. Instead, he cocked his head to the side and smiled slowly. "You left it loose."

"Excuse me?"

"Your hair. Slipping up again, huh?"

She lifted her hand, startled to realize she'd forgotten to style her hair into its usual twist. She looked around for her pins.

"No, leave it how it is," he said. "I like it that way." He straightened up from the door frame and grasped the pointed ends of her vest. "You're not wearing one of your suits," he said, tugging her forward. "Just as well, for what I've got planned."

She brushed away his hands and stepped back. "We should be working on breaking Duxbury's alibi."

"But that's exactly what I'm talking about. You'll need to wear something comfortable. We might be gone all day."

"What do you mean?"

"We're going out."

"Out?" she repeated, clutching the briefcase to her chest.

"How else are we going to follow up on the real estate Duxbury owns near that parking garage?"

"Oh," she said. "But it's broad daylight. You're bound to be recognized."

"Not if we're careful. Besides," he added, turning toward the hall. "I have a theory."

His limp didn't slow him down much anymore, she thought, watching his progress as she followed him to the table where he'd spread out the map. He was starting to move with the same long, loose-limbed stride she'd first noticed on the plane, like a cross between a strut and a prowl. The rest of his injuries no longer seemed to bother him, either, considering the way he hadn't flinched when he'd leaned back on the couch and pulled her down on top of him.

No, she wasn't going to think about that. She detoured to the kitchen to pour herself a mug of coffee, then she settled into the chair across the table from Nick. "What's your theory?"

He waited until she passed him the updated file of Duxbury's properties, then ran his index finger down the list of addresses. "I'm betting he has a girlfriend."

"He's been married for almost twenty years...." She paused. As she knew, marriage vows didn't have much effect on faithfulness.

"He married in order to get his hands on his wife's money and family name," Nick said, echoing the direction of her thoughts. "It wasn't a love match."

"Probably not." She looked at the yellow circle he'd highlighted on the map. "But he wouldn't be careless enough to leave a paper trail to his mistress, even if he has one."

"That's why we need to do some hands-on investigating, Lauren. And if there's a woman involved, I'm going to need your help."

"Why?"

"Whoever she is, she'd probably be more co-operative talking to another woman."

"That makes sense."

"And there's another reason. Since I'm sup-posed to be dead, I can't go around flashing my badge when I question people."

"That's right." Her brow furrowed. "You have to be careful about your questions, too. If it gets back to Duxbury that someone's still in-vestigating your partner's death, he might get suspicious."

"Yeah. I can't afford to make him nervous. We'll have to cook up some kind of cover story when we find his girlfriend."

"Well, I'll help any way I can."

"You already have."

"Gathering that information wasn't diffi-cult."

"That's not what I meant." He reached for a chocolate-glazed doughnut that he'd left on the edge of the map. He glanced at the sugary ring on the paper, then wiped it up with his finger. "It's because of you that I stayed awake most of the night thinking about sex."

She choked on her coffee. Coughing, she looked at him over the rim of her cup. "Nick!"

He grinned, deepening the dimples beside his mouth. "Surprised?"

No, she wasn't surprised. If anything, she'd been expecting him to mention it before this. "I thought we'd agreed—"

"We didn't agree on anything, if I remember right." He licked the sugar off his finger. "But while I was lying around feeling frustrated, I realized that the urge to have sex is one of the strongest in the species. Why should Duxbury be any different?"

"I can't believe we're having this discussion."

"So I thought that maybe I'd been approaching things from the wrong direction," he continued. "We've been concentrating on his business deals, but his reasons for being in that neighborhood might have been strictly personal."

She shifted, recrossing her legs and forcing herself to take a more controlled sip of her coffee. "We'd assumed that because it was the middle of a business day."

He took a bite of his doughnut. "There's no telling when people can get the urge. It's not always convenient."

That much was true, she thought, watching the way his freshly shaved jaw flexed as he chewed. Urges definitely weren't convenient.

"You want some?" he asked, offering her his doughnut.

"No, thank you."

"Can't risk slipping up again, huh?"

As a matter of fact, she couldn't, she thought as he bit into his high-calorie, high-sugar, non-nutritious breakfast. She had always preferred fruit or yogurt in the morning, yet today she felt tempted to do something she hadn't felt like doing in years. "Those doughnuts are terrible for you."

"That's what makes them so good. Usually we enjoy the very thing we know is bad for us."

Her gaze moved over his face. "That's why it's so important to maintain our self-control."

He smiled. "Uh-huh."

Her gaze was drawn to his mouth. "You have chocolate icing on your upper lip."

With the tip of his tongue, he licked it off.

Instantly she remembered what it had felt like last night, when his mouth had covered hers and his tongue had slipped so boldly past her lips. A shiver of anticipation rippled through her frame.

"Do you like chocolate, Lauren?"

"Depends on what kind."

"Let me guess. You'd like it fancy, something like expensive, imported ice cream. Cold on the outside but with the kind of taste that invites you to take your time and savor the experience."

She swallowed. "Good guess. What about you?"

"I'm a simple man, easy to please." His voice dropped. "I like the hot fudge sauce that covers the ice cream."

Fudge sauce. Maraschino cherries and whipped cream. Since when had food taken on this extra significance?

"You're looking hungry, Lauren."

"Nick..."

"How about sharing my breakfast?"

"Not a good idea."

"Why not? I like the taste of something...sweet. Anytime. Day or night."

"It'll rot your teeth."

His smile grew. "Not so far. And despite what you might have heard, overindulgence doesn't make you go blind."

She gave a startled laugh. "I haven't heard that since I was a teenager."

"Yeah? I bet the subject wasn't chocolate."

Lauren shook her head. "Nick, you're impossible."

"No, just hungry." He broke off a chunk of his doughnut and reached across the table to offer it to Lauren.

She eyed the piece of icing-covered calories for a few seconds before she took it from his hand and popped it into her mouth. The sugar burst across her taste buds like one of Nick's kisses.

"Have you thought about what I said last night?" he asked.

She nodded as she chewed. She swallowed, then removed the napkin from her lap and carefully wiped her lips. "You said we'd continue to work together. I agree with that. Our priorities haven't altered."

"No, they haven't."

"As for the thing…I mean, about what happened between us personally, I'm not going to be a hypocrite about it. I've already admitted I'm attracted to you. I'm just not sure I'm ready to do anything more about it."

He leaned back in his chair, lacing his fingers behind his head. "What about during our time off?"

"Don't rush me, Nick. I've managed just fine for six years. You can't expect me to change simply because we've been thrown together like this and you happen to be hungry."

His smile faded. "If I thought for one second that it was one-sided, I'd leave you alone. But it's not, Lauren. And if you want me to take it slow, I'll try. Other than that, neither one of us wants any promises."

For a long minute he continued to look at her, his expression sober. Then he reached for the printout she'd passed to him earlier and started to read.

The trail had been skillfully buried. It took most of the morning to wade through the layers, but eventually they had the address of a condominium that was in a building on the same block as the parking garage. It was officially owned by one of Duxbury's subsidiary companies, which in turn leased it to another company. At the end of the chain was a business that as far as Lauren's research showed had only one employee, Wanda Smith.

Nick knew in his gut this was the break he'd been waiting for. It all fit. If Duxbury had been visiting his girlfriend the afternoon Joey had been killed, that would have put him in the right place at the right time. It would also explain the ease with which he'd put together that phony alibi—if cheating on his wife was a regular occurrence, he'd probably had flunkies like Kohl swear to countless fictitious meetings over the years.

Wanda Smith wasn't home when they visited her condominium, but thanks to Lauren's cool, low-key persuasion, they'd learned from the building's superintendent that she was a singer. And thanks to the information Lauren had compiled, they also learned that the nightclub where Wanda worked happened to be owned by another tangle of subsidiary companies that led back to Duxbury.

Drumming his fingers on the dashboard, Nick glanced at Lauren's profile as she drove through the midafternoon traffic. He was starting to depend more and more on her help. And the closer they worked together, the more difficult it was to concentrate on work.

He liked to see her hair down like that. It fell in soft waves to her shoulders, framing her face in a sensual caress, making him remember the silky feel of it through his fingers. But he liked to see it twisted up on the back of her head, too. Hell, he'd still like it if she cut it short and dyed it red.

Of course, she'd probably claim that she'd never consider doing anything so reckless or spontaneous. Before last night, he'd have probably agreed. But as he'd said, that kiss had changed everything.

Angling his long legs into a more comfortable position, he leaned against the door, propping his elbow on the base of the window as he let his gaze move to her lips. He'd focused on her mouth more times than he could count today. Technically, all they had done was kiss, but he'd never known a kiss could be so...involving.

He knew she had a hang-up about marriage. It was understandable, considering her childhood and that bastard who had left her at the altar. He wasn't interested in talking her out of it, anyway, since he wasn't about to risk another commitment like that again, either. They both knew their association was only temporary, and that was fine, too. So exactly what was it that he wanted?

Unlike the other questions that plagued him lately, the answer to that one was easy. One night with her. To get her out of his system. To release all this restless energy she inspired. To take up the challenge she'd been offering from the moment they'd met. To see her lying naked on that cool green satin bedspread.

Oh, yeah, he thought. If she had melted in his arms with just a kiss, what would happen if they made love?

No, it wouldn't be *if* they made love. It would be *when*.

Groaning under his breath, he shifted on the seat again.

"Is it your knee?" Lauren asked as she pulled to a stop at a red light.

"No," he muttered. The source of his discomfort was somewhere else entirely. It was his own fault, for letting his focus wander. Trying to force his thoughts back to the task at hand, he looked at the intersection they had reached. They were only a few minutes away from the Painted Pony, the nightclub where Wanda Smith worked.

"Nick, I've been thinking about what we need to do."

"Oh, yeah," he murmured. "So have I."

"And we might be better off using a direct approach."

"I did. You said it was too fast."

She drew in a sudden breath. "I'm talking about what we should do when we get to the Painted Pony."

"Right." He rubbed the back of his neck, trying to ease the tension that knotted his muscles. "Okay, what's your idea?"

"We have a ready-made cover story. I'm a journalist working on a story, and I want to interview Wanda. I'll say I'm putting together a piece on local entertainers."

He considered it in silence for a moment. "She'll tell Duxbury."

"It doesn't matter. He'll think it's just coincidence, as long as I'm careful to be subtle with my questions.''

''How do you explain the lack of a camera?''

''I'm doing background interviews. I'll say I'll arrange for a taping later.''

''Okay, sounds good. Where do I fit in?''

''Well, we could say you're my assistant.''

He glanced down at his jeans. ''Think anyone will buy it?''

''Gord dresses casually all the time. Just put on that jacket I brought home yesterday.''

Twisting around, he dug through the bag of props she'd left in the back seat until he found the tweed jacket she meant. He shrugged it on, then leaned against the door again and scratched the corner of his jaw.

They had made some adjustments to the phony beard before they'd left the apartment, trimming it to make it look less disreputable, but it was still as itchy as ever. Lauren had talked him into adding a pair of glasses as an extra precaution against being recognized, and he'd eventually agreed, but he found the necessity annoying. Some of his colleagues thrived on changing personas and going deep undercover, but he'd always hated it. He'd be glad when this charade was over.

But when it was over he'd no longer have any reason to keep staying with Lauren.

"What's wrong?" she asked.

Good question. They were making progress. The case was his priority, right? He should be happy. At least, as happy as a dead man could be. But every minute he spent with Lauren his body reminded him vividly that he was very much alive.

"Nick?"

"Nothing. Just impatient, I guess."

The Painted Pony was in an old brick building, flanked on one side by a sporting goods store and on the other by a travel agency. A blue awning arched over the pair of frosted glass doors at the entrance, shadowing the already dim interior. Recorded music of some old show tune floated from speakers recessed into the ceiling and a deep blue carpet speckled with gold stars covered the floor. It was still early, so only a small scattering of customers occupied the tables and the velvet-covered stools at the bar.

Lauren's idea to pose as herself was a good one—the bow-tied manager, no doubt sensing free publicity for his nightclub, was all smiles and affability as he ushered them past the stage that jutted into the main room. He led them down a narrow hall to a door decorated with a pink painted heart and knocked smartly. "Wanda? You have visitors."

A few minutes later, the door swung open. Nick had already decided it would be best to let Lauren do most of the talking, but one look at her face told him she had been struck speechless.

Nick followed her gaze. On the wall directly in front of them was a life-size, full-color poster. According to the glittering letters across the top, the woman pictured there was Wanda Smith. And aside from a pair of scarlet high heels and a strategically placed ostrich feather, the smiling image of Wanda Smith was completely nude.

Chapter 9

Lauren had been prepared to dislike Wanda Smith. Considering what she now knew about Duxbury's character, she'd expected any woman who associated with him to be thoroughly unpleasant. She'd been wrong.

There was something very likable about this earthy, uninhibited woman. In her late thirties or early forties, she had long, layered hair that was bleached the color of brass. Although there were signs of hard living in the lines beside her eyes and mouth, her dark brown gaze was honest and direct, and at times her smile seemed touchingly childlike.

"So you see, I got my first big break in St. Andrew's Church choir," Wanda said, her face moving into another ready smile. She crossed her legs, swinging her foot through the gap in the front of her feather-trimmed pink dressing gown. The high-heeled slipper that dangled from the tips of her toes was trimmed with feathers, too. It seemed to be her trademark fashion statement.

"And after that?" Lauren prompted.

"Well, that was when I met my first husband. I used to dance as well as sing back then, so Ted took me down to Vegas, said he knew some people who could get me into one of those shows there." She extended her leg, turning her ankle to admire it, then sighed and let it drop. "I was too short for the chorus lines, so I took up stripping."

Lauren's gaze went to the poster on the opposite wall. What Wanda lacked in height, she certainly made up for in her other dimensions. Voluptuous was the best way to describe her. Had it been a lack of self-esteem that had led her into allowing her body to be exploited that way, or had she been too young and innocent to know any better?

"I looked great there, eh?" Wanda stated. "That was six years ago."

"You're very pretty," Lauren said.

"That's what my Dad always said. He said,

'Wanda, it's a good thing you got looks, 'cause you sure don't have brains.'"

The cruel comment had been spoken in the same matter-of-fact tone as everything else. Lauren felt her sympathy for this woman grow. "I'm sure he didn't mean—"

"Oh, sure, he did. He was a real bastard." She recrossed her legs. "I don't care. I was a double-D cup from the time I was thirteen, and I was good at stripping. It's 'cause of this body that I didn't need to do any of that stuff with live snakes or with those poles that are stuck into the stage."

Snakes and poles? Lauren gripped her pen more tightly. "When did you begin singing professionally?"

"When Ted and I split and I moved back home. I gave up stripping for good when I got this job—it's a real classy place, so all I have to do is sing. I always wanted to be a singer."

"And now you are."

She nodded, drawing in a deep breath that widened the gap in her robe. Without hesitation, she sang a few bars of a popular ballad in a soft, throaty contralto. Her voice held the same touching mixture of hard living and innocence that was reflected in her face.

"That was lovely," Lauren said when she had finished.

"Thanks." She glanced at Nick. "Did you like it?"

Since Lauren and Wanda were occupying the room's only chairs, Nick was leaning against the door, his arms crossed over his chest, his weight on his good leg. Although he'd managed to disguise his looks to the casual observer, he hadn't been able to suppress the aura of masculinity that always surrounded him. Despite the glasses and gray beard, he was still an attractive man.

At least, he was attractive to Lauren.

Beneath his beard, his cheeks moved into a smile. "You sound as pretty as you look, Wanda."

Her earthy laughter filled the small dressing room. "Thank you, Mr. Sweeny."

Nick held on to his smile while Wanda chattered on, but he started to drum his fingers against his elbow. "I suppose a girl as pretty as you must have a dozen boyfriends," he asked when she paused for a breath.

Not subtle, Lauren thought, frowning when she caught Nick's eye. He lifted a shoulder in an almost imperceptible shrug, then tapped lightly at the watch on his wrist.

At the gesture, Lauren felt her pulse accelerate. He was right. They couldn't afford to stay here much longer. There was no telling when Duxbury might show up. She dipped her head in agreement and looked back at Wanda.

Evidently, Wanda had missed the silent byplay. She stroked her palm down the feather trim that floated over her bosom in a slow, sensual movement. "Not a dozen, just one."

"Lucky man," he said.

"Lucky Ducky," she said, her ready smile returning. "That's what I call him."

Ducky? Lauren thought. If there had been any doubt before, the nickname clinched it. She would have to tread carefully here, not let Wanda know the true aim of their interview. "How do you manage to balance your personal life with your singing career?" she asked.

"Oh, my boyfriend's really busy. He can't get away to see me that often because of his job."

"That's a shame," Nick said. "What does he think of your singing? Does he come to all your shows?"

"Oh, no, but he loves my singing. That's how we met. He's..." She hesitated, a shuttered look coming into her eyes. "He's wonderful. I'm really the lucky one." She looked at the clock over the door and uncrossed her legs to rise to her feet. "Shoot. I've got to get ready. Will you excuse me?"

Nick's gaze was riveted to the widening gap of Wanda's robe. Lauren felt a sudden stab of...what? Impatience? Disgust? Or jealousy? Clearing her throat, she took out one of her business cards and wrote her home phone number on the back. "I'd like to continue this conversation some other time, Wanda. Would tomorrow be more convenient?"

She pursed her lips, her brow furrowing. "Tomorrow? Um, how about next week?"

"Do you have a rehearsal tomorrow?" Nick asked, continuing his scrutiny of her visible flesh.

"No, I get Sundays off, but I'll be, um, busy in the morning."

"We'll be taping interviews in the afternoon with some of the other local singers I'm profiling," Lauren improvised. "I wanted to get footage of everyone's home as well as where they work. Could we come over with the camera crew in the afternoon, Wanda?"

At the mention of the camera, Wanda's brow cleared. "Hey, this is gonna be great for my career. Sure. I'll be free by the afternoon."

"Wonderful. We'll see you then."

"Don't you need my address?"

She smiled, hoping Wanda hadn't noticed the inadvertent slip. "Oh, Mr. Sweeny takes care of those details. You can give it to him."

Nick pushed away from the door and walked over to Wanda. He shoved the scribbled address she gave him into his pocket, then paused to shake her hand. It didn't appear to bother her that he took advantage of their height difference to stare down her cleavage.

Lauren felt another stab that was uncomfortably close to jealousy. What should it matter if Nick decided to ogle another woman? Someone like Wanda was probably more his type, anyway. Her straightforward sensuality would suit Nick, with his impatient fingers and his blunt way of speaking. So it wasn't her concern.

He finished his inspection of Wanda's breasts and glanced at Lauren, catching her gaze. The expression in his eyes surprised her. She had seen desire there often enough by now to know that wasn't what he was feeling. No, judging by that steely blue glint, and the tight line of his mouth, he was angry.

Angry? Why would ogling a former stripper's cleavage inspire anger?

It wasn't until Wanda walked them to the door and said goodbye that Lauren saw what Nick must have been studying. The feather trim of Wanda's robe stirred in the draft from the hall. On the upper curve of her breast, standing out starkly against her creamy white skin, was the edge of an ugly blue bruise.

"I'm going to get him," Nick stated. He raked his fingers through his hair impatiently, then jammed his hands into the pockets of his jeans. "He thinks he can get away with anything, but I'm going to bring him down."

Lauren watched him move restlessly across the living room. He'd been like this since they'd returned three hours ago, using physical activity to channel the energy that always simmered just below the surface, like a panther measuring the confines of his cage. With every day since the crash, his strength and his vitality had been steadily increasing. And each day the apartment had been steadily shrinking.

"He'll be at her place tomorrow," he said. "That's why she doesn't want us over there in the morning."

"Probably."

His frustration was evident in the tension that corded the muscles in his arms and hardened his jaw. He kicked aside a crumpled wad of paper as he limped back to where she was sitting on the couch. "This is going to be tougher than I thought. Even if we can get Wanda to break Duxbury's alibi, she probably won't testify against him in court.''

''She might eventually,'' Lauren said.

''I wouldn't hold my breath. He has her right where he wants her. Not only is he footing the bill for her rent, he owns the place where she works.''

''He's made her dependent on him,'' she agreed. ''That, combined with the low self-esteem she grew up with makes her doubly vulnerable to an abusive relationship.'' She paused, drawing her legs beneath her as she curled more tightly into the corner of the couch. ''I saw the bruise on her breast.''

''There are lots of reasons a person can get bruises, as we both know.''

''So, do you think it was nothing?''

''No,'' he said. ''I don't.''

''You think Duxbury was responsible, don't you?''

''I wouldn't put anything past him. We're talking about a man who killed a complete stranger with his car and put a price on the heads of five innocent women. He wouldn't think twice about knocking around his girl-friend.''

"Poor Wanda. We have to find a way to help her."

"Putting Duxbury away is the first step."

"Maybe I should go over alone tomorrow, try to get her to open up to me. I could give her some information on places she could go for help."

He pulled his hands out of his pockets, leaning over quickly to grasp her by the shoulders. "I'm not letting you go alone, Lauren. Don't underestimate him."

"But the more you go out in public, the more chance there is that you'll be recognized."

"Even if Duxbury doesn't connect you to my investigation, the fact that you're continuing to talk to his girlfriend is bound to make him nervous. We stick together, okay?"

His touch was making it difficult to concentrate. She inhaled shakily. "You don't need to worry about me, Nick."

"I've already brought enough trouble to my family. I don't want you in danger, too."

"I'll be fine."

He looked at where he held her shoulders and gradually eased his grip. "You didn't want to get involved in the first place."

"No, but I am now, and I intend to see this through."

"Duxbury hasn't been down to the station again, has he?"

"No. Will you relax? From what we've learned about him, he might be ruthless and have absolutely no conscience, but he's not stupid. He's not going to risk harming a member of the press. The pen is mightier than the sword and all that."

"I wouldn't rely on a pen being much of a weapon, Lauren. Or a TV camera, either."

Her gaze went to the end table. He'd gotten into the habit of storing his gun in the drawer there. His knife was probably still in his boot, wherever that might be—he tended to pull them off and leave them lying around anywhere. He was different from her in so many ways. He was a man who was familiar with violence, someone who dealt with all the things she preferred to view at a distance.

"Lauren?"

"All right, Nick. I won't go over without you."

"Good." He watched her for a moment in silence, then he withdrew his hands and sat beside her. The couch dipped with his weight, bringing her knee against his thigh.

"Nick, why did you become a cop?"

"Where did that question come from?"

"I'm curious." She turned to face him, propping her elbow on the back of the couch. "Was it because of your father?"

"In a way. I probably inherited his temperament, but I'd like to think it was my own decision."

She looked at the wound on his forehead. It continued to heal at an impressive rate, but there was no doubt it would leave a scar. Her gaze moved to the curving white line on his temple, the one he'd said had happened when he'd fallen out of his sisters' tree house. "What was it like, growing up with all those sisters?"

"Busy. Intense. It's hard to describe. What comes to mind first is the noise."

"Noise?"

"We all tended to have strong opinions."

"More inherited tendencies?"

"Oh, yeah. My mother traces her ancestry back to a long line of cossacks. They weren't known for their diplomacy." He propped his feet on the coffee table and crossed his arms, settling into a more comfortable position. "My dad's heritage was just as distinctive. He maintained that the first Strada in North America was a conquistador. He didn't have any proof, but it made for some interesting dinner table discussions."

"I can imagine."

"My parents were quite the pair. Married since they were teenagers and still crazy about each other. It wasn't until I was older that I realized how rare that was."

"You must have had a wonderful childhood...." She broke off, not wanting to bring up his father's death. He'd said he'd grown up fast then, and in a way she understood what he meant. Her childhood had essentially ended when she was eight. "Would you mind answering another question for me?"

"Ask away."

"It's a bit...personal."

He raised one eyebrow, his lips quirking. "We've lived together for more than a week. You mean there's something you *don't* know?"

"I was wondering about your marriage."

"It was a mistake. It's over."

"But why did you get married in the first place? You don't strike me as the type who would want to be tied down."

"I suppose I was looking for the same kind of happiness my parents had, that soul-deep, till-death-do-us-part kind of love. What Gloria and I had sure wasn't that. When the sex cooled off, there was nothing left."

Although his words were deliberately light,

there was a note of pain in his voice. Lauren knew it couldn't have been easy for Nick to admit defeat. He was so stubborn and passionate about everything he did. If he had thought he'd loved this woman...

A sudden wave of jealousy took her by surprise. It was ten times worse than what she'd felt when she'd thought Nick had been ogling Wanda. What was wrong with her? She didn't have any claim on him, and she certainly didn't intend to make one.

"It was a simple divorce," he continued. "Last I heard, she was living in Seattle with her new husband and a couple of kids."

"And that was four years ago?"

"I see Duxbury's not the only one you've been investigating."

She lifted her shoulder. "Gord told me."

"What's all this about, Lauren?" He tilted his head, studying her keenly for a moment. "Is this a roundabout way of asking me about my love life?"

Instant warmth rushed to her cheeks. Annoyed with herself, she decided to be as blunt as he was. "You don't need to go into detail. I found something else in your pocket besides your keys, so I already know you're no monk."

He looked puzzled. "My pocket?"

"Your leather jacket. The one you gave me after the crash."

Comprehension spread across his face, along with a slow, knowing grin. "Damn, were they still in there? I must have been carrying those around since O'Hara's party."

"Please," she said quickly, holding up her palm. "It's really none of my business."

"We threw a stag for Epstein. Those were O'Hara's idea of decorations instead of regular balloons."

She blinked. "Balloons? You mean he... inflated..."

Nick laughed at her expression. "What a waste of good condoms, huh? The ones in my pocket were leftovers."

She moved her hand to her mouth, muffling a giggle. She'd thought Angela's shower was bad.

"Now, as for the question you say you didn't want to ask—"

"Nick, it's okay. It's not my concern."

"Wrong. You have a right to know. I'm not currently involved with anyone, Lauren. Only you."

"We're not involved, Nick."

He extended his arm and clamped his hand on her thigh. "What would you call it?"

Through the linen fabric of her slacks, the warm strength of his fingers sent awareness tingling across her skin. Her laughter tapered off. What would she call it? "Dangerous."

"Uh-uh," he murmured, sliding closer. "What we're doing when we're working together is dangerous. We're not working now."

Lauren pulled away from his touch and stood up. "I'm going to fix some tea," she said.

Nick sighed noisily and yanked his feet from the table. "That was too fast again, right?"

Walking toward the kitchen, she spoke to him over her shoulder. "I have no intention of debating this with you."

"Okay by me," he said, following her. "I'm a hands-on kind of guy. I don't have much patience with talking all the time, either."

She did her best to ignore him as she moved around the kitchen, but he was a difficult man to ignore. Of course, she already knew that. Lord, did she know that.

He leaned a hip against the edge of the sink, folding his arms over his chest and crossing his ankles in a pose that made him look all long legs and muscle.

Picking up the kettle from the counter, she leaned past him to turn on the tap.

"You don't really want any tea, do you, Lauren?"

No, she didn't. Not with him standing so close to her. What she really wanted was to turn into his arms, feel his heat and his strength once more. She wanted to let the sparks that jumped between them make her forget all those logical, reasonable arguments that kept them apart. For a breathless second she hesitated. But then she filled the kettle resolutely and turned to put it on the stove. "Let's stick to business, okay? What do you think we should do next?"

"Now, that's a leading question if ever I heard one."

She kept her back to him, watching the element beneath the kettle turn orange, then red. "I mean about Duxbury."

"Short of staking out Wanda's condo and trying to get some incriminating pictures of them together?"

"Would that help?"

"It wouldn't prove anything. We need her testimony to break his alibi for the night Joey was killed." He moved behind her, slipping his arms around her waist. His breath stirred the hair over her ear. "You were great today," he said. "You handled that interview with Wanda like a real pro."

"That's because I am a pro."

"Good point." He tightened his arms gradually, drawing her toward him until her back nudged his chest. "I really appreciate the help you've given me so far. Have I told you that?"

"There's no need to thank me. I'm doing it for my story."

"Uh-huh. That nude poster threw you for a second, though, didn't it?"

"It was unexpected, that's all."

He lowered his head, rubbing his chin lightly across the top of her shoulder. "You know what I thought of when I saw it?"

Even though she knew it was crazy, Lauren couldn't help feeling another stab of jealousy. He'd been studying Wanda's bosom because of the bruise. He'd probably had a good reason for studying that poster, too. "No, what?"

"I was picturing you dressed in nothing but high heels and a feather."

The quiver of excitement that tiptoed through her stomach at his words was a shock. So was the image that sprang to her mind. "Nick..."

"You could use a green feather, to match your eyes."

"You're being ridiculous."

"Yeah. Forget the heels and the feather." He nuzzled the side of her neck. His lips were warm and firm, sending tendrils of sensation curling over her skin. "I'd rather see you naked."

Lauren grasped his forearms as her knees suddenly went weak. "When we visit Wanda tomorrow, we'll have to take a camera along if we want to keep to our cover story," she said quickly, struggling to concentrate.

"You'll have to show me how to work it." He splayed his fingers along her ribs. Sliding his palm across her midriff, he dragged the knuckle of his thumb along the underside of her breast. "I'm a fast learner. Real good working with my hands."

"I'll try to borrow...one of the...big ones...." She broke off, her chest heaving. "Nick..."

He moved his hand higher, cupping her gently. "Uh-huh?"

"Nick, my kettle's boiling."

A chuckle rumbled from his chest. "Oh, yeah. Mine, too."

"No, really. It's boiling."

Steam was shooting toward the ceiling from the kettle that was on the front burner of the stove as a high-pitched whistle filled the air.

Nick dropped his hand and reached past her to switch off the stove, then turned her around in his arms until she faced him. "Now, where were we?"

Tipping back her head, she looked into his face. It was a mistake. He was smiling, and the lines beside his mouth had deepened into those adorable dimples. In the sober illumination from the overhead track lighting, there was no mistaking the gleam in his eyes.

The passion and energy that had been crackling around him all evening had found another outlet. And it was clear that the physical activity he had in mind wasn't another hour of pacing the living room. Lauren felt her pulse thud in response, helpless to control the thrill she felt. There were so many things she could say, starting with no.

Yet she couldn't make a sound.

"Remember when I told you last night that there'd be a next time?" he murmured, his voice laced with the same anticipation that tingled through her veins.

She moistened her lips, nodding once.

"I think the next time is now, Lauren."

She raised her hand and touched his face with her fingertips, tracing the square jaw and high cheekbones, skimming the edge of the healing wound on his forehead. A lock of hair had fallen forward again. This time she didn't restrain the impulse to push it back. Giving in to temptation, she ran her fingers through his hair.

She felt his embrace enclose her, but she had no urge to escape. She should be afraid, but she wasn't. Love, dependency, vulnerability, all that she feared had nothing to do with the desire she felt at this moment.

"We'll take it as slow as you want, Lauren." He lowered his head, his smile fading. "But if I don't kiss you in the next minute—"

Sensation burst through her at the first touch of his lips on hers. Closing her eyes, she lifted her other hand and locked her fingers together behind his neck.

She hadn't believed it could be any better than the last time, but it was. His lips were familiar now. She knew the pleasure he could give her, and she reached for it with the mindless instinct of a flower turning toward the sun. His tongue traced the seam of her lips, and she parted them eagerly, seeking more of what she had tasted last night.

At her silent invitation he didn't hesitate, deepening the kiss with a steady mastery that turned her knees to jelly. Tightening his arms, he anchored her to the front of his body and kissed her until she had to gasp for breath.

"I've been waiting all day to do this," he

whispered, tracing his lips down the side of her neck. He nosed her collar aside and nibbled at the spot where her shoulder began.

His warmth and his scent surrounded her, melting her restraint. She leaned back in his arms, feeling her hair swing loose behind her, shivering as his teeth scraped gently over her collarbone.

Step by step, he backed her as far as the kitchen counter and lifted her up to sit on the edge. He pulled the hem of her blouse loose from her pants with two firm yanks, then slid his hands upward and began to unfasten the buttons—she should have known that whatever she chose to wear wouldn't stop him. Not Nick, not when he got that determined glint in his eyes. Before the last button was out of its hole, he was already parting the fabric.

Lauren waited for his touch, her pulse pounding. Cool air brushed her skin, then the slide of silk as he eased the blouse and her vest past her shoulders. Slowly, oh-so-slowly, the tickle of his breath on the curve of her breast became the brush of his lips.

She shuddered, wanting more, wishing she'd never told him he was too fast. Her nipples tightened against her bra and she moved restlessly, needing to soothe the ache he was creating. She thrust her fingers into his hair, urging him on wordlessly.

With a muted groan, he lowered his head to the swollen tip and dragged his tongue across the thin barrier of lace. His hands unsteady, he reached behind her and unhooked the clasp of her bra. Tossing the wispy scrap to the floor behind him, he cupped one breast in his palm and lifted it to his lips.

The pleasure that shot through her was so intense she moaned aloud. She heard the sound distantly, but was too immersed in sensation to care. She swayed forward, cradling his head in her arms, shamelessly taking everything he was willing to give.

"Beautiful," he whispered, letting her nipple slide from his mouth. "And delicious." He flicked it with his tongue, then tugged it into his mouth again.

"Oh, Nick. Oh, that feels…"

He turned his head, meeting her gaze. "Mmm?"

The primitive desire she saw in his face made her shudder. "Good. It feels so good."

His smile a devastating combination of arrogance and promise, he switched to her other breast. For long, maddening minutes, he squeezed and suckled until she was mindless with delight.

Placing his hands on her thighs, he parted her legs and urged her closer to the edge of the counter. With excruciating slowness, he straightened to his full height, letting her swollen flesh rub inch by inch over his lean, hard body. "Lauren?" he asked hoarsely.

She swayed, hooking one foot behind him to keep herself steady. It was hard to focus on his face, on anything, when every nerve was thrumming. "I can't believe this," she said.

"Why?"

"This. Us. We're in the kitchen, for God's sake."

"So?"

His reply was so typical, so male, so...Nick, that she felt her lips curve into a trembling smile. "We can't—"

"Hey." He raised his arms, flattening his palms against the cupboards above her head as he brought his face to hers. "We already are."

"We're already what?"

He nipped at her lower lip, then paused for a more thorough kiss. "We're enjoying each other," he answered finally.

Enjoying each other? Could it really be that simple? If this is what he made her feel like when she was sitting on a linoleum counter under the glare of an overhead fluorescent light, what would happen if they ever made it to the bedroom? She lifted her hands to his arms, curling her fingers around his rock-hard biceps, and a tremor of anticipation rippled down her spine.

"Is that a yes?"

She barely heard his question over the pounding of her pulse in her ears.

Nick cursed under his breath and glanced over his shoulder.

"It isn't a no," she murmured, spreading her fingers, marveling at the sleek skin over the firm muscle.

"Damn! It couldn't be your sister again, could it?"

She felt his tension in the stiffening of his arms. It took a moment to realize it wasn't because of what they were doing. The pulse in her ears grew louder, sharper, as if someone were knocking on... She drew in her breath. "Someone's at the door."

He swore again and turned to face her. "Of all the times to—"

"Lauren?"

At the hesitant call, Lauren's blood froze. "Oh, my God."

Nick snatched her blouse from the counter

and thrust it into her hands. "Why the hell didn't we chain that door?"

Clutching her blouse over her bare breasts, Lauren looked toward the kitchen door. "Nick, you have to hide," she whispered desperately.

Grasping her by the waist, he helped her down, steadying her as her feet hit the floor. "Too late."

"No, it's not. I'll head her off and—"

The kitchen door swung open. Nick turned around, stepping in front of Lauren to shield her with his body.

Angela moved into the room, her breath hitching on a sob as she dropped her suitcase to the floor and rubbed her eyes. Tears glistened on her cheeks and her chin trembled. "Lauren, I don't know what to do," she said, fumbling in her pocket to withdraw a tissue. "We had a terrible fight and..." Her words trailed off as she raised her gaze. The tissue fluttered to the floor. "Good Lord. *Lauren?*"

Her cheeks burning, her body still throbbing with unfulfilled desire, she closed her eyes and dropped her forehead against Nick's back.

Chapter 10

It didn't happen immediately, probably because Angela's vision was still blurred with tears. For a split second, Nick considered bolting past her before she had a chance to recognize him. But he didn't move. The harm had probably already been done, and it would be better to deal with this now when they still had an opportunity to control the damage.

And there was another reason he didn't move, one that had nothing to do with this hoax he was playing. He couldn't leave Lauren to face this alone. Not like this, not when she was so vulnerable and exposed. If they hadn't been interrupted...

This wouldn't have happened if he'd been able to keep his hands off her. He should have heard that knocking at the door earlier. It could have been anyone. What was it about Lauren that made him lose his sense of caution? Was it only their circumstances, a natural consequence of being cooped up together? Was it the same for her?

Nick fought down his frustration and crossed his arms over his chest, watching Angela's changing expressions, knowing it was only a matter of time.

"Oh, I'm sorry," she said, taking a step back. "I never should have barged in like this. I never dreamed…oh, I'm so sorry."

He heard the soft rustle of silk behind his back and guessed that Lauren was pulling on her blouse. She cleared her throat, but her voice when she spoke was far from steady. "Hello, Angela."

"I'm sorry," she repeated again, backing toward the kitchen door.

"You had no way of knowing," Lauren said, moving to Nick's side as she fastened her last button.

"No, I…" Angela inhaled shakily, wiping her eyes with the back of her hand. "Oh, Lord, I feel so stupid."

Nick glanced at Lauren, taking in her tangled hair and her swollen lips. She was struggling hard to regain her usual composure, but it was no use. She looked like a woman who had been long and thoroughly kissed. A surge of protectiveness took him off guard. "Are you all right?" he asked quietly.

She smoothed back her hair, pressing her lips together as she met his gaze. She looked as frustrated as he felt, yet there was something more in her eyes. Confusion. Regret. And a need that wouldn't be satisfied by merely a quick release.

He put his arm around her shoulders and pulled her securely against his side before looking back to Angela. "Could you give us a minute?" he asked.

"Oh, of course. I'll just go in the other room and…" Her words trailed off. For a moment she didn't move.

"Angela," Lauren began, "I think we should—"

"Oh, my God," she whispered, the shock on her face slowly giving way to recognition. "Oh…my…God. I know who you are. You're…you're…him."

"Angela, please," Lauren said. "I can explain."

"You're the hero, the one from the crash. I saw you on TV." She pressed her hand to her mouth. "Oh, Lord," she mumbled, twisting around quickly and heading for the living room.

"Wait," Lauren called, slipping out of Nick's embrace to go after her sister. "Angela!"

Nick watched them go, then raked his hands through his hair. He spotted the crumpled lace of Lauren's bra, still lying on the floor where he'd tossed it. Less than a foot away was the suitcase Angela had dropped. Through the swinging door to the living room came the sound of feminine voices raised in rapid conversation.

Hell, when things started to go wrong, they just didn't know when to stop.

Lauren sat on the edge of the bed, drawing her legs beneath her as she turned to face her sister. Angela had propped a pillow behind her back and sat cross-legged against the headboard, the same way she had liked to do more than twenty years ago when they'd shared their childhood secrets.

Resolving to be completely honest, Lauren kept her explanation as short as possible. She gave only the barest details of the crime Nick was investigating, and she didn't reveal Duxbury's name. By the time she had finished, Lauren was relieved to see that Angela seemed to accept her sister's participation in Nick's hoax relatively easily. From the sidelong glances she continued to give her, it was clear that it was the scene she'd interrupted in the kitchen that shocked her the most.

"How long has he been staying here?" Angela asked.

Lauren sighed, pleating the hem of her blouse between her fingers. "A week."

"A *week?*" Her curls bounced as she shook her head in disbelief. "You mean he was here when I came over the day after the crash? And last night, during my shower?"

"He went out last night."

"But how could you do this? What about your job? And if his life is in danger, is it safe for you to be involved?"

She dropped the ends of her blouse and leaned forward to take Angela's hands in hers. "Don't worry about my job. This story is going to be worth it. And the danger's minimal as long as no one knows Nick's alive. You can't tell anyone, Angela," she said firmly. "Please, promise me."

"Of course, if that's what you want."

"I mean it. No one. Not even Eddy."

At the mention of Eddy's name, her chin

trembled. She pressed her lips together and nodded.

"I'm trusting you, Angela. We're hoping this won't go on for much longer, but until Nick can get some firm evidence in his case, we can't end the hoax."

"I understand."

Lauren squeezed her fingers. "Thank you."

"I'm sorry about...walking in on you."

Warmth tingled into her cheeks. "Please, forget it."

"I simply had no idea...." She shook her head again. "I should have known it would happen sooner or later, though."

"What are you talking about?"

"You. Meeting a man."

She dropped her hands and slipped off the bed. "I'd hardly consider going through a plane crash as a good way to meet men."

"I don't mean to trivialize what happened, but—"

"Don't let what you saw give you the wrong idea. Nick and I are working together, that's all."

"It's more than that."

"Okay, we find each other attractive, but it's nothing serious."

"Where's he sleeping?"

Sucking in her breath, she tucked her blouse back into her pants. ''On the couch. Let's drop the subject, all right?''

''I know it's none of my business, but this is the first time since Harper that you've shown any interest in anyone.''

Shown any interest? Lauren thought, glancing down at the way the silk fabric clung revealingly to her breasts. That was putting it mildly. She pulled a light cotton sweater from her closet and slipped it on to preserve what was left of her modesty. ''I'd really prefer not to talk about this, Angela.''

She slumped back against the headboard. ''Sorry.''

''What happened tonight with Eddy?''

''We had a fight.'' She pulled a tissue from the pocket of her skirt and blew her nose. ''I thought I could stay with you, but I'll find a hotel.''

Lauren returned to the side of the bed. Now that Angela's initial shock was wearing off, her tears were returning. ''Oh, Angie, is it that bad?''

''I don't know. I just needed some time to think.''

''Do you want to talk about it?''

"It's not that complicated. I'm just not sure I'm ready to get married."

Lauren sank down heavily on the edge of the bed, her jaw going slack. Angela? Not wanting to get married? She and Eddy had been engaged for almost a year. They'd bought a house together. They'd been living with each other for the past six months. Of all people, she was the last one Lauren would have expected to get cold feet.

Angela gave a watery laugh that ended on a sob. "Now it's my turn to shock you."

"But you two are so...happy together."

"I love him so much it scares me. All my life, I wanted to belong with someone. Now that I think I've found him, I keep remembering what happened to Mom. What happens if he leaves me? What happens if we have kids and he abandons them?"

"Is this about Dad? I thought you understood—"

"Sure, I understand why he left, but it still hurt."

"He did the best he could, but his job kept him away most of the time even before he divorced Mom. Those two were never meant to be married. They made each other miserable and were happier apart. Are you saying that's how it is for you and Eddy?''

''No, of course not.''

''Then what's wrong?''

She hesitated. ''All this started over that big band music he listens to. He keeps changing the station on my car radio.''

''Is his different taste in music that important to you?''

''I know it sounds petty, but that's how it began. One thing led to another and then we were yelling at each other. Oh, Lord,'' she mumbled, covering her eyes. ''I thought I knew what I wanted.''

Lauren stared at her helplessly. She was scarcely qualified to give advice on problems of the heart. And she was no advocate of marriage, so she certainly wouldn't try to talk Angela into going back to Eddy.

And she'd never forget how her sister had been there for her when she'd had nowhere else to go.

''Stay here as long as you want, Angela,'' she said finally. ''It's a big bed. It'll be like when we were kids.''

''I don't think an all-night pajama party is going to solve my problems,'' she said on another choked laugh.

"You need to talk. We should have done this earlier." She leaned forward, handing Angela a fresh tissue. "I've just been so wrapped up in my work lately, and then there was the crash and all this business with Nick...." She stopped, realizing she was only making excuses. She'd been avoiding Angela the same way she'd been avoiding dealing with her feelings about the wedding. "I'm sorry."

"Maybe it's the permanency that's scaring me. Maybe Eddy and I should forget the whole wedding and go on living together the way we were. We were getting along fine until now."

"Perhaps you're just getting overwhelmed by all the wedding details."

"Do you know what a mess it would be if I backed out at this point?"

"Actually, I know exactly what a mess it would be."

"Oh, I'm sorry. Of course you'd know," Angela said hurriedly. "I didn't mean to bring that up."

"Canceling the ceremony and everything that goes with it is only a matter of a few phone calls."

"But it's taken months to plan. Eddy's parents are flying in from Dallas. Uncle Jim and Aunt Kate said they'd be here by Friday, along with all their kids. It took me weeks to track Dad down, and I don't even know if I'd be able to contact him to tell him not to come. And as if that weren't enough, everyone from work is talking about the reception we've got planned, and—''

''It still can be stopped,'' she said firmly. ''Don't let what other people might think force you into doing something you don't want to do.''

It sounded so easy, the way she said it. For Angela's sake, she didn't mention the rest of what canceling a wedding entailed. She didn't bring up the humiliation, the awkward explanations or the looks of pity she'd had to endure afterward. She omitted the crushing blow she'd felt to her pride, and how she'd had to accept a large part of the blame for her failure.

She also didn't mention the six years of self-imposed celibacy that had followed her fiancé's betrayal. Six years of refusing to let herself get close to another man, doubting her judgment, fearing her own emotional inadequacy too much to free the natural, physical reactions of her body.

But as Nick had said, there was a big difference between marriage and…and what? Fooling around? *Enjoying* each other?

She drew her lower lip between her teeth, rubbing the tip of her tongue over the still-sensitive flesh. Despite the time that had passed, it felt slightly swollen from the kisses they had shared.

There hadn't been time to think about what they had done together, or where it had been leading. It was just as well they had been interrupted. If Angela hadn't pushed open that door when she had...

It isn't a no. That's what Lauren had said. She'd been half naked and wanting more. All her caution, all her common sense had simply melted away when his lips had touched hers. No, it had happened sooner than that. All he needed to do was to look at her in that certain way. Or stand close enough for those pheromones of his to short-circuit her reason.

"God, I wish I knew what I wanted," Angela said on a sob.

Lauren brought her attention back to her sister with a guilty start. "Give yourself more time away from Eddy. You might be able to think more clearly."

"You're right. I can never think too clearly whenever he's around. His idea of solving an argument is to..." She halted, her cheeks going pink. "Well, he makes me forget what I wanted to say."

Some men have a talent for that, Lauren thought wryly.

As usual, Nick was already up and dressed in his customary T-shirt and jeans by the time Lauren walked into the living room. Morning light bathed his strong features and highlighted his lean body where he was standing beside the window. With one arm braced against the edge of the frame, his body angled so that he wouldn't be visible from the street, he gulped a mouthful of coffee and glanced at her over his shoulder. "Is your sister calmer now?" he asked.

"Yes, she's feeling much more herself this morning," Lauren replied, coming over to stand on the other side of the window.

"Is she going to keep quiet about me?"

"I explained the situation to her, and she said she would."

"Do you trust her?"

"Of course."

He drained his coffee and tapped his fingers against the empty mug. "You sure?"

"Yes, I'm sure. But we don't have much choice."

"Who was on the phone?"

"Eddy." She tipped her head toward the bedroom. "They're still talking."

"Is there going to be a wedding?"

"I don't know. I think so."

"My parents used to argue," he said. "Their fights were legendary in our neighborhood. Mom would lapse into Russian and Dad would answer in Spanish, and they both had enough lung power to vibrate the windowpanes."

"But you said they had a happy marriage."

"They did. They were just the kind of people who needed to let off steam every now and then, their way of not letting the little things build up."

"I see."

"The way they made up afterward used to vibrate the windowpanes, too," he said, his mouth curving into a smile. "It wasn't until I was a teenager that I figured out why."

"There's a lot more to marriage than physical compatibility. Angela has some very real, very valid doubts about what she's getting into."

His smile faded. "Yeah, I can understand that."

"She'll be staying here for a while, at least until she comes to a decision."

"When I saw the suitcase, I figured that's what she'd had in mind."

"We'll find some way to manage. As I said, she won't reveal your presence."

His jaw tensed as he turned his gaze back to the window. "This whole thing is getting too damn complicated."

There was no disputing that, Lauren thought.

He set down his mug on the windowsill and pushed his hand into the back pocket of his jeans. Seconds later he had withdrawn the bra she had been wearing last night. He looked at it for a moment, then hooked his forefinger through one strap and held it out toward her. "Here," he said.

She'd told herself she wasn't going to dwell on what had happened. She'd almost convinced herself that they could continue with business as usual. But at her first sight of that cream-colored lace against his strong fingers, her mouth went dry. "Where..." She cleared her throat. "Where was it?"

"On the floor. I picked it up so you'd have fewer questions to answer. Your vest's in the front closet."

"Thank you," she said, reaching out to take the underwear from his hand.

Instead of releasing his hold on the bra, he

caught her hand in his and tugged her toward him. "About last night," he began.

"Nick, considering our situation now, with my sister staying here and all, I don't think there's any point discussing it."

He twined their fingers together, the silky strap sliding between them. It was a tangible reminder that went beyond words, instantly evoking the feelings that had raged last night. Holding her gaze, he leaned forward slowly and covered her mouth with his.

It was a brief kiss, filled with tender restraint. Apart from their hands, they didn't touch anywhere else, yet when he lifted his head, Lauren's body was humming.

For a long, silent moment he remained motionless. Then he released her fingers and took a step back. "We're going to have to do something about that one of these days."

She crumpled her bra between her hands. "What are you talking about?"

"I think you know," he said, reaching out to rub her lower lip gently with his thumb.

Oh, yes. She knew. Any woman with a pulse would know. His light caress was creating waves of warmth, softening her resistance more swiftly than she would have believed possible. "Nick..."

"Next time I'll make sure we won't be interrupted." He dropped his hand and turned away before she could form a reply.

Next time. How often had he said that now? He was largely responsible for all this upheaval in her normally comfortable, predictable life. So why did her pulse thud and her palms sweat simply because he'd made another one of his arrogant, macho boasts?

Only, it wasn't a boast. It was a statement. And the confusion she felt over her reaction was as much due to the prospect that there *would* be a next time…as it was due to the growing possibility that there *wouldn't*.

The rest of the morning passed with painful slowness. Angela spent most of the time on the phone in the bedroom while Nick alternated between pacing the length of the living room and staring out the window. Lauren tried to concentrate on the work she had brought home, but it was no use. Between hearing her sister's tearful voice through the bedroom door and watching Nick try to work off his barely controlled restlessness, Lauren felt the tension in the apartment steadily increase to a level that was almost unbearable. It was with a sense of relief that they finally left for their meeting with Wanda Smith.

The condominium that Duxbury kept for his

mistress was in a tall, gleaming white building. Access from the parking garage that served the block was through a locked, tenants-only basement corridor, so as they'd done on their previous visit, they entered through the marble-tiled lobby that faced the street.

Lauren hesitated, unable to resist the urge to glance nervously over her shoulder.

"He wouldn't be here," Nick said, pausing beside the building directory. "He's always at his in-laws on Sunday afternoons, remember?"

"So it wasn't a useless piece of information after all," she murmured.

"What a guy, huh? Spends the morning with his girlfriend and then makes nice with his wife's folks the rest of the day."

She tightened her grip on her purse, trying to control her anxiety. "Wanda wouldn't have agreed to a time when we'd run into him, anyway. And even if something goes wrong, we'll be able to bluff our way through."

Nick pivoted to face her, laying his hand on her shoulder. "Say the word, Lauren. If you want to call this off, it's okay. I'll try something else."

"No, this is our best chance. I'm fine."

"You sure?"

"Yes. But all this might be useless, anyway.

She might not open up. She might be too scared of him to answer any questions.''

''Then we'll talk to her neighbors. Or I'll track down the garage attendant who was working the day Joey was killed. Or I'll talk to every person I see on the street between here and the accident scene until someone does answer my questions. I won't give up.''

No, Nick wouldn't give up, she thought. He hadn't yet. About anything.

He'd added a baseball cap to his disguise, and along with the beard and the heavy glasses, his features were well concealed. Lauren had to remind herself that simply because *she* was always conscious of the man beneath the disguise didn't mean that everyone else was.

She glanced at the camera he held by his side. They had stopped at the station before coming here, and the heavy video camera leant a much needed note of authenticity. She'd given Nick a brief course in its operation and he'd proved to be a fast learner. As he'd said, he was good with his hands.

Stiffening her spine, Lauren picked up the telephone receiver and punched in the code beside Wanda's name. She listened to the phone ring on the other end seven times, then pressed the reset button and tried again. This time she waited for ten rings before she disconnected.

''She said two-thirty,'' Nick said, glancing at his watch.

''Maybe she reconsidered,'' Lauren said.

He scowled. ''No way. She was eager to get this free publicity.''

Lauren tried the phone again, cradling it against her shoulder as she listened to it ring. Despite the sunlight that streamed brightly through the glass entrance, she felt a chill. ''Something must have happened,'' she said.

Turning toward the lobby door, he tried unsuccessfully to pull it open, then stooped over to reach into his boot. Seconds later, there was a muted click and the sound of metal scraping on metal.

''Nick!'' she exclaimed. ''What are you doing?''

He worked the tip of his switchblade between the latch and the lock plate. ''You're right. Something must have happened. I'm going to check it out.''

''For heaven's sake, someone's bound to come through here sooner or later. Or we could call the superintendent.''

''Don't think we should wait,'' he said tersely.

Dread curled in her stomach at his tone. In the next instant, the phone was finally picked up. Lauren cleared her throat. "Hello? Wanda?"

There was a long pause during which the only sound was labored breathing. Then a quiet voice came on. "Who is it?"

"Wanda, it's Lauren Abbot. We'd arranged to meet this afternoon."

Another long pause. "I'm sorry," Wanda said. "I tried to call you all day, but your line was busy. I, um, changed my mind."

"We could come back later, if that would be better. If you have company, I wouldn't dream of intruding."

"No, I'm alone. I just..." She hesitated. "I changed my mind," she repeated.

Maybe the tension of the last week had made her more attuned to other people's emotions, or perhaps it was because she'd lost her own professional detachment somewhere in Lake Michigan. Whatever the reason, Lauren knew that Wanda was in trouble. "Could I help, Wanda?" she asked softly. "Off the record. You might feel better if you could talk to someone."

"I, um, need to go out."

There was a sudden click from the lock, then Nick swung the lobby door open. He shoved his knife back into his boot and gestured to Lauren with a jerk of his head. "Come on," he mouthed.

"I could drive you, Wanda. We could talk in the car. Where do you need to go?"

"You wouldn't put this in your story, would you?" There was the same note of innocence in her voice that had been so touching before.

"Absolutely not," she said, the feeling of dread growing. "I like you, Wanda, and I really do want to help you however I can."

This time the pause was long enough to raise the fine hairs on the back of Lauren's neck. Finally Wanda sighed and told her what she wanted. For a split second, Lauren remained motionless, stunned, not wanting to believe what she had heard. Then she slammed the phone down and hurried through the door Nick was holding open.

He limped behind her to the elevator. "What did she say?"

Lauren jabbed the button with enough force to snap her fingernail. "She wants me to drive her to a hospital."

There was no response to Lauren's first knock on Wanda's door. Nick shifted impatiently, then backed up a step and raised his foot to kick it in, but Lauren stopped him with a touch on his arm. "Don't," she said, knocking again. "I suspect she's already seen enough violence."

The door swung open to a shadowed interior. Wanda retreated quickly until she was no more than a curvy silhouette against the light that filtered through the closed curtains. "I'm sorry for messing up your plans, Miss Abbot," she said. "It was really dumb. I fell in the bathtub."

Lauren walked toward her, giving her vision time to adjust to the dim lighting. "It'll be all right. My assistant and I will take you to the emergency room...." Her words trailed off as outrage closed her throat.

The right side of Wanda's face was swollen and mottled with purple. More swelling had blackened and closed her right eye to no more than a slit. She held her arms crossed over her breasts, her shoulders curled as if to protect her from more blows.

It was one thing to sit in the safety of her comfortable apartment and speculate about the possibility of Wanda's being abused, or to read articles or view photographs of victims, or to share public anger when wealthy abusers escaped punishment. But it was something else entirely to confront such incontrovertible evidence of cruelty.

This was no story. There was no safe distance, no protective aloofness possible. With no other thought than to give comfort, Lauren moved to Wanda's side and slipped her arm carefully around her shoulders.

"That bastard," Nick said, striding forward. "He did this to you, didn't he?"

At the vehemence in his voice, Wanda started nervously. "I...don't know who you mean. I fell, that's all."

He stalked past her, doing a quick check of the other rooms before he returned and switched on a lamp. His breath hissed between his teeth as he took another look at Wanda. "Duxbury's going to pay for this. For everything."

She glanced at Lauren, her good eye widening with fear. "I never told you his name. Oh, God. He's going to think I told. I didn't. I wasn't going to say anything about him. He's so good to me, I'd never tell."

In the revealing light from the lamp, Wanda's injuries looked ten times worse. "Let's get you to a doctor," Lauren said, gently steering her toward the door. "That's the first priority."

There was a mirrored door on the front closet. When Wanda saw her reflection, she gave a sudden sob and turned into Lauren's loose embrace. "It shows this time," she cried. "I'll have to miss work. He never did it so it showed before.''

Lauren's outrage became tinged with fury. She raised her hand to Wanda's head, her fingers shaking as she smoothed the brassy blond, baby-fine hair. ''We'll help you. I promise. It'll be all right.''

''Wanda, you need to file charges,'' Nick said. ''We'll help you do that, too.''

''I thought he'd be proud of me, that he'd want to see me on TV. He got so mad,'' she said, her voice muffled against Lauren's shoulder. ''It was all my fault. I've never seen him so mad.''

Nick met Lauren's gaze over Wanda's head, his expression mirroring the sudden guilt she felt. ''It was nobody's fault except Duxbury's,'' he said. ''It would have happened eventually. That's the pattern of abusers. They keep getting worse unless they're stopped.''

''But he loves me. He's always sor...sorry.'' Wanda hiccuped, nestling more tightly against Lauren. ''I know I'm not smart, but he should have trusted me. I wasn't going to tell anyone. I didn't before. He didn't mean to hurt me. He didn't mean to hurt that man....''

''What man?'' Nick asked, cutting through her rambling words. ''Who else did he hurt?''

"He didn't mean to. That was my fault, too, 'cause he was driving me home from rehearsal."

His entire body tensing, Nick stepped closer. He swung the camera up and switched it on. "Adam Duxbury was driving you home from your job at the Painted Pony?"

"Ducky is so good to me," she repeated, her voice growing more high-pitched, like a little girl's. "He loves me so much."

Nick ground his teeth, his nostrils flaring. "He just beat you up, Wanda."

"He couldn't help it. I got him mad. He didn't want me talking to any reporters."

"There's no justification for the way he hurt you," Lauren said. "None at all. It's his fault, not yours."

"What happened in the accident," Nick persisted, "when he was driving you home?"

For a moment it seemed as if she wouldn't respond. She shuddered, her shoulders trembling beneath Lauren's light embrace. Finally, she lifted her head and turned her battered face toward Nick. "He was in a hurry," she said brokenly. "We only had an hour before he had to go to some banquet or something, but he took care of me, got ice for my head and everything.

He knew how I didn't want a bruise on my face.''

Banquet? Lauren thought. Duxbury had attended a fund-raising dinner the day Joey was killed. ''What was wrong with your head, Wanda?'' Lauren asked.

''I was trying to find the earring I dropped. He doesn't like me to leave stuff in his car. It was my fault I was bent over like that so I bumped the gear shift real hard when he hit that guy.''

As the halting story gradually took shape, Lauren saw the flare of triumph in Nick's eyes. It was better than they had hoped. Wanda could do more than break Duxbury's alibi, she was a witness to the hit-and-run.

Chapter 11

"She'll be all right," Nick said, coming up behind Lauren where she stood by the coffee machine in the visitors' lounge. "The fractured ribs will heal themselves, and there wasn't any permanent damage done to her face."

Lauren pressed her lips together, watching the cup drop to the grate, waiting while the stream of liquid gurgled downward. "We're responsible, you know. It was because he didn't want her talking to a journalist that this happened. If we'd left her alone—"

"Don't start that again," Nick said fiercely. "Do you think she'd be better off if things had gone on the way they were? She had to make the break from Duxbury eventually, and at least we were there to help."

She lifted her cup and sipped without tasting. Yes, at least they'd been there. "Is the counselor still with her?"

"Just left. Wanda's agreed to talk to the police."

"Thank God. It's the only way out for her."

"The doctor checked her over again and discharged her, so I'm taking her down to the station as soon as she's dressed."

Just like that, it was all coming to an end. Lauren took another gulp of whatever it was that had filled her cup and turned to face him. "No matter what she's been led to believe, she isn't stupid. It didn't take her that long to realize her safety depends on testifying...." Her head snapped up when she caught sight of his face. "You got rid of the beard."

He rubbed his jaw. "That glue was itchy as hell."

The hat and glasses were gone as well. Of course. He didn't need to hide his face, he didn't need to hide at all. Now that Wanda had agreed to testify, this whole incredible situation was almost over.

"Once Wanda gives her statement, Joey's case is going to be reopened," Nick said, echoing the direction of her thoughts. "And once my captain sees the job Duxbury did on her face, he'll have to provide protection not only for her but for my family.''

"You accomplished what you set out to do," Lauren said. "You won't need to hide anymore."

"No."

"It's time to end the hoax."

"I already called my Mom and the captain. The rest is up to you."

"What do you mean?"

"We made a deal, remember? It's your story, so you get to break it however you want."

She set down her coffee, her fingers suddenly cold.

"What's the matter?" he asked, covering her hands with his. "This is what you wanted, isn't it?"

"Yes, it is. I suppose I hadn't expected it to end so...fast."

He smiled. "I've been told that's one of my faults, being too fast."

One of his faults? She wouldn't call it that. His tendency to rush ahead, to prefer action to idleness, was a part of his nature. It was one of the things that was so attractive about him.

God, he *was* an attractive man, she thought, looking at the way the lines beside his mouth deepened into those adorable dimples. At last he no longer needed to hide his face when they went out in public. She was free to look at him as much as she wanted. It didn't matter where they were, or whether his expression was tense with anger or sparkling with that boyish glint of teasing, she loved to look at him....

She drew herself up, struggling to control the impulse she felt to sway into his arms. She couldn't afford to think about that now. Once they made an appearance at the police station with Wanda, the news of Nick's resurrection was going to spread. If she wanted to be the one to break the story, she would need to work quickly. Her personal feelings couldn't be allowed to interfere with the work that she had to do.

After all, the story was really all she wanted, right?

Pulling her hands from his, she reached into her purse for her notebook and pen.

The graveyard shift was just coming on duty when Nick ushered Lauren and Wanda up the worn wooden stairs to the second floor. He'd already called Captain Gilmour from the hospital. As he'd expected, the captain had recovered rapidly from the shock of hearing his voice and had agreed to meet them downtown. What

Nick hadn't expected was the group of people who were waiting for him in the captain's office.

"Strada!" Epstein slapped him hard on the back as he stepped through the door. "Should have known you were too stubborn to die."

Nick staggered, grabbing the edge of a filing cabinet to keep his balance. "Damn, Epstein. You been bench-pressing engine blocks again?"

"Nah, just doing push-ups with the wife."

O'Hara laughed as he reached for Nick's hand. "Welcome back, Strada."

"Thanks, Phil."

"Does this mean I still have to pay you the twenty-five bucks I owe you?"

"Why else do you think I came back?"

Ramona Brill pushed O'Hara aside and punched Nick in the shoulder. "You rat! I can't believe I actually cried at that memorial service."

Grinning, Nick lifted his hand and tugged lightly on her red ponytail. "And I can't believe you missed me, pest."

She shook her head. "Neither can I, pain." Grasping his arms, she stretched up to plant a smacking kiss on his mouth.

The captain's gruff voice cut through the whistles that followed Ramona's kiss. "All right, all right This can wait until after we take care of business. Everybody out.''

As Nick's colleagues grumbled and filed out the door, Gilmour frowned at Lauren. ''Miss Abbot, we'll make a statement to the media after—''

''She stays,'' Nick said, putting his hand on her shoulder.

''You're in no position to give any orders, Strada.''

''I can vouch for Lauren's trustworthiness, Captain. And she already knows more about this than you do.''

Without further delay, Gilmour directed Wanda to the chair in front of his desk. Between the long day and the painkillers she'd been given at the hospital, she was obviously close to exhaustion. Still, she repeated her story about the night Joey had been killed, reciting the details in her wavering earthy-innocent voice.

By the time she had finished, the captain's scowl had deepened. He opened the door and waved Ramona inside. ''Detective Brill will take care of you now, Miss Smith. Thank you for your cooperation.''

''You'll be fine now,'' Lauren said, giving Wanda's hand a squeeze. You have a beautiful voice, and if you need any help when you're well enough to get back to work, you still have my number.''

''Thanks, Miss Abbot.''

Lauren stepped back to let her walk past. ''Even if you just want to talk, call me, okay?''

Ramona put her hand on the small of Wanda's back and gently ushered her out of the office. ''Come on, honey. Let's get you to bed. I guarantee everything's going to look a lot better in the morning.'' She paused to smile at Nick, then clicked the door shut behind them.

Gilmour raked his hand through his thinning hair as he moved back behind his desk. ''You really opened up a can of worms this time, didn't you, Strada,'' he muttered. ''Adam Duxbury. You were right after all.''

''We have another eyewitness to back up my story,'' Nick said, counting off the points on his fingers. ''We have documented proof of Duxbury's capacity for violence. We have enough background information on Duxbury's dirty business deals to destroy the squeaky-clean image he's been hiding behind. And once I'm back on the case full time, it's a sure bet I'll find more evidence.''

''We have enough for a warrant now, but you can forget about working on the case. Epstein and O'Hara will take it from here.''

"What?"

"After the stunt you pulled? Your hot-dog tactics are going to do more damage to this department's credibility than one of those cheap detective shows."

"It'll blow over. Besides, it was the only way to protect my family."

"That's not necessary anymore. With your death, the contract was lifted."

Nick clenched his fists, leaning forward. "So you knew about Duxbury's contract all along. You said there wasn't any proof."

"There still isn't. Epstein heard about the contract through one of his informers after the plane crash. And now that we have an eyewitness, Duxbury has nothing to gain by renewing his threats."

"Then it worked. They'll be all right."

"Just because things worked out this time doesn't mean I'll tolerate conduct like yours again. And don't hold your breath about getting back on the payroll. Until personnel updates the computer files again, you're still dead."

"Gee, thanks, Captain."

"I have a good mind to leave you that way." Gilmour braced his hands on his desk and glared at Nick. "If you ever pull another stunt like this

I'll bust you down to kindergarten crossing guard.''

Nick took Lauren's elbow and started for the office door. ''Since I'm not getting paid, there's no point hanging around to listen to this crap.''

''Strada!''

He paused, glancing over his shoulder. ''Yeah?''

''Leave Duxbury to Epstein and O'Hara. That's an order. We need to do the rest of this by the book or his lawyers will find a way for him to get off. Have I made myself clear?''

''Perfectly.''

Gilmour transferred his glare to Lauren. ''Be aware that this is still an ongoing investigation. If you reveal information prematurely, it could jeopardize our success.''

Lauren nodded once to acknowledge the advice. ''It's Lieutenant Strada's miraculous return that will be the focus of my story, Captain Gilmour. After seeing what Adam Duxbury is capable of, I have no intention of doing anything that might prevent him from being brought to justice.''

''If that's true, then you'll wait until he's arrested before you go public.''

''I won't wait indefinitely.''

''Twenty-four hours. That's all it should be.''

She nodded again, then pulled a card from her purse and handed it to Gilmour. ''Please call me if it's sooner. I assisted Lieutenant Strada in this deception on the clear understanding that I would have the right to break his story. If you want my continued cooperation, then I expect to have yours in return.''

Nick listened to her words, marveling at how cool and composed she sounded. Evidently she had impressed the captain, and that was no easy feat.

From the moment they'd left the hospital, she had slipped back into her professional mode, staying in the background, silently observing. More often than not, whenever he'd look at her, she'd be jotting down points in the small spiral notebook she kept in her purse.

He knew what she was doing. She'd thrown those icy barriers back up around her and was doing her best to submerge all the warmth and passion he'd come to know. She said she wanted his story, and she was making damn sure that's the only thing he was going to be able to give her.

But this wasn't over yet. No, not by a long shot. They had unfinished business between them that had nothing to do with the story that would eventually hit the airwaves.

"How long do you think it will take?" Lauren asked as they left the police station twenty minutes later.

He watched the way her hair turned silver in the stark lighting of the street lamp, thinking about how she'd looked last night under the fluorescent light in her kitchen. He'd lost track of the time the moment he'd kissed her, so he had no idea how long it would take—

"Nick? Do you think it will take another day before Duxbury's arrested?"

"Maybe. Epstein and O'Hara are solid, dependable cops. Considering what I've already given them, they'll get him."

"All right." She stopped beside her car, her keys already in her hand. "That will give me a chance to put my notes in order before we go on the air."

"We?"

"I'd like to do a live interview at the station with you the moment Captain Gilmour gives me the go-ahead."

"Before I go on the air, I want to see my family."

"Oh. Of course. I'll drop you off at your mother's house and then go back to my place to pack up your things. I'll bring them to the studio, so you can pick them up then."

"Hey, for someone who likes to take things slow, you're sure in a hurry to get rid of me," he said, moving closer.

"Nick, it's pointless to prolong this."

Trailing his fingertips down her arm, he covered her hand with his. "I don't think so."

"We both have lives to get back to. We both have jobs to do. I'm happy that everything turned out well for you, but it's over."

"No, it isn't."

"Nick..."

"My family was the reason I had to play dead while I went after Duxbury. And it's because of your help that they're going to be safe now. They'll want to meet you, Lauren. Besides..." he added, taking the keys from her hand to unlock the car door. "My story isn't over yet. You've been with me from the start, so you might as well stick around and see how it ends."

Although the rest of the tree-lined street was sleepily dark and quiet, the Strada house was ablaze with lights, the inside door standing open in welcome. Lauren tried to stay a few steps behind Nick as he headed up the walk, but he grinned and grasped her hand, tugging her along with him with his usual impatient energy.

He'd just reached the doorstep when there was a shriek from inside the house. In the next instant, the screen door banged against the wall and two fifteen-year-olds barreled through the doorway and flung themselves against him. He staggered backward, releasing Lauren's hand as he caught his sisters in a tight embrace.

"Nick!" Tina stretched up on her tiptoes to kiss his cheek. "Nick, it's true. You're all right."

"I knew you couldn't be dead," Barb said, laughing as she slid her arms around his waist. "I knew it."

"We missed you so much. Barb wouldn't stop crying—"

"Neither did Tina."

His smile faltered. "I'm sorry. I know it must have been tough for everyone—"

"Oh, I can't believe this," Tina said, wiping her eyes against his shirt. "It's like a dream. You're really here."

Barb wriggled out of his embrace, catching his arm to urge him inside. "Why didn't you let anyone know before? Where have you been?"

He tipped his head toward Lauren. "I've been with her."

Tina ducked under his arm, looking toward

the shadows beside the doorstep. "Oh! I saw you on TV. You're the lady who—"

"You saved Nick's life!" Barb finished. "You dragged him out of the plane."

To Lauren's surprise, Tina sprang forward and caught her hands. She pulled her into the house with the kind of reckless enthusiasm typical of her brother. "You saved him," she said, her smile radiant. "I saw you talk about it on the news."

"Mom wanted to call you, to thank you for trying to help. Wow, and Nick was with you all along!"

"What happened, Nick?" Tina demanded. "How come everyone thought you were dead?"

Before either of them could reply, his other two sisters strode forward to join the group in the front hall. Rose's dark eyes were bright with tears as she threw her arms around Nick. "Thank God," she said, her voice choking with emotion. "It's true."

"When Mom called, I thought she'd cracked from the strain," Juanita said, taking her turn as soon as Rose loosened her hold. "I had to come and see for myself."

"I'm perfectly fine," Nick said. "As long as I don't get smothered by all this affection."

Rose swatted his arm, then stretched to give

him another kiss. "We can't help it, Nick. When we thought you were gone—" She sniffed hard, shaking her head. "This is stupid. I cried when I thought you were dead. Now I'm doing it again because I know you're not."

"And she never cries," Barb said.

"Where's Mom?" Nick asked, looking past them. "Is she all right?"

"She's been on the phone since I got here, trying to reach the rest of the family," Juanita said. "I think she's—"

"Nicholai!"

At the authoritative voice, Nick's sisters laughed and swept him down the hallway to the living room. Lauren followed, then hung back in the doorway as Natasha Strada came forward to greet her son.

The face that had been so brittle with grief looked years younger. Tears softened the steel blue of her gaze and a smile framed by dimples stretched her hollow cheeks. "Nicholai," she repeated, holding out her arms.

He broke away from his sisters and stepped into her embrace. "Hi, Mom."

Her lips trembling, Natasha closed her eyes and pressed the side of her face to his. She repeated his name, her voice barely above a whisper. "I thought never to hold you again," she said. "Nico, Nico. You're alive. Really alive."

"I'm sorry," Nick murmured. "Sorry for putting you through this."

Lauren felt a lump form in her throat as she watched the poignant reunion. Some men might be embarrassed by such an outpouring of emotion, but not Nick. No, his masculinity seemed all the more powerful as he returned his mother's embrace.

This was a facet of him she hadn't seen before. It was the flip side to his protectiveness, a capacity to love that was as deep and as intense as everything else about him. Yet it didn't surprise her. The straight-ahead, blunt-talking, stubborn, determined man she'd come to know would be as honest about his emotions as he was about everything else.

She took a step back, suddenly uncomfortable, feeling like an intruder. There was so much warmth in this family, so much love. They were all so open about it, they made it look... easy.

"So what happened after the crash?" Tina asked, coming up to her before she could leave the room. "How come Nick stayed with you instead of going home?"

Nick draped his arm around his mother's

shoulders and led her over to introduce her to Lauren. Natasha looked at her for a long moment, then smiled and kissed her cheeks. She said that she, too, had seen the newscast and she thanked Lauren for saving Nick's life.

The questions that Tina had begun escalated as the rest of Nick's sisters demanded to know the reasons for his deception. Lauren soon found herself squeezed onto a sofa between Juanita and the twins while she helped Nick explain everything that had happened since she'd pulled him out of the lake.

Well, not everything, she thought, following Nick with her gaze as he walked back from the kitchen with a handful of chocolate chip cookies. He sat on the arm of Natasha's chair, smiling at something Rose said before he bit into a cookie. No, Lauren didn't mention the more disturbing things that had happened during the time they'd been together in her apartment. She didn't say anything about the feelings that he stirred...or the way she was going to miss him.

The idea shook her more than she cared to admit. Why now? She had managed to keep her distance for more than a week. Why now, when she was about to be free of his disturbing presence, did she feel this sudden yearning to keep him?

Barb reached past her to grab the photograph album that Juanita had pulled from a shelf. Once they'd understood the reasons, Nick's family had been quick to forgive him for the pain he'd caused them. Amid laughter and good-natured teasing, the women launched into stories of his past escapades, their love clear in every word they spoke.

From across the room Nick met Lauren's gaze, his eyes sparkling with vitality. He watched her in silence while the conversation swirled around them and gradually his expression changed. Although he still smiled, it wasn't a smile of amusement. His mouth curved sensuously as his gaze dropped to her lips in a look that was as intimate as a kiss.

The photograph album landed in her lap with a thud that made her jump as Tina leaned over to point out a picture of a tree house. Lauren looked down, trying to force her attention back to what Barb was saying.

It was no use. When Nick got to his feet and walked across the room to her, all she was aware of was how close he was standing. He leaned down to shut the album and pass it to Juanita, then took Lauren's hand and pulled her gently to her feet. "Do me one last favor?" he asked, tugging her away from the sofa.

She felt his thumb move lightly over her knuckles, and awareness glowed over her skin. "What?"

"Give me a ride home?"

"Rose can do that," Tina said. "She said she had to give you back the mail she picked up—oof." She rubbed the side of her ribs and turned to glare at Juanita. "What'd you do that for?"

"I think the mail can wait," Juanita said, winking at Rose.

Nodding, Rose dug into the pocket of her overalls, then tossed a set of keys to Nick. "Here. The landlord gave them to me, told me to clear out your stuff by the end of the month. Good thing I haven't started yet."

Although the goodbyes were heartfelt and lingering, Nick walked to the car with Lauren less than five minutes later. She kept her speed under the limit on the darkened streets, yet the trip to Nick's apartment passed quickly. As she pulled to the curb and set the parking brake, she thought of what Nick had said to her outside the police station. She'd been with him at the start. She might as well stick around and see how it ends.

Oh, God. She didn't *want* it to end. Not yet. It was so obvious to her, and it must have been obvious to Nick. Because without any discussion, he reached past her to shut off the engine, then got out of the car and walked around to her side and opened her door.

His apartment looked the same as it had a week ago. And yet she saw it differently, because now she knew the man who lived here. The big, comfortable furniture, the scattered papers, the photograph of his family and the stack of country music CDs...all the traces of his personality seemed familiar now, offering her a private welcome.

There was a click and the rattle of a chain as Nick locked the door. A few moments later, the plaintive strains of a saxophone drifted from the stereo. Lauren trailed her hand along the back of the sofa, tracing the ridges of chocolate brown corduroy as she watched him straighten up from the tuner. "I thought you didn't like jazz," she said.

He lifted his shoulders in a shrug that tightened his shirt across the broad expanse of muscle. "I suppose I'm getting used to it. When I first heard your taste in music, I was surprised, though."

"Really? Why?"

"At first I would have guessed that you would prefer something more formal, like long-hair, classical stuff. But once I got to know you, I realized this music suited you better.''

''Oh?''

''On the surface it can be elegant and sophisticated, but with a bit of practice, a person can find a whole lot of unexpected levels. Over the last nine days, I've had a lot of practice.''

''Country music isn't all that bad, either. It's honest and straightforward. I suppose I've started to get used to it, too.''

''Listen to that beat,'' he said, moving toward her. ''It's sexy as hell, isn't it?''

''I never thought of it.''

''No, you wouldn't. You probably never thought that those stiff business suits you like to wear are sexy, either, but they are.''

''They're not meant to be.''

''That's my point. I like it that other men don't know about that dynamite body underneath your suit. I like knowing about the woman no one else sees, Lauren. And despite all the differences between us, we've made a pretty good team.''

''I wouldn't have predicted it at first.''

''Me, neither.'' He stopped in front of her. For a moment he simply looked at her, his gaze filled with the same anticipation that sparkled along her nerves. ''The last time we were here, when I woke up and saw you standing in my kitchen, I didn't hold out much hope that you'd help me, but I was wrong.''

''Considering the situation, it was my only choice.''

''You could have walked away.''

''No. You needed me.''

''I still need you, Lauren. Stay the night, just this once. Let's finish what we started. No promises or strings, just two people doing what comes naturally.''

There it was, out in the open at last, a proposition that was as blunt as it was honest.

What on earth was she doing here? Lauren thought belatedly, a last spurt of reason trying to cut through the sensual fog she was enveloped in. It was late, almost morning. She should—

''Don't,'' Nick said, lifting his hands to cradle her cheeks. ''Please, Lauren. Don't go back yet.''

''I need to get home. I have to work tomorrow.''

''That's not what I meant. Don't go back behind that ice wall yet. I want...'' His mouth lifted in a lopsided smile. ''Damn, I'm not good with words.''

She felt his palms move over her skin,

leashed strength in his restrained touch. She made her living with words, but right now she knew she wouldn't be any good with them, either. Sighing, she pressed her cheek into his hand.

"Do you want to leave?"

No, she didn't want to retreat behind her walls yet. They'd been through this last night. This had been building from the moment she'd first seen him. Neither of them had any illusions about what this meant, so neither of them would be hurt.

Why shouldn't she take what he was offering?

And why was she hesitating, anyway? She'd already made her decision. She'd known what was going to happen since they'd left the police station three hours ago.

"Lauren?"

"No, I want to stay."

He smiled one of his eye-crinkling, cheek-dimpling smiles, the kind that always made her go weak. "Good," he said, sliding his fingers into her hair. Carefully he eased out the pins that held what was left of her twist in place. His smile grew as he watched her hair tumble over his wrists. "God, I like doing that."

It felt wonderful to have him touching her. If

it was a mistake, then perhaps it would be worth it. She couldn't handle emotional intimacy, but this was sex, that's all. No strings, no promises.

Swaying forward, she clasped her hands behind his neck and nestled closer. She nuzzled her nose against his throat and inhaled greedily, filling her senses with his unique scent. "I like your after-shave."

"I don't use any."

She shook her head, smiling into his collar. "I was afraid of that."

Nick stroked his hands down her back, anchoring them at her waist as he swayed from side to side with her to the music that filled the quiet room. It was a moment out of time, as if everything that had happened, and everything they had yet to face, simply faded away. Moving in harmony, they danced together, their hearts keeping perfect rhythm.

"Lauren?"

She tilted back her head to look into his face. "Mmm?"

Bracing his legs apart, he cupped her bottom and lifted her against him, showing her without words the effect she was having on his body.

At the feel of him, so hard, so large, the warm glow of awareness blazed to passion. Lauren responded instantly, her breath catching, a shudder of longing rippling through her. "Oh, Nick," she whispered, clutching his shoulders, pressing her breasts to his chest, trying to get closer.

He lowered his head, catching her earlobe between his teeth. He tugged gently, then sucked it into his mouth, swirling his tongue over the sensitive skin until she shuddered. Still holding her against him, he took a step backward, bringing them beside the sofa. In one smooth movement, he carried her down to the cushions.

Lauren felt his weight settle over her and sighed with pleasure. She thrust her fingers into his hair, guiding his face downward, needing his kiss. His lips were warm and firm and possessive as they molded to hers. They had kissed before, but this time it was different. She sensed it in the pressure, in the way he angled his head. She tasted it in his urgency as he plunged his tongue past her lips. It was different, because this time they wouldn't stop.

The certainty didn't frighten her. It freed her. With a sound that was half moan, half cry, she slipped her hands between them and groped for the buttons of his shirt.

At the touch of her fingers on his flesh, Nick felt his teetering control slip another notch. He didn't want to rush her. He wanted to savor every moment, make the night last, give them both a chance to quench the need once and for all. But she was the one who was rushing. She was the one whose hands were trembling. Those throaty sounds, the writhing of her soft body, the delicate, womanly scent that rose from her heated skin were driving him wild.

Wrenching his mouth from hers, he straddled her thighs, raising himself up so he could get rid of his shirt. He tossed it to the floor, then reached for the hem of Lauren's sweater. Without hesitation, she arched her back off the cushions, helping him strip off her bra as well. Her eyes gleaming, her hair tangled in abandon, she smiled and unbuckled his belt.

The desire that shot through him made him throb to the brink of pain. Never had he wanted a woman as much as he wanted Lauren. All thoughts of control fled from his mind as the rest of their clothes were discarded in a flurry of sliding, ripping fabric.

Skin against skin, they feasted on what they had merely tasted before. She was sweet, and she was slick. Parting her legs with his knees, Nick stroked her until she gasped and reached out, her delicate fingers curling firmly around his length in a demand neither of them could deny any longer. His pulse racing, his hands shaking, he took a condom from the pocket of his jeans and smoothed it into place. Grasping her hips, he held her steady as she guided him inside.

''Oh, Nick,'' she breathed. Her eyelids fluttered shut, her lips parted on another gasp as he pushed forward. She wrapped her legs around his waist, instinctively finding the angle that would bring him deeper. ''Oh, Nick, hurry.''

Her whispered plea sent him over the edge. Reaching past her, he braced his hands against the arm of the sofa, flexed his legs and drove himself hard and fast.

She clutched his shoulders, her nails raking his skin, her breasts heaving with the rhythm of his thrusts. Tension built and coiled and built, spiraling upward with dizzying speed. Lauren stiffened, clenching her entire body as she flung back her head and cried out.

Dipping his head, Nick slanted his mouth across hers, sealing their joining in a kiss as the intimate tremors of her release triggered his own.

Gradually her grip on his shoulders loosened. She lowered her legs, sliding the soles of her feet down his thighs, and another shudder shook them both. He lifted his head, looking into her flushed face. He'd always thought that she was beautiful, but seeing her like this made him wish he had the eloquence of a poet. He wanted to say something. After the incredible power of what had happened here between them, he felt he *should* say something.

But what? He wasn't a man who made promises. And she wasn't the kind of woman who wanted any.

Lauren blinked and looked up at him. Her lips were still moist and parted, her expression bordering on…surprise.

"You okay?" he asked, his voice hoarse.

She shifted, sliding her hands over his back. "That was…" Her breath stirred his hair as she sighed. "I don't know what to say."

"That makes two of us."

The radio still played softly, the music moody and subdued. The corduroy ridges of the sofa dug uncomfortably into his bad knee. On the floor beside them their clothes lay in a heap like the tangled wreckage after a storm.

He'd thought once they made love she would be out of his system.

He'd been wrong.

Oh, it had been good. Better than he had imagined. Better than he'd known possible. He should have been satisfied.

Instead, the desire that still coursed through his veins shook him to his very core.

It must have been because they'd gone so fast. Or maybe they'd let the tension between them build too high for too long. Considering all the time they'd been forced to spend together, it was only natural the fire wouldn't be snuffed out that quickly.

He trailed his fingertips down her cheek to her neck, then lowered his hand to her chest, spreading his fingers, absorbing the lingering heat of the flush that tinged her skin. He traced the upper curves of her breasts, remembering her taste, her texture, the sound of their bodies sliding together....

"Lauren?"

"Mmm?"

"I changed my mind," he said. "Once isn't going to be enough."

"What do you..." Her gaze met his, her eyes widening as he eased back inside. "Oh, my," she whispered. "Already?"

Wrapping his arms around her, he shifted to his back, positioning her above him. "Yeah. That okay?"

She ran her tongue across her lower lip, licking the moisture he'd left from his kiss, then smiled and rotated her hips.

She didn't reply aloud. There was no need. For the rest of the night, they let their bodies express what words could not.

Chapter 12

Holding her hands stiffly, Lauren patted the loose papers into a neat stack, closed the folder and slipped it into her briefcase. The silence that followed dragged on for a full minute, hovering in the station manager's office like a thick fog.

She'd known this meeting was going to be difficult. She'd seen what Nick had gone through when he'd finally revealed the situation to his captain. Although Victoria Sandowsky didn't resemble the portly Captain Gilmour in appearance, their temperaments were remarkably similar.

"I can't believe you sat on this story for ten days," Victoria said, folding her arms on the edge of her desk and glaring at Lauren over the rims of her glasses.

Lauren smoothed her damp palms over her skirt and crossed her legs, striving to maintain her facade of calm as Gord Skinner fidgeted in the chair beside her. "As I explained, it was essential to the safety of Lieutenant Strada's family to maintain my silence."

"And you let me make an ass of myself on network TV," Gord said, twisting to face her. "You let me go ahead with that special, even let me interview you and you never let on that it was a lie."

"I understand your anger," Lauren said. "But if you calm down and think about it for a minute, it's not all that bad."

"Not that bad?" he repeated incredulously. "The guy I built up into a hero is a fake. I've been had."

"Just because he's not dead doesn't change who he is or what he did. He still saved those people after the crash."

"Then the least you can do is let me take it from here," he said. He turned toward Victoria. "Let me go on the air, do the live interview myself. My credibility as a journalist is at stake because of this hoax Lauren took part in. It's only fair that I should be the one to break this story."

"What do you think, Lauren?" Victoria asked. "He has a good point."

She clasped her hands more tightly, her damp fingertips sliding over knuckles that went white. Give up her story? How could she walk away from it now? It was the reason she'd put herself through all of this in the first place. It was what had kept her going. It was all she had left now that the charade was over and Nick was gone....

"Lauren?"

Pressing her lips together, she slowly shook her head. "I've tracked this story from the beginning," she said firmly. "I'd like to see it through to the end."

Victoria took off her glasses and polished them on a fold of her skirt, letting the silence draw out before she spoke again. "While I understand your desire to follow through, I'm concerned about the damage that has been done here, not only to Gord's credibility, but to the station's. You should have let us know the moment you discovered Lieutenant Strada was alive."

"It wasn't an option. As I said, it was essential to his investigation that I maintain my silence."

"Your priority should have been *your* job, not his. Even if the news couldn't be aired, we should have been informed. We never would have milked Gord's dead-hero story if we'd known the truth.''

''I apologize if you feel I acted unprofessionally.''

''You were probably in shock after surviving that crash. Your judgment was clouded.'' She fitted her glasses back on and crossed her arms with an air of finality. ''But whatever the reasons behind your lapse, we have to present a united front to our viewers. Therefore I've decided that Gord will be the one to break the news to the public.''

Lauren felt her breath rush from her lungs as if someone had punched her. She shook her head. ''What?''

''You'll be included in the interview, of course, but you will be one of the subjects, not the interviewer.''

''But I've been working on this for—''

''By providing shelter to Lieutenant Strada and assisting him in his investigation, you involved yourself too closely with your subject,'' Victoria went on relentlessly. ''You can't report the news properly when you're part of the story.''

''You can't do this,'' Lauren said. Curling her fingers into her palms, she rose to her feet. ''I made a deal with Captain Gilmour as well as Nick. I've been given an exclusive—''

''Which I'm positive you'll be happy to pass on to your colleague.''

She looked at Gord. He was rubbing his chin, trying to look appropriately grave, but he could barely contain his glee. She set her jaw, feeling a sudden wave of anger. ''I did all the work. I turned my life upside down. And now you expect me to simply hand everything over to him on a silver platter?''

''You're too close to this, and the way you're reacting now only proves my point.''

''Well, I'm afraid the bulk of the information I've gathered is in the hands of the police, so I'm unable to give it to you at this time.''

''Lauren, this isn't like you,'' Victoria said. ''If you refuse to cooperate, I won't find it so easy to excuse the damage you've done to this station's integrity.''

The anger was rapidly deepening, pushing against her crumbling facade of calm. She placed her hands on the edge of Victoria's desk, leaned forward and matched her glare for glare. ''This isn't fair, and you know it.''

''I really have no choice. We have to do what's best for everyone.''

''If Gord and this station hadn't been so eager

to cash in on what he thought was a dead hero, there wouldn't be any damage done to your integrity in the first place.''

''Hey, don't go blaming this on me,'' Gord said.

She whirled around. ''It was disgusting the way you were so happy over capturing the moment of Nick's death. And the way you intruded on his family's grief was obscene. They're not just stories, they're people.''

He held up his hands. ''That's the nature of the business, Lauren. You know that as well as I do.''

''Just because we report the news doesn't mean we have to lose touch with our humanity. Don't condemn me because for once I decided to be human.''

A stunned silence followed her outburst. In disbelief, Lauren realized she'd been shouting.

''Lauren, you've obviously been under a great deal of strain,'' Victoria said. ''After you do the interview with Gord and Lieutenant Strada, I'd like you to take the rest of the week off.''

She breathed deeply a few times before she was able to reply. ''I can still do my job, Victoria.''

"I shouldn't have believed you last week when you said you were fit to work."

"Is this a punishment? Is that why you're giving the story to Gord and getting rid of me?"

"Of course not, Lauren. This is for the good of everyone concerned."

"But—"

"It's just a temporary leave of absence," she continued implacably. "Give yourself some time to put things back in perspective."

Lauren nodded curtly, picked up her briefcase and left the room. It was good advice, she decided, using all of her self-control to keep from slamming the door behind her. She definitely needed to put things in perspective before she said or did something that would get her fired.

She took the stairs instead of the elevator, hoping to work off the rest of her anger. Yet when she reached the privacy of her office, the emotion was still there. Before she could stop herself, she stepped over the threshold and threw her briefcase against the nearest wall.

The impact produced a loud, satisfying thud and sprang open the latches. Papers and file folders spewed out in a fluttering arc. The pen that Lauren had been using ricocheted off the filing cabinet and bounced across the dingy gray carpet, coming to rest against the toe of her shoe.

Pressing her hands to her cheeks, she stared at the mess she had created.

Lauren, this isn't like you.

Victoria was right. This *wasn't* like her. She'd had disagreements over stories in the past, yet during the nine years that she'd worked here, she had never once lost her temper. Her method of dealing with unpleasantness had been to retreat from the situation, to distance herself, to maintain her control at all costs.

That's the way she dealt with everything, from a business dispute to an unfaithful fiancé. She made compromises and accepted blame and always managed to push aside her feelings. Behind a wall of ice. That's what Nick called it. Her wall of ice.

"Oh, God," she whispered, fumbling for the office door. She swung it closed, then picked her way across the littered carpet until she reached her desk and sank bonelessly into her chair.

What was the matter with her? What had happened to the sense of detachment that always protected her?

The answer was obvious. Nick Strada had happened. He'd done this. He'd shaken her out of her safe cocoon. He'd barged into her nicely ordered existence and made her do things and feel things that she'd spent most of her life avoiding.

She had become involved. She was too close. Victoria had been right to pull her off this story, because when it came to Nick, Lauren had stopped acting like a journalist long ago.

And after what had happened last night…

Groaning, Lauren dropped her head into her hands. She and Nick had made love. Oh, they'd agreed it would be only the one night, and they'd parted without any awkward promises. She'd thought she could handle that.

But how could she possibly have thought she'd be able to sit next to him in front of the studio cameras? How was she going to be able to listen to his voice and feel the heat of his body and breathe in his scent without reaching out to touch him? How could she look into his eyes without remembering the things they'd done on the sofa…and on his bed…and in the shower….

After last night, she knew there was another reason why he would need to carry around five condoms in his pocket, and it certainly had nothing to do with using them for party decorations.

Sex, pure and simple, right? That's all it was.

It shouldn't have been that big a deal. Other people did it all the time.

Yet for someone who had lived without it for as long as she had, making love with Nick had been more than merely quenching a thirst. It had been like diving into the clear, cool water of a mountain lake after wandering for days in a desert.

But last night was over. Everything was over. And what did she have to show for it? A professional slap in the face from the station manager, a boost to the career of her most ambitious colleague, a forced leave of absence...

And some subtle, residual tingles in some extremely intimate parts of her body.

He'd shared his passion, and the strength of it had freed her own. But she didn't want her passion freed. She wanted it controlled. That's how she dealt with life. It was so much safer. Less painful.

There was a sharp knock at her door. Lauren looked up quickly, smoothing her hair with her hands as she cleared her throat. "Come in."

The door swung open and Nick stepped inside, a dimpled grin on his face. "Hi, gorgeous."

Oh, God, she thought. Why him? Why now? She didn't return his smile. "Hello, Nick."

His grin faded as he noticed the papers that had spilled from the open briefcase. He nudged the door shut and took the three steps that brought him to her desk. "What's wrong?" he asked.

She leaned back in her chair to look at him. For the first time since they'd met, he was wearing something besides jeans and cowboy boots. His leather shoes were polished to a deep luster, his tan chinos were neatly pressed. The classic masculine lines of his body were emphasized by a perfectly fitted sport coat. A tie was knotted snugly against the collar of his white shirt, his cheeks were freshly shaved and his dark hair was tamed into a sleek, slicked-back style.

He looked well-dressed and civilized...and handsome enough to make her mouth water.

And for some reason, that only made her anger rekindle. "What are you doing here, Nick?"

"You invited me, remember?"

"We can't go on air until Duxbury's in custody, remember?"

He pushed aside a stack of computer printouts and sat on the corner of her desk. "I came early in case you need any help with your boss."

"What?"

"I thought she might give you a rough time about what you did for me."

She laughed without humor. "You're about half an hour too late. Gord got the story. I got a week's leave of absence."

His jaw tightened. "I'll back you up. So will Epstein and O'Hara if I ask them. We won't talk to anyone but you."

"Thanks for the offer, but it's better this way."

"Why?" he asked. "I know how important your job is to you. If I've caused you problems, I want to fix them."

"If you've caused me problems?" she repeated, her voice rising. "You've caused me nothing but trouble from the moment we met. I knew it with my first whiff of your after-shave."

"I don't wear after-shave."

She shoved her chair back and stood up. "Don't you think I know that!"

"Why are you yelling at me? I offered to make them give the story back."

Gritting her teeth, she moved past him and began to gather up the notes that were spread across the carpet. "You might as well go find Gord. He'll tell you what's expected when we go on air."

Instead of leaving, he came over to crouch beside her to help her pick up the scattered papers. "What happened here?"

"I threw my briefcase at the wall," she answered tersely.

"Did it feel good?"

"Yes." She paused, bracing her fingertips against the floor as she turned her head to look at him. "Yes, as a matter of fact, it felt great."

He knelt on the carpet in front of her and cradled her face in his palms. "Want to know something else that might help?"

"What?"

"This," he said, leaning forward. His kiss was swift and hard, knocking her back on her heels.

She grasped his lapels for balance and inhaled sharply. "Nick!"

"Good, huh?"

"What was that for?"

"I don't want to argue."

"Kissing isn't going to solve my problems."

"Then tell me what else I can do to help." He rested his hands on her shoulders. "Want me to try calling Captain Gilmour? Your boss might change her mind if he puts pressure on her."

"No, Victoria was right. I shouldn't be reporting the story if I'm part of it. I got too involved."

"So you're angry at yourself for making a mistake."

"Yes, of course I am. I should have known better."

"You're only human, Lauren," he said. "We all make mistakes."

"Thanks for the news flash."

His gaze didn't waver. "And you're also angry at me for dragging you into all of this."

As usual, his perceptions were swift and accurate. "I don't want to talk about it."

"Hey, that suits me." He moved his hands to her back and kissed her again, gentler this time, waiting while her lips softened and warmed beneath his. Pulling her closer, he slipped his tongue inside in a smooth, breathtaking plunge.

Her response shocked her. The simmering emotion that she'd taken for anger transformed instantly to desire. Her pulse thudded, her breathing turned ragged and all the lingering, intimate tingles she'd felt since last night suddenly flared to life.

Paper crumpled as she shifted to her knees and pressed the front of her body to his. Tilting her head so that their mouths meshed more closely, she stroked his tongue with her own.

The sound he made in his throat was close to a growl, sending a shiver of anticipation streak-

ing down her spine. He gathered her closer, his
muscles tensing, his thighs hard against hers.
With another low, wordless rumble, he unfastened the button that held her jacket closed and
slipped his hand inside.

Lauren gasped, pulling back to look into his
face. "Nick!" she whispered.

He met her gaze boldly and raised his hand
to cup her breast, rubbing his thumb over her
nipple. Even through layers of silk and lace his
caress had the power to raise the delicate nub to
aching sensitivity.

Her breath hitched on a sudden sob of need.
"Nick, I can't think when you touch me there."

"Hey, join the club," he said, lowering his
head until his lips settled over hers once again.
The kiss was firm and possessive, familiar and
knowing. His thumb mimicked the movement of
his mouth, circling, pressing, making her throb
with remembered passion, making her hungry
for more.

Lauren parted her lips and arched her back,
inviting him to deepen both his kiss and his caress. He readily complied. She could feel his
control slipping, and a reckless excitement
swept through her body.

"Is there a lock on that office door?" he
whispered against her mouth.

"No."

"Then we'll have to be quick."

"Nick, for heaven's sake, we can't."

"Can't what?"

"Make love here."

"Give me one more minute and we will be."

She bit back a moan of frustration. What on earth were they doing? They were in her office. On the *floor*. Anyone could walk in and find them like this.

And yet she knew that she was close, very close, to the point of not caring.

Muttering an oath, he raised his head. He breathed hard through his nose, his nostrils flaring. "Stand up with me."

"What?"

"We'll do it against the door. No one will come in."

The image sprang full blown into her mind. Against the door, her skirt hiked up, his pants undone. Yes, oh, yes. It would work.

He moved his hand to her thigh, his fingers impatient as he pushed his hand between her legs. He murmured her name on a groan as he brushed her dampness.

It was the sound of her own voice crying out that finally shocked her into action. Grasping the last remnants of her sanity, she pushed hard on his chest. "Nick, no!"

A shudder shook his frame and his fingers stilled. He tipped back his head, clenching his jaw, the tendons along the sides of his neck standing out as he fought for control.

Lauren bit her lip to stop herself from protesting as she felt him withdraw his hand. She sat back on her heels, her heart racing, her nerves thrumming. Pressing her hands to her cheeks, she gulped for air.

"Damn," Nick muttered. "How do you do this to me?"

"What?"

"Make me crazy." He exhaled harshly and looked at her. "You make me absolutely crazy."

"I can't believe...I...we..." She swallowed. "I've never done anything like this in my life."

"I only meant to kiss you."

"I hadn't meant to do anything at all. I thought we were arguing."

"Hell of a way to make up." His gaze dropped to her open jacket. "I shouldn't have started this," he said, reaching out to place his hand on her breast once more.

She groaned softly. "Please, Nick, we can't."

"I know." He kept his palm motionless. "I

had to leave you like this once before, I don't want to again. Let me help.''

Lauren looked into his eyes, seeing the regret and the barely leashed desire, and she felt the warmth of his hand slowly ease her swollen flesh. Gradually her breathing steadied until the sharp ache he had created dulled to a throb.

He refastened her jacket, then pushed himself to his feet and extended his hand to help her up.

As she reached for his hand, her gaze strayed to where the crisp fabric of his chinos was stretched across his groin. Her cheeks burned at the sight of the blatant, unmistakable bulge. And her palm tingled.

''It wouldn't help, Lauren,'' he said tightly. ''If you touch me there now...''

Grasping his fingers, she stood up quickly, then dropped his hand and stepped back. She brushed at the wrinkles in her skirt. ''I don't know what to say, Nick.''

''I do. One night wasn't enough.''

Startled, she met his gaze. ''What do you mean?''

''It's obvious, isn't it? One time or one night. It's going to take more than that to get this out of our systems. I want more, Lauren.''

''More?''

''We've got something special going on between us. Why don't we give it a chance, see where it leads?''

''But we agreed—''

''So we made a mistake.''

She glanced at the scattered papers that still littered the floor. A mistake. That's what it was, all right. She'd been angry when he'd come in. Angry over losing her story, and over losing control of her emotions. Yet all he'd needed to do was touch her and she'd lost control again.

She'd been a fool to think she could handle this. She'd known from the start what kind of man he was, and she should have known better than to get involved. Even a no-strings, no-future, one-night affair was enough to mess up the smooth pattern of her life.

And he was asking for more?

Crossing her arms tightly, she shook her head. ''I think it would be best if we limit our relationship to a professional capacity. Even though it appears I won't be doing your story anymore, we'll probably still be coming into contact with each other—''

''Dammit, Lauren! Don't pull that ice princess act on me. Last night I tasted your sweat and heard you scream.''

''I'm not denying the sex was good, but I

made it clear from the start that I'm not interested in a more serious relationship.''

"Yeah, you made it clear, all right. I should get it tattooed on my arm to remind me.''

"Then we don't really have anything more to discuss.''

"So that's it? You're not even willing to give us a chance?''

She shook her head again, unable to reply.

He raked his fingers through his hair, destroying the carefully combed style. A dark lock fell across his forehead and he flicked it back impatiently. "We're good together, Lauren. And I'm not only talking about when we're in bed.''

"Yes, we did manage to work well together, but it's over now.''

"It wasn't over three minutes ago.''

A quiver tickled through her stomach at the intimate timbre of his voice. She steeled herself against the involuntary response. "Please, Nick. Let's leave this alone before one of us gets hurt.''

He raked his hair again, then scowled and rubbed the back of his neck. "I wouldn't hurt you, Lauren.''

"You wouldn't mean to. But this physical thing is going to wear off, and then you're going to recognize all the differences between us.''

"What? You mean the way you like neatness and cantaloupes? The way you squeeze the toothpaste in the middle? I already know all those things. We've lived together for more than a week. We didn't have any big problems adjusting to each other."

"It's more than that, Nick. It's your honesty, and your bluntness, and the way you're so... intense about everything."

"And that bothers you."

"Yes."

"Because I don't let you hide."

She swallowed against the sudden lump in her throat. "Please. Just leave me alone."

He shoved his hands into the pockets of his pants and looked at her without speaking, his gaze snapping with all the emotions she didn't want to acknowledge. All the emotions she wanted to hide from.

This was why she couldn't handle another night with him, or even another minute. He had never let her hide. And once he saw that she wasn't capable of returning those emotions, he'd leave her, anyway.

"I guess I really did make a mistake here, Lauren," he said finally, turning away to open the door. "I thought you were someone I knew."

* * *

The mural of the Chicago skyline looked exactly as it always did. The flurry of activity as the crew did the last-minute lighting and sound checks was as familiar as it always was. Lauren had watched these preparations countless times, yet what had once seemed comfortably secure now felt stifling. She didn't want to do this. She didn't know how she *could* do this.

But the studio was already filling up. Word of what was happening had spread, and more and more of the station's employees were gathering in the shadows beyond the lights. The cameras were rolling into position and the producer was waving frantically from the other side of the set, indicating to Lauren that it was time to take her place.

Focusing on the empty chair, concentrating on moving one foot in front of the other, Lauren walked across the floor and sat down beside Nick.

The monitor on the edge of the set flickered silently, showing the scene at the police station. One of the other videographers had been sent there to cover Adam Duxbury's arrest. Lauren clasped her hands in her lap, watching the silver-haired, affable face fill the screen for a moment as the camera zoomed in. Duxbury was smiling, his perfectly capped teeth and cherubic face gleaming like a campaign poster. He appeared relaxed, unworried, as if being charged with a hit-and-run death as well as assault was nothing but a minor misunderstanding.

Nick shifted restlessly beside her, propping his ankle on his opposite knee and drumming his fingers against the arm of his chair. Lauren angled her legs the other way, easing her body as far away as the chair would allow, doing her best to ignore him.

It wasn't any use. She was aware of every breath he took and every frown that crossed his face. She knew he didn't like waiting. She also knew that he wished he could be the one who put the handcuffs on Duxbury. It was ironic, the way this story had worked out. Nick had been reduced to the role of an observer while she'd become a participant.

Epstein didn't let Duxbury linger in front of the camera for long. He guided him out of sight, leaving O'Hara to make an official statement. One of Duxbury's lawyers spoke next, his demeanor more sober than his client's but still projecting an aura of calm confidence.

Lauren hoped the confidence was as phony as Duxbury's smile. This time his lawyers wouldn't be able to sweep away the charges. And once all the facts came out, Duxbury's wealthy wife and influential in-laws might not want to fund his defense.

Gord held a finger against his earpiece, concentrating on the audio that was being transmitted to him. "Okay, they're winding up. Lauren, you ready?"

She lifted her chin. "You're in charge, Gord."

"Come on, Lauren. No hard feelings, okay? If I'm willing to forgive and forget what you did to me, you can loosen up a bit, can't you?"

"I'll cooperate, Gord. The rest is up to you."

"Hey, you're all right, aren't you? We're going to be live, so if there's anything you need to straighten out with me beforehand, better tell me now."

"I'm fine."

"Okay. Good. Lieutenant Strada?"

Nick stopped drumming his fingers. "Yeah?"

"We'll be on in one minute."

"Fine." For the first time since he'd walked out of her office, his gaze met Lauren's. "Might as well get this over with."

She'd wondered how she was going to sit beside him and function normally under the scrutiny of the camera. Well, she'd just found out.

She'd never seen him so distant before. Oh, the passion and energy that always crackled around him were still there, but none of it was directed toward her.

And that was good. As he'd said, they might as well get this over with.

The news director shouted for quiet, then counted down from five and cued Gord. He straightened the cards he had written his notes on, pasted on an earnest smile and looked into the camera with the red light.

"Good afternoon. This is Gordon Skinner coming to you live from the Channel Ten studio. It is my privilege to bring you the conclusion to a very special story about courage, heroism and one man's dedication to his duty."

He transferred his gaze to the other camera. It aimed just to the left of his shoulder, allowing space to roll the tape of Nick's "drowning." "Ten days ago, most of the country watched in horror as I presented this moving footage of the tragic crash of Flight 703. We watched Lieutenant Nicholai Strada of the Chicago police risk his life to assist his fellow survivors to reach safety, and we watched him as he faltered and slipped under the water."

He paused as the camera moved back to widen the angle of the shot. "But the crash of Flight 703 claimed one less victim than had been believed. Lieutenant Strada did not die. We are now able to reveal that for the past ten days, he has been working undercover in order to gather the evidence that led to the arrest of Adam Duxbury.''

Over the next few minutes, Gord methodically guided Nick and Lauren through questions that revealed the scope of their hoax. He was careful to leave the impression that he had known all along, and he was even more careful to punctuate any statements about Duxbury with words such as *alleged* and *suspected*. Once the framework of the story was established, though, Gord's questions grew more personal.

''Lieutenant Strada, what led you to trust Miss Abbot not to reveal your secret?''

''Miss Abbot is a real professional,'' he replied. ''Everything she did was for the sake of her story.''

Lauren braced herself against a wave of cold. They were her words. It was what she'd always told him. Yet hearing him state it so clearly only widened the gulf between them.

''And Lauren,'' Gord said, turning his smile toward her. ''It must have been challenging to conceal a strange man in your home for more than a week without anyone discovering his presence. Tell me about the close calls you had.''

She thought of that first night, how she'd had to help Nick to her bedroom and had ended up in his arms. And she thought about the night that Angela had found them in the kitchen, and about what they had been doing....

Looking Gord in the eye, she chose her words carefully. ''Lieutenant Strada is very resourceful and has a flair for improvisation. He was able to adapt quickly to changing situations.''

''What was the most difficult aspect of sharing your home with Lieutenant Strada?''

''We each were very busy compiling information for his investigation, so where we worked wasn't an issue.''

A hint of annoyance flickered across Gord's face at the way she was sidestepping the questions. ''What about your personal relationship? There must have been a good deal of tension with two complete strangers forced into such...intimate circumstances.''

She heard the chair beside her creak as Nick shifted. She fought the temptation to look at him as she answered. ''Despite the unusual circumstances, we managed remarkably well.''

''Is there any truth to the rumors about a budding romance between the two of you?''

''None whatsoever,'' she answered quickly,

hoping the microphone didn't pick up the tremor in her voice or the short oath that Nick muttered.

At a signal from the director, Gord turned his gaze back to the camera. "I'll have more on this fast-breaking story on our regular newscast this evening. Until then, this is Gordon Skinner, live from the Channel Ten studios."

As soon as the lights were switched off, Gord leaned forward to speak with Nick. "Thanks, Lieutenant. You did great. I'd like to do a follow-up sometime this week, so when would you be able to come in?"

Nick unclipped the mike from his lapel and handed it to the technician who was waiting behind them. "No more," he said, getting to his feet. "I think I've had enough of journalists." He looked at Lauren. "Did you pack my stuff?"

"Yes. It's in a blue flight bag in my office closet."

"I'll get it."

"All right."

"Thanks for your help. I'll reimburse you for the groceries and all that."

"Don't bother. It was a business expense."

His jaw hardened. "Yeah. How could I forget?"

"Good luck with the trial."

"Thanks." He lifted his hand, paused, then

shoved it into his pocket and stepped back. "See you around, Lauren."

Too fast. It was happening too fast. Just like everything when it came to this man, there was no way to stop or even slow down the rush of events. The crew was already moving away the cameras, the buzz of the onlookers was growing. After ten days of being alone with Nick, now their last moments together were going to be spent in front of a crowd.

But perhaps it was better this way. They had already postponed this too long. Swallowing hard, she lifted her chin and forced her lips into a professional smile. "Goodbye, Nick."

The passion was gone from his eyes, and in its place there was regret and a flash of something else, something that looked far too much like...pain.

Lauren curled her fingers around the arm of her chair, fighting the urge to reach out to him. Oh, God. She'd thought that by ending things now neither one of them would get hurt.

She'd been wrong about that, too.

Chapter 13

The muted hum of conversation and clinking cutlery blended in the air with the perky strains of Mozart. White wicker furniture and cool blue tile gave the restaurant a relaxed, inviting atmosphere. Normally Lauren enjoyed dining here, but she hadn't tried to fool herself into thinking she'd enjoy it today. The most she'd hoped for was that by getting out of her apartment she might start to dislodge the bleak mood that had enveloped her since Nick had left yesterday. Yet ten minutes into her lunch, she knew she wouldn't be able to swallow a single bite.

She set down her fork carefully and stared across the table at her sister. "What did you say?"

"I said, I've decided to go back to Eddy."

"You mean you're going to go through with the wedding after all?"

Angela nodded, giving her a wobbly smile. "It's kind of late to call the whole thing off. Saturday's only four days away."

"Don't worry about the details. It would be a lot easier to cancel a wedding than to dissolve a marriage. If that's the only reason you've reconsidered..."

"No, it's not the only one. I have to admit it gave me a push, but this is what I want to do."

Lauren bit the inside of her lip to keep from arguing. She'd promised herself that she wouldn't interfere with her sister's decision, but it was difficult not to. She had to keep reminding herself that Angela was a different person, that she was a mature, rational adult, that perhaps she and Eddy would beat the odds and make their marriage work.

"Thank you," Angela said.

"What for?"

"For not trying to talk me out of it. I know what you're thinking. I can see it by the look on your face."

She sighed. "All right, you know how I feel, but you should ignore it. It's no secret that I'm not exactly the poster girl for the institution of marriage."

Angela chuckled. "No, really?"

"I do have to admit that I'm a bit curious about what tipped the balance in Eddy's favor."

"Ah, besides the fact that he's six feet tall and handsome as sin?"

Eddy? Handsome? Lauren pictured his face in her mind. While his cultured features and sandy hair were certainly pleasant, she wouldn't describe him as handsome. As sin. No, for that a man would need to have more drama, more animal appeal, maybe a few more inches in height and a hard, muscled body. And dark brown hair that curled at the nape of his neck, and piercing steel blue eyes and a smile that dimpled with hidden, sensual knowledge...

It had been almost a day since she'd said goodbye to Nick. How much longer would it take for her to accept the fact that he was gone? Reaching for her water glass, she forced her thoughts away from him. Again. "Yes, besides that."

"Well, I've spent the last three days and nights trying to figure it out and this morning while I was at work it all hit me. I realized I was looking for a guarantee that everything would be fine. I wanted to know that my life would be wonderful and trouble-free once I said 'I do,' and that the kind of happiness we've known will last forever. And about the time I realized that, I decided I'd been a fool.''

''I wouldn't have thought so. There's nothing unreasonable about exercising caution when you're making such a major decision.''

''But that's the point,'' she said, leaning forward. ''Life won't be perfect. We'll probably always argue about the music on the car radio and a hundred other things over the years. As long as we can talk through our problems, we'll be able to solve them.''

''Didn't you and Eddy talk before?''

''Not enough. It seems silly, considering the fact that we've been living together, but sometimes the day-to-day stuff gets in the way and we talk to each other without really saying what's important.''

''You're both individuals, with jobs and lives of your own, so it's understandable.''

''Sure, but we shouldn't let things slide. If two people love each other, they should put that before their careers. I mean, my job isn't going to keep me warm at night, or grow old with me, or listen to my problems.''

''No, but it's not good to be completely dependent, Angela, either financially or emotionally.''

"I know how Mom was, and I know how scared you've always been of being like her—"

"Me? Scared of being like Mom? Angela, I'm in no danger of that. I've always taken after our father."

She shook her head. "I know I was only five when he left, but I understood more than you think. You saw how unhappy Mom's bad luck with men made her, and you saw how Dad thrived on his freedom, so you deliberately modeled yourself on his example. But we can't let what happened with our parents hold us back from living our own lives."

"It didn't hold me back. I was willing to give marriage a try, but Harper showed me how unsuitable I am."

"Unsuitable? Why? Because you didn't approve of infidelity?"

"No, because I drove him to it."

Her eyebrows shot up. "What?"

"You're such a warm, open person, Angela. Your ease in dealing with emotions is something I've always admired. I'm not like that. I didn't give enough of my heart to Harper, so it was understandable that—"

"That's a load of bull," Angela interrupted. "Harper was an idiot, and he did what he did because of *him,* not you. I never knew you've blamed yourself all these years."

"The infidelity was only a symptom of the underlying problem. And it's not a matter of blame. It's accepting the type of person I am."

"That's your problem. You *don't* accept the type of person you are."

Her sister was wrong, Lauren thought. Look how disastrously things had turned out because she'd believed she could handle the involvement with Nick. Instead, she'd lost control of her emotions, lost her objectivity and her good sense. Unless she straightened herself out, she might end up losing her job. No, she accepted her limitations, all right.

So it was for the best that she ended things with Nick before he saw how unsuited they were. Yes, it had been the right choice, the logical, sensible choice.

But if it was so logical and sensible, why did her heart feel as if it had been torn in half? He was gone, so why couldn't she stuff all those feelings he'd unleashed back behind her barriers? Why did the past day seem so empty, and why did the days to come seem so...what? Hollow. Meaningless. Like the neat, distant, perfect pictures on a postcard.

"I'm sorry, Lauren. I wasn't trying to criticize you."

She cleared her throat, pulling herself back to the conversation. "It's okay. But I'd much rather talk about your wedding than dredge up everything that went wrong with mine. Now, since the ceremony is on for sure...?" She paused, lifting her eyebrows to punctuate the question.

Angela nodded firmly. "For sure."

"Then I have to get busy. What's left to do?"

"I guess for starters I'd better reschedule that final dress fitting I canceled last Saturday. And I was supposed to get back to the caterers about the appetizers because of Eddy's cousin's allergies. There was a problem with the church, too, but I was waiting until I'd decided for sure before I found out what it was."

Lauren held up her palm. "Good thing I have the rest of the week off."

"Have I ever told you what a great sister you are?"

"Angela..."

"Okay, okay. You don't like getting mushy, but I really appreciate everything you've done for me. And I owe you big time for letting me stay with you these past few days."

"You don't owe me a thing. You were there for me when I needed you."

"Well, I can't thank you enough. The time away from Eddy really helped. Seeing what life would have been like without him was a good way to realize how much I have to lose."

"I'm glad I could help."

"Oh, you did. Considering everything that was going on with you, I guess I couldn't have shown up at a worse time."

"Well, everything's back to normal now. Or it will be once I get back to work."

There was a pause. "Are you going to see Nick again?"

"They gave the story to Gord. I might run into him if I'm called to testify at Duxbury's trial."

"That's not what I mean. I was kind of hoping you and Nick...well, with so many sparks flying whenever you two are in the same room—"

"That's irrelevant," Lauren said. "Any relationship needs more than that."

"Sure, but it's a good start. And you two spent a lot of intensive time together, so you had the opportunity to see beyond the physical thing."

"It wouldn't have gone anywhere. We're just

too different. Besides, he wasn't looking for something serious or permanent any more than I was.''

''Then why aren't you eating your salad?''

She pushed aside her untouched plate. ''I had a late breakfast.''

''I remember you weren't up when I left for work this morning.''

''I have the week off, so I slept in.''

''Lauren, if you want to talk about it, I'm willing to listen. Lord knows I'm no expert, since I've barely settled my own love life, but if there's anything I can do to help....'' Her words trailed off as she looked past Lauren's shoulder. ''What on earth is he doing here?''

Lauren glanced behind her and her empty stomach turned over.

Dressed like the upstanding, conservative businessman he purported to be, his navy blue suit projecting a calm solidity, Adam Duxbury was making his way through the busy restaurant. His silver hair flashed as often as his smile as he paused to say a few words to acquaintances as he progressed across the room. He looked as relaxed today as he had when Epstein had arrested him.

''I thought he was supposed to be in jail,'' Angela said.

Lauren quickly straightened to face her. "He must be out on bail already."

"After what he did?"

"Allegedly did," she said. "He was just arrested, not convicted."

"But...isn't he dangerous? He threatened the lives of Nick's family, didn't he?"

"That was only to keep him from gathering more evidence. The threats would be useless now, since matters are out of Nick's hands." From the corner of her eye she saw Duxbury continue on a path that would lead him directly toward them. "He should know he has nothing to gain by harming anyone at this stage."

"He gives me the creeps," Angela muttered.

That was putting it mildly, Lauren thought. Into her mind came an image of Wanda's face, the swollen jaw, the blackened eye, and she thought about Nick's partner, Duxbury's other victim. And how many more were there that no one knew about?

"Why, hello, Miss Abbot."

At the smooth voice, Lauren lifted her chin and turned her head. Duxbury had stopped beside their table. She made herself nod a greeting.

From this close, she could see deep lines of strain around his forced smile. His tailored suit couldn't hide the brittle tension that surrounded his solid frame, and his baby blue eyes had a glazed, distant look. He seemed like a man teetering on the edge.

Lauren had a sudden, completely irrational impulse to flee. She fought it down, reminding herself that they were in a public place, that he couldn't hurt her, that he had no reason to hurt her.

Duxbury slipped a hand into his pocket, striking a relaxed, casual pose. "I'm glad I ran into you today, Miss Abbot. I'd like to have the chance to correct some misconceptions you have about me."

"This is neither the time nor the place for an interview. Why don't you contact the Channel 10 news department and—"

"But it's you I'd like to talk to. You're the one responsible for all this—" he paused, as if searching for the word "—negative publicity."

"No, it's you that's responsible. You are a criminal, Mr. Duxbury. You deserve everything you get."

He lost his smile. "You have no idea what you've done, do you. You and that damn cop."

"We were only doing our jobs. Now, if you'll excuse me, I'd like to finish my lunch."

For a moment he stared at her, and the affability he usually projected dimmed. "Some other time, then, Miss Abbot.'' He tipped his head and turned away. ''Enjoy your meal.''

Lauren watched him walk to a table beside the window and join a pair of men already there. The knot in her stomach tightened. She shouldn't have let her own revulsion to that man overwhelm her judgment. He'd wanted to talk, that's all. As a journalist, she should have jumped at the chance to present his side of the story, no matter what her personal feelings were. Gord wouldn't have hesitated. What was wrong with her?

Nick would have understood her reaction. He wouldn't have sat down for a civilized chat with the man who had killed his partner and threatened his family. He would have…

God, he was out of her life. So when would she be able to get him out of her mind?

Nick slouched in his chair, propping his feet on an open drawer of his desk as he listened to O'Hara bring him up-to-date on Duxbury. It had been four days since the arrest, and Duxbury's carefully woven public image was seriously unraveling.

''It's confirmed now that his wife took their kid for an extended visit to some relatives in New York,'' O'Hara said.

"She left him?"

"Yup. She obviously complained to Mummy and Daddy before she did, though. Now the Vanwhatevers are bailing out faster than you can say Dow Jones."

Nick whistled softly. "They obviously don't believe he'll be acquitted."

"Looks like the in-laws want to put as much distance as possible between themselves and Duxbury before he drags them down with him."

"What a family."

"Oh, yeah. They have about as much loyalty as rats do to a sinking ship."

Nick nodded. "I have a feeling this is going to hurt Duxbury more than the trouble with his wife. Most of his companies rely heavily on financing from his in-laws."

"There were some pretty convoluted connections between them, all right. That lady reporter of yours did some impressive work with her background research. Epstein told me all the juicy material's giving the D.A. hot flashes."

"Lauren's very good at her job."

"Easy on the eyes, too. I wouldn't have minded shacking up with her for a week, that's for sure."

Nick's boots thudded to the floor. His body

tensing, he rose to his feet. "What did you say?"

"Take it easy, Nick. No harm in a man thinking about it, is there? And it's not as if you staked your claim or anything."

"She's not your type, Phil."

"Why not? Sometimes those classy types really go for some down and dirty—"

"Shut up, O'Hara."

"Geez, what's wrong with you?"

What was wrong with him? That was a simple one to answer. Lauren Abbot. The ice princess who made him burn. He'd thought he would have cooled off by now. After all, the woman had told him in no uncertain terms to get lost.

Scowling, Nick slammed the desk drawer shut. "This isn't a damn locker room, so watch your mouth."

O'Hara smiled. "Cranky today, aren't we."

Nick ground his teeth, realizing O'Hara had been trying to get a rise out of him. And he hadn't needed to try too hard, either. "Go annoy someone else," he muttered, sitting down behind his desk once more. "I've got better things to do than listen to your fantasies."

For the next half hour, Nick read over the reports Epstein had slipped him on Duxbury.

Officially he shouldn't be here, since according to Gilmour he was still dead, but he was too restless to sit around doing nothing. He'd been on edge all week, and it was only getting worse.

Once the story about his hoax had hit the media, he'd been bombarded with demands for more interviews. He'd refused them all. He'd told himself it was because he'd had his fill of reporters, but he knew it was out of a sense of fairness to Lauren. She'd worked hard to help bring Duxbury to justice, and she was the one who had gained the least. If she wasn't going to profit from his story, then no one would.

Was he a fool for continuing to care? Time and distance should have begun to dull the feelings he still had for her, and yet his desire to see her, to hear her voice and to feel the warmth of her arms around him hadn't faded.

Since his divorce, he'd never been with any woman long enough for her to have the chance to push him away. His involvements had been brief and the endings had been mutually agreeable. It wasn't like him to hang on to someone who didn't want him anymore.

She had made herself perfectly clear. She'd even looked straight into a camera on live TV and stated there was nothing romantic between them. Maybe she really did have ice water in her veins if she could say something like that after the way she'd been so hot for him....

He dropped his head into his hands, rubbing his eyes hard with the tips of his fingers. Sure, the sex had been great, but most of the time when he thought about her it wasn't only her body that he missed. It was everything. The entire complex, maddening, fascinating woman.

The phone on the desk shrilled suddenly. He frowned at it, knowing that the voice wouldn't be the one he really wanted to hear. And he was angry at himself because he still wanted to hear it. God, he was a mess.

Snatching up the receiver, he snarled a hello.

"Whoa, better cut back on the coffee, big brother."

Nick rubbed his face with his free hand in an effort to ease his scowl. "Hi, One-up. How're you doing?"

"Better than you, by the sound of it," Juanita answered. "Hasn't Gilmour forgiven you yet?"

"He's thinking about it. What bothers him most are the nice things he said about me at the memorial service."

"I guess you're anxious to get reinstated, huh?"

"The rumors are that personnel is working on

it. I'll be back on the street by next week at the latest.''

''A hero's work is never done. Speaking of which, I heard that the twins have become extremely popular lately, thanks to you. All their friends want to meet their famous relative.''

''That's all I need,'' he grumbled.

''I bet.'' She paused. ''By the way, I haven't seen Lauren Abbot on TV this week. How's she doing?''

''How would I know?''

The pause was longer this time. ''Ah. So it's not the coffee. I figured there was something going on between the two of you. She's a nice lady.''

''She doesn't want anything to do with me.''

''Like I said, she's a nice lady.''

''If you called me up just to razz me, don't bother. I'm doing a good enough job of that myself.''

''I'm sorry, Nick. If you feel like talking…''

''Thanks, One-up, but I'll sort it out.''

''I hope so.'' She cleared her throat. ''Anyway, the reason I phoned is that I was wondering how the case against Adam Duxbury is progressing.''

''Fine. Looks solid.''

''Do you think he'll be convicted?''

"It's out of my hands. I'll have to trust the courts now, but yeah, I think he'll be convicted."

"And those rumors about the contract he had out on you and the rest of the family? They weren't true after all?"

Nick tightened his grip on the phone. "They were true, but the contract was lifted as soon as Duxbury believed I'd died. Why?"

"Oh, nothing to get alarmed about. I was just wondering whether there was an undercover cop assigned to watch us, that's all."

"No one's assigned. What happened?"

"Well, when I went over to Mom's this afternoon, I noticed a guy sitting in a parked car across the road. He was gone by the time I left."

"Did you get a look at the man?"

"No, it was the car that caught my eye. It wasn't the kind of bland sedan the plainclothes guys usually use, so that's why I thought I'd ask."

"What kind of car was it?"

"A silver Jag."

A chill washed over him. Duxbury's car. Epstein had been in constant contact with his snitch all week, and if there had been any rumors about another contract, he would have known immediately. Besides, Duxbury had nothing to gain by renewing his threats.

So what logical reason could he have for watching Nick's mother's house?

The chill coalesced into a hard lump in his gut. There *was* no logical reason, but was Duxbury thinking logically? The man's life was falling down around his ears. He'd lost his family and his financing. What if he'd finally cracked?

What if he wasn't seeking to intimidate anymore and instead was simply seeking revenge? What better way to get even with Nick than to hurt him through the people he loved?

"Where are you now?" Nick asked sharply.

"I'm at home."

"Is Rose there, too?"

"Yes, she just got in. Nick, I—"

"Stay there. Lock your door. I'm going to have them send a unit over."

"Just because I saw a strange car? Nick, you're overreacting."

"Don't argue with me, One-up. I'm not taking any chances."

His phone call to his mother was as brief as he could manage. They'd been through this before. He'd thought they wouldn't need to do it again. Despite her protestations that he was blowing the potential threat out of proportion, she finally agreed to keep the twins at home until she heard from him.

Captain Gilmour wasn't as cooperative. "Come on, Strada. I can't go sending someone over just because Duxbury drove through the neighborhood. You're jumping at shadows."

Nick struggled to control his temper. "You didn't believe me before and I was right. I'm right this time, too. I feel it."

"All you have are suspicions and a vague theory about retribution. That's even less than the last time."

"You know he's dangerous, or you wouldn't have Wanda in protective custody."

"That's different and you know it."

"Then at least put Duxbury under surveillance. Hell, I'll do it myself, make sure he doesn't go anywhere near—"

"You stay away from him or his lawyers will be screaming harassment. We have to handle this by the book from here or risk having the case thrown out of court."

Epstein and O'Hara were waiting for Nick when he strode out of the captain's office a minute later. O'Hara put a restraining hand on Nick's arm and tugged him aside. "We heard what you were saying. Epstein and I are going off duty now, so we're on our own time. I'll go to your mother's. I haven't had any of her borscht in years.''

''And I'll cover Rose and Juanita,'' Epstein said. ''If you're wrong, Rose can always give my car a tune-up.''

''You two believe me?''

They looked at each other briefly. It was Epstein who answered. ''You were right before. I wouldn't want to underestimate Duxbury again, either.''

Nick raked his hands through his hair in frustration. ''I should have seen this coming. It was going too easily. I should have—'' He stopped suddenly. This time the fear that surged through him chilled him down to his bones. ''Lauren.''

''What?''

''If Duxbury's seeking vengeance, he's going to blame her as much as me,'' he said, racing for the phone on his desk. He punched Lauren's home number. All he got was her answering machine.

No, she wouldn't be home tonight. It was Friday. If Angela's wedding was still on, they'd be at the church for the rehearsal.

The church. What was its name? He ground his teeth as he yanked the phone directory out from underneath a pile of paper. Saint something or other. Started with a *P*. He ran his finger down the listings, stopping at St. Paul. Heart thudding, he dialed the number. He let it ring twelve times before he handed the phone to Epstein and asked him to keep trying. Pausing only long enough to grab his jacket and check to make sure his gun was loaded, he headed for the stairs.

By the time he hit the parking lot, he was running. There was no proof that his fears were justified. Maybe he really was jumping at shadows as Gilmour had said. But somehow, he knew he was right.

This was the reason behind the restlessness that had been plaguing him all week. Some part of him had known from the time he'd watched the coverage of Duxbury's arrest. The man shouldn't have been smiling like that. It should have tipped Nick off, but he'd been too tangled up in his feelings for Lauren to listen to his instincts.

Nick reached his car and was turning the key in the ignition before he'd shut the door. The powerful engine of the vintage Mustang came to life with a satisfying growl. Jamming it into gear, he muscled onto the street.

This was too much like the last time. The entire pattern seemed to be repeating itself. The anxiety and the protectiveness he felt was the same as it had been two weeks ago. He had to warn Lauren. He had to make sure she was safe. Because when it came to the people he loved...

His hands jerked on the wheel. He corrected the skid with a quick tug and pressed harder on the accelerator.

The people he loved? Lauren?

Of course, he was in love with her. The fact had been staring him in the face for days. It was about time that he finally admitted it. He loved her smiles, and her frowns, and the way she angled her chin when she got stubborn. He loved her intelligence and her compassion, her wit and her sensitivity. He loved the way she fit into his arms....

They did fit, despite their differences. Or maybe because of them. They were good for each other. To the rest of the world he'd been dead, but he'd never felt more alive than when he'd been living with her. And she'd started to feel it, too. She must have. The passion that had exploded between them had come from a source that was far deeper than physical.

Yet she'd pushed him away.

She didn't want love. She didn't want to feel anything. She wanted to wall herself up behind her professional objectivity and go through the rest of her life without risking involvement with anyone. Especially him. That's what she'd said. She didn't want him.

Well, that was just too damn bad, wasn't it. He loved her, and he wasn't going to let her push him away again. He wasn't going to give up. He'd camp on her doorstep, or he'd climb through her balcony window and beg if that's what it took. Somehow he had to make her see...

But first he had to find her.

Tires squealing, he braked to a stop in front of the church. He took the steps three at a time, his pulse drumming in his ears as he pulled open the front door.

A small group of people was gathered at the end of the aisle, their voices echoing distantly in the hushed high-ceilinged interior. Nick recognized Angela immediately. She was holding hands with a thin, sandy-haired man, the two of them smiling into each other's eyes. Another couple was being directed into position by a black-garbed minister, while several other people stood to either side of the altar.

Everything seemed calm and completely normal. Yet Nick's pulse hadn't slowed down. His boots thudded hollowly as he strode up the aisle and searched the group for a glimpse of Lauren.

Angela turned her head, her eyes widening in surprise as she caught sight of him. "Nick?"

Other heads turned toward him, but none of the faces were familiar. Nick scanned the other side of the church, his pace increasing.

"Nick, what are you doing here?" Angela asked when he reached her.

"I'm looking for Lauren. Is she here?"

"No, you must have missed her on the way." She tilted her head, peering at him oddly. "Are you all right? I thought it was serious."

He stepped closer, his muscles knotting. "Me? What are you talking about?"

"She left as soon as she got the call. The doctor said you had gone into surgery—"

"*What?*"

"Someone told her you'd been in an accident."

"Where did she go?"

"To the hospital, I assume. She didn't tell me which one. Nick, what's going on?"

But he didn't stay long enough to reply. He was already running back toward the door.

Someone had lured Lauren away with a phony story.

He was afraid that he knew who.

And he was terrified that he knew why.

Chapter 14

She'd been conned. And it hadn't even been a very good con. Yet she'd walked right into it. She should have known Nick could take care of himself. And even if he had been injured, she should have known better than to believe he'd have been asking for her. Yes, she should have stopped to think for a minute instead of letting panic and gut-deep fear rule her actions.

It had been just plain stupid not to look around the darkened parking lot before she'd jumped out of her car. She'd lived and worked in the city for more than ten years, so she should have exercised some caution. But her sense of self-preservation seemed to have short-circuited, because all she had been able to think about was

Nick, and how he was in pain, and how he wanted to see her....

Lauren winced as the car hit a bump. Or maybe a curb. She pressed her feet against the curve of the wheel well, trying to steady herself as best she could in the pitching darkness, fighting off the hysteria that was waiting to claim her. Look at this logically, she told herself. Think of it as a story.

Right. Great story. Gord would have a field day. Incompetent journalist travels to her last interview in the trunk of a silver Jag.

Duxbury said he only wanted to talk. He'd sounded eerily reasonable, his voice as smooth, his manners as polished, as always. He'd even apologized for the gun he'd been holding. But when she'd tried to break away, she'd felt the strength of madness in his hands.

She was going to miss the wedding rehearsal. And unless she figured some way out of this, it was a pretty good bet that she was going to miss the wedding. That's what she'd hoped for two weeks ago. A plane crash hadn't been enough to stop it. Neither had Angela's last minute doubts. Maybe being abducted at gun point would do the trick—

Swallowing against a bubble of hysteria, she twisted her wrists, hoping to weaken the tape that bound them. Before she could make any progress, the car stopped suddenly, rocking her hard against the spare tire. Seconds later, the trunk popped open. Lauren blinked at the dim, gray light of a parking garage. She drew in a lungful of cool, cement-dank air and screamed for help.

In the next instant, Duxbury was leaning over the trunk and the hard, cold muzzle of the gun was pressed to Lauren's temple. "Really, Miss Abbot," he said softly. "I was hoping to avoid this." He ripped off a length of the same duct tape he'd used on her wrists and pressed it over her mouth.

Lauren shuddered in revulsion at his touch as he pulled her out of the trunk and brushed the dust from her skirt and sweater. Still holding the gun, he used his free hand to pull the pins from her hair. She jerked away, her shoes slipping on a patch of oil.

He shook his head as he hauled her back toward him. "I'm not going to hurt you. We just need to loosen your hair. From the back, one blonde looks the same as another," he said, guiding her across the garage to a short, iron-railed staircase. He unlocked the door at the top and led her down a narrow corridor, through another door and into what appeared to be the basement of a building. Keeping a painfully tight grip on her arm, he nudged her toward an elevator.

The moment the doors slid open, she recognized where they were. This was Wanda's building. But Wanda wouldn't be here. She had been too nervous to return home, and according to Ramona Brill, she was staying elsewhere until the trial. Was Duxbury really mad enough to think anyone could mistake Lauren for his girlfriend?

Evidently he was. With the gun nestled tightly beneath her breast, he held her face against his shoulder in an obscene parody of a loving embrace as the elevator sped upward.

The moment they reached Wanda's condominium, Duxbury led Lauren to the couch in the living room and pushed her to sit. "It won't do you any good to call for help here," he said. "The neighbors are accustomed to noise and know how to mind their own business."

Lauren tried not to imagine the noises the neighbors might have heard—and ignored. Anger wasn't going to help her now. She nodded sharply to show she understood.

"Fine. I'll let you remove the gag."

With movements made clumsy by her bound wrists, she lifted her hands and worked the edge of her thumb under the tape that covered her mouth, then cautiously eased it off.

Duxbury walked around the room, switching on all the lamps before he stopped in front of a tripod that held a small video camera. "I do apologize for the necessity of bringing you here like this," he said. "But it's only fair that you have the chance to correct the mistakes you've broadcast about me."

She looked at the camera. It had been positioned to one side so that it would cover anyone sitting on the living room furniture. Oh, God. This was crazy. "You can't really expect me to...interview you."

"Of course. The setup is regrettably primitive, but it should produce some adequate footage."

She watched the gun barrel waver and assessed her chances of reaching the door before he could pull the trigger. They weren't good. Could she take the risk that he wouldn't shoot?

He switched on the camera and walked over to sit in the chair across from her. Crossing his legs, he rested the gun on his thigh and gave her a smile that raised the hairs on her arms.

No, she couldn't take the risk. If he was irrational enough to think he could restore his reputation through an amateur video of a gun-point conversation, then it would probably be safest to humor him for now. She'd simply have to tamp down the panic, wait for a better opportunity to escape and hope that somehow Nick would find her....

She steadied herself against a wave of despair. Nick. It wasn't reasonable or logical to expect him to help her. No, this sharp yearning she felt for him was beyond reason and deeper than logic. It was a longing that came straight from the heart.

The panic was growing, clawing at Nick's insides like a hungry animal. It had been more than an hour since Lauren's white compact had been found. There was no longer any doubt that she'd been abducted. An intern who had gone out to the hospital parking lot for a cigarette had witnessed the entire event. The patrol cars had already arrived at the scene by the time Nick had gotten there, and the descriptions of the abductor and his car had been unmistakable. Within minutes, the APB on Duxbury had gone out. Every patrol car in the city would be watching for him, and Gilmour maintained it was only a matter of time.

But Nick didn't want to put his faith in the random chance that someone might spot them.

No, Duxbury might have gone off the deep end, but he still wasn't an idiot. He'd have planned his destination with care. He would want to stay in familiar territory, go someplace that would insure privacy for whatever he intended....

Swearing under his breath, Nick gunned the engine and sped through an amber light. He couldn't let himself think about what might be happening to Lauren or he'd be unable to think at all. It was his idea to check out the list that Lauren had compiled, the one that detailed the properties belonging to Duxbury's companies. Gilmour had agreed to the approach, and people were already on the way to several warehouses that would be ideal locations for a criminal to go undetected.

The condominium that Wanda had been using was on the list of properties, too. So when Nick stopped his car under the arching white canopy in front of the building, he had a logical reason to be there. But as he stepped into the elevator and pressed the button for the sixteenth floor, the sudden clutching in his gut had nothing to do with logic.

There was a faint shadow on the carpet in the back corner of the elevator car, a fresh smear of oil in a shape that vaguely resembled a woman's shoe. But the shoeprint was facing backward.

There was another trace of oil in the hall outside Wanda's condo. Holding his breath, Nick pressed his ear to the door.

There was a man's voice inside. The words were indistinguishable, but the tone was harsh. He hadn't heard Duxbury often enough to be certain it was him, but who else would have access to the condo?

Nick's breath hissed out when he heard another voice. It was Lauren's.

Moving as silently as possible, he retreated to the stairwell at the other end of the hall and used his cell phone to call for backup. When he returned, he could no longer hear anything.

Damn! What was going on in there? In the time it took for the backup to arrive, Duxbury could—

Nick refused to let the image take hold. Pulling out his badge, he went to knock quietly on the next door down the hall.

Lauren shifted on the couch, trying to ease the cramp that was forming in her calf as she watched Duxbury adjust the video camera. She knew the truth about his background and his unscrupulous rise to success, but his version was nauseatingly sugar-coated. He had excuses for everything, including the accident that killed

Joey McMillan. In his own warped thinking he found ways to justify everything he did, including this bizarre interview.

At another time, she might have found the progressive deterioration of his grasp on reality quite interesting. Yes, the mixture of rational and irrational thought would probably provide rich fodder for a discussion among mental health professionals.

But at that moment, Lauren wasn't feeling the remotest bit like a professional of any kind. The strain of maintaining her poise was taking its toll. She was starting to imagine things. She moved her gaze to Duxbury's reflection in the balcony doors. Beyond the glare of the living room lights, the shadows outside appeared to be moving.

''Well, that should do it,'' Duxbury said suddenly, stepping away from the video camera. ''I think we've covered all the important points.''

Lauren swallowed hard, her mouth suddenly dry. ''I can edit that tape down at the station. I'd like to present as polished an interview as possible, so I'll need to—''

''Oh, you've done quite enough,'' he said, his lips forming another one of his hair-raising smiles. ''I've appreciated your cooperation, Miss Abbot. You've gone a long way toward repairing the damage you've done to my reputation.''

''Then I'm pleased that we had this opportunity to talk. After you drop me off at my car, I'll—''

He laughed harshly. ''We haven't finished yet. We're waiting for your friend.''

''What friend?''

''Oh, come now, Miss Abbot, why so coy? You were eager enough to see him when you thought he was about to die. I'm sure he'll do the same for you. Why do you think I made no effort to hide my identity? I didn't make it easy, but I'm sure a cop like Strada will figure out where we are eventually.''

The hope that flashed through her at his certainty was quickly followed by dread. ''Why do you want him to find us? What have you planned?''

His smile grew. ''I plan to finish your story for you. You're both going to confess that you conspired together to ruin me. There will be a lovers' quarrel, and then...'' He shook his head in mock commiseration. ''A tragic end for a tarnished hero, but at least my reputation will be restored.''

''You're sick. You'll never get away with it.''

''Such clichéd phrases, and from a journalist,'' he said, shaking his head again as he checked the ammunition clip in the handle of his gun. He snapped it back into place and sat in the chair across from her, positioning himself so that he could watch the front door. "You disappoint me, Miss Abbot. Now, why don't you relax and make yourself comfortable while we wait.''

With a cold certainty, Lauren knew that he intended to kill them. There was no point in arguing, because he would probably find a way to justify whatever he did. She looked desperately around the room, hoping to see something she could use as a weapon, but with her wrists still taped together, there wouldn't be much she could do even if—

The glass of the patio door behind him exploded inward as a white wrought-iron chair hurtled into the room.

Springing to his feet, Duxbury whirled around to face the balcony and leveled his gun at the darkness outside.

A shadow moved on the balcony, a tall, lean silhouette that Lauren recognized instantly. *Nick.* He *did* come. Somehow he was already here.

And Duxbury intended to kill him.

The fear she'd been barely managing to keep

at bay surged over her in a breath-stealing instant. Duxbury was going to kill Nick. Without pausing to think, Lauren lunged off the couch and dove for the video camera. She grasped the legs of the tripod between her hands and swung it in an arc toward Duxbury.

The camera connected with the back of his head a split second before the gun went off. The tripod broke in half with the impact and the camera snapped loose, skittering across the floor to smack into the wall, but the momentum of Lauren's blow was enough to knock Duxbury to his knees. She staggered, tightening her grip on what was left of her makeshift weapon.

Glass crunched beneath the soles of Nick's boots as he strode through the shattered door. ''Don't move, Duxbury,'' he said, aiming the large pistol he held at the fallen man.

Groaning, Duxbury looked at the destruction around him, then suddenly lifted his gun.

Without breaking stride, Nick kicked the gun from his fingers. The weapon went flying, landing with a dull thud on the other side of the couch.

Duxbury sat back on his heels, cradling his hand to his chest as his groans strengthened. A cool breeze ruffled his silver hair, bringing the distant whine of sirens.

Her knees trembling, Lauren slowly lowered her arms and looked at Nick.

He was standing with his feet braced apart, his gun held steady between both hands. Every muscle in his body was tensed. Although he remained motionless, the air around him seemed to crackle with energy.

It was like the first time she had seen him. He wore the same battered leather jacket, the same fierce stare. And the same primitive aura of masculine power surrounded him, wrenching an equally primitive response from her exhausted emotions.

God help her, she didn't care where they were, or what was happening. She wanted to fly across the space that separated them and fling herself into his arms and tell him she'd been wrong to send him away. She wanted to revel in the strength of the feelings she'd done her best to deny. She wanted to—

"You all right, Lauren?" he asked hoarsely.

Swallowing hard, she managed to nod. She'd maintained her composure this long. Why did she feel this sudden urge to cry now that she was safe?

"He didn't hurt you? You're okay?"

The note of suppressed violence in his voice jarred her. She spread her fingers and the broken tripod dropped to the floor with a clatter "Yes, I'm fine."

Duxbury twisted around to glare up at her. "You broke my camera, you stupid bitch."

Nick reacted instantly. With movements too swift to follow, he pushed Duxbury face down, pressed his knee between his shoulder blades and snapped a pair of handcuffs on his wrists. "Consider yourself lucky that she got to you before I could," Nick said.

"You can't treat me like this. I'm an innocent man. Once the truth is broadcast—"

"You have the right to remain silent," Nick said, shifting more of his weight to his knee. "You'd better use it."

Through the broken window, the noise of the sirens strengthened. Lauren looked at the video camera and suppressed a shudder. She'd probably never be able to look at any camera the same way again. She'd probably never be able to look at her job or herself or Nick the same way again, either.

Everything happened quickly after that. Within minutes, Wanda's condo was filled with people. A pair of uniformed officers led Duxbury away while two more questioned Lauren about the events of the evening.

Throughout it all, Nick stayed with her, a

solid, imposing presence by her side. His touch was efficient but gentle as he eased the last of the duct tape from her wrists. His warmth was comforting as he draped his arm around her shoulders. And when Lauren swayed, the tension of the last few hours finally catching up with her, Nick tightened his hold and announced he was driving her home.

She fell asleep in his car, rousing only when she felt herself being lifted against his chest. Her cheek rubbed his jacket, and she inhaled the scent of leather and...Nick.

She blinked and struggled to focus on his face. "I'm all right," she said. "I can walk."

"I'm sure you can," he said, settling her securely in his arms. He nudged the car door closed with his hip and began to walk forward.

"Nick, really. I'm fine. He didn't hurt me. There's no need for you to—"

"Lauren, *you* might not need this, but *I* do." He had the key to her building ready in his hand, so when he reached the front entrance, he was able to carry her through.

It was late, almost morning, so there was no one else around to witness her unusual mode of transport, but Lauren wouldn't have cared even if there was. After the terror of the last few hours, and the misery of the last few days, being close to Nick felt so right she wasn't going to object further. She hooked her arm behind his neck, enjoying the strength of his embrace.

He hit the button for the elevator with his elbow, then stepped inside. "I almost went crazy when I thought I might have lost you. I'm sorry I didn't warn you about Duxbury in time. I should have—"

"It wasn't your fault. You couldn't have known. No one could."

"I got you involved in this case. You didn't want to be. I should have taken better care of you."

"If you're feeling some misplaced sense of guilt—"

"It's not guilt," he said firmly. When they reached her apartment, he unlocked her door as smoothly as he'd managed the first one, then carried her across the threshold and kicked the door shut with his heel. Only then did he loosen his hold enough to let her slide down to stand in front of him.

She could have stepped away and broken the contact between them, but she didn't want to. Not yet. After what they had been through, she didn't think she'd want to let him go again. Grasping the edges of his jacket, she tipped back her head to meet his gaze.

The tenderness in his eyes surprised her. Tension still hardened the line of his jaw and flattened his lips, but his gaze was soft with a poignant mix of emotions. "It's not guilt," he repeated. "That's not what I feel for you."

"Nick..."

He lifted his hands, framing her face in a gesture as tender as his gaze. Slowly he stroked his thumbs across her skin, tracing her cheekbones, her brows, the corners of her mouth. "Angela told me how you raced to the hospital because you thought I'd been hurt."

"I didn't know it was a lie."

"Doesn't matter. You told me we were through, but your actions say something else."

"I didn't really stop to think—"

"Exactly. And when you swung that camera at Duxbury's head, you didn't stop to think about ruining a tape that could scoop every news show in the country."

"My career didn't matter, Nick. He could have shot you."

"And you were willing to risk your life for mine. Again."

"I appreciate your gratitude, but—"

"It's not gratitude that I feel, either, Lauren. That's not why I brought you home, and that's not why I plan to stay with you."

"You can't stay."

"Then why are you hanging on to me?"

She tightened her grip on his jacket and leaned her forehead against his chest. "I don't know. I don't want to talk about it now, okay?"

He pressed his cheek to the top of her head, holding her until his tensed muscles gradually relaxed. Slowly he eased away from her and grasped her hands. He looked at her wrists, then bent forward and kissed the reddened skin.

In disbelief, Lauren felt a tear slide hotly down her cheek. "Nick..."

"Sh," he said, straightening up. "You're right. This isn't the time to talk." He turned to slide the chain into its slot on the door, then shrugged out of his jacket and his shoulder holster, dropping them to the floor. He twined his fingers with hers and led her across the living room and down the hall to the bathroom.

Wiping her eyes with the back of her hand, Lauren watched numbly as Nick opened the faucets on the bathtub, picked up a bottle of bubble bath and poured half of it into the running water. With a smile that brought on another spurt of tears, he turned toward her and began to unbutton her blouse. Although his nostrils flared and his hands weren't quite steady, he kept his gaze on her face as he took off her clothes and helped her into the tub.

The warm water and the bubbles were like an extension of being carried in Nick's arms. Bit by bit the remnants of fear that she hadn't even wanted to acknowledge seeped from her body. Leaning her head back against the tub, she breathed in the fragrant steam and looked at Nick.

He was sitting on the toilet seat lid, a towel clutched tightly between his hands. His hair, damp from the heat in the room, clung in dark strands to his forehead and curled wildly at the nape of his neck. The expression on his face was so fiercely protective it sent awareness rippling over her skin. Yet the second he caught her gaze, his expression softened and he rose to hold out the towel.

The wave of desire took Lauren by surprise. He'd seen her naked five nights ago, and the pleasure they had brought each other had been more than she'd imagined was possible. Yet the longing she felt now was deeper, stronger and somehow more intimate than anything she'd experienced before. She stepped out of the tub, took the towel from his hands and pressed herself full length to the front of his body.

For a breathless moment he didn't move, the

water from her bath soaking into his clothes. But then he exhaled harshly and dropped his head to the side of her neck. "Maybe we'd better talk, after all," he said.

She slipped her arms around his waist. "No."

"I want to do what's best for you, to make you feel better."

"Oh, you are," she said, curling her leg behind his to rub her foot along his calf.

"I wanted to prove that there's more than this between us. There are things I planned to say—"

"Later." She lifted her head, brushing a kiss across his ear. "Make love to me, Nick," she whispered.

Although she couldn't see his face, she knew he smiled. She felt it in the warmth that flowed into her. Without any more hesitation, he scooped her into his arms and carried her to the bedroom.

No words were spoken as he discarded his clothes and tumbled to the mattress with her. The passion that flared between them was as powerful as it had always been. And yet Lauren knew there was a difference this time. In the same way she had been able to feel Nick's unseen smile, she felt something new in his touch.

They didn't spend long on preliminaries.

They didn't need to. The lingering adrenaline from the evening transformed to desire in a dizzying rush. With a swift, fierce tenderness, Nick joined his body to hers.

She clasped him to her, every nerve screaming for completion. He moved once, twice, hard and sure, sending her spiraling over the edge, catching her cry of delight with a kiss.

Even when the tremors began to fade, the kiss continued. Lauren was suffused with a satisfaction deeper than anything she'd felt before. Satisfaction and belonging and...rightness.

Nick rolled to his side, hooking his leg over hers to keep her with him. He drew up the sheet and pressed her tightly to his chest as his lips grazed her cheek. For long, delicious minutes they remained motionless, their hearts beating in unison.

"I think my ancestors had the right idea," Nick murmured, trailing his hand down her back in a slow caress.

"Mmm?"

"It would be a lot simpler if I could toss you in front of my saddle and gallop away with you in my arms."

She arched her back so that she could look at him. "What are you talking about?"

Surrounded by his lush, dark lashes, his blue

eyes sparkled. "Cossacks and conquistadors, remember?"

Lauren stroked a lock of hair from his forehead, then tunneled her fingers into the silky curls at his nape. "How could I forget? You had to get the macho streak of heroism from somewhere."

"I'm no hero."

"So you keep telling me. I knew you would find me tonight. I don't know how, or why, but I did."

"Yeah, well, my ancestors wouldn't have let anyone mess with their women, either."

From someone else, the comment would have been outrageous. But not from Nick. "You're completely serious, aren't you," she said.

"That's right."

"Am I your woman?"

He lowered his hand and splayed his fingers over her hip. "Feels like it to me."

His tone was as possessive as his hold on her body. She caught her breath. "Nick..."

"You're mine, Lauren," he said, tightening his grip. "And if I could whisk you off to our own private horizon, I would. I'd take you away from all the hurt in your past. I'd show you that you don't have to be afraid to trust your feelings. I'd prove that what we have isn't going to burn out in one night or one year or one century—''

She pressed her fingers to his lips to stop his words. She knew where this was leading. She'd known it from the moment she'd felt the difference in his touch tonight. She'd known it for days. That's why she'd sent him away. That's why she'd been so frightened of the feelings he stirred....

But she wasn't frightened now, even though she knew that the intimacy they were sharing went far beyond the physical union of their flesh. No, this time she didn't want to hide from the emotion that was rushing through her. With a trembling smile, she dropped her hand to his chest.

The sparkle in his eyes became a determined glow. He returned her smile with one that was positively dazzling, then covered her fingers with his and pressed her palm over his heart. ''Feel that? It's yours.''

''Oh, Nick.''

''I love you, Lauren.''

The declaration was as simple and direct as everything else about him. And it was just as impossible to resist. She curled forward, nudging their hands aside in order to brush a kiss over the spot where her palm had been.

Love. She had always associated it with weakness and vulnerability. Yet she didn't feel weak. She felt strong, capable of anything. Maybe even loving in return.

Maybe?

She turned her head, listening to the steady throb of his heart beneath her ear. Yes, she loved him. She'd been fighting against it from the moment she'd first looked into his eyes, and sometime during the past two weeks, the battle had been thoroughly lost.

He threaded his fingers through her hair, guiding her face upward until her mouth was a breath away from his. "It's all right. You don't need to say anything."

"But—"

"I pushed you too hard before. If you need more time to get used to the idea, it's okay. But I'm giving you fair warning, Lauren."

"About what?"

"I don't intend to give up."

"So I've noticed. It's just one of the reasons I love you, Nick."

He reacted instantly, rolling on top of her and lifting his head to look into her eyes. "Say it again."

She smiled. ''I love you, Nick.''

A quiver traveled through his brought his mouth down on hers, words with a kiss that said it all.

A quiver traveled through his body as he brought his mouth down on hers, sealing her words with a kiss that said it all.

Chapter 15

Sunshine slanted through the stained glass window, casting whimsical patterns on the sober wooden pews. The dark green floor, the golden pulpit and the white altar cloth were alive with dapples of color. Organ music mingled with the sunshine, wafting through the air in a joyful babble of tones. From the back of the church, Lauren scanned the people who were already seated, then picked up her skirt to keep from tripping and hurried to the room where Angela and her bridesmaids were waiting.

"Did you see Dad anywhere?" Angela asked, her forehead wrinkled with concern.

"No, but I'm sure he'll turn up. He still has—" she glanced at the clock on the wall "—five minutes."

"The minister said they can't wait. They've got three more ceremonies booked after this one."

Lauren picked up the white veil and fitted it on Angela's head, fluffing the gauzy lace over her sister's vibrant curls. "Will you stop worrying? Everything's going to be fine."

"If I were superstitious, I'd suspect that this wedding was cursed."

"Relax. We've had some bad luck, but—"

"Bad luck?" Angela interrupted, her voice rising. "Is that what you call having my maid of honor kidnapped from the wedding rehearsal?"

"Angie, that's over. I'm fine. Nothing's going to stop this now."

She shook her head, knocking her veil askew. "I know you're right. I do. I wish I could get my nerves under control."

"It's your wedding day. You're entitled to be nervous," she said. "Just remember what this is for. Think about walking down the aisle to Eddy, and about how wonderful it's going to be to share your life with the man you love."

"We should have eloped."

"No, I think you're doing the right thing." She reached up to straighten Angela's veil, anchoring it in place with a pair of hairpins.

"There's something very special about the ritual of the wedding ceremony. To stand up in front of your family and friends and publicly vow to love, honor and cherish one man for the rest of your days...well, that's the kind of courage and commitment you'll be able to build a life on."

Angela smiled shakily. "What a beautiful thing to say."

"And you're a beautiful bride," Lauren said, taking a step back to look at her. Despite all the delays and the re-scheduled fitting, the dressmaker had produced a gown that made Angela look radiant. No, it was more than the softly gathered white satin that made her glow. Shining through the layer of last-minute jitters, there was an eagerness and the kind of steady certainty that could only come from love.

Lauren didn't question her ability to recognize it. She'd seen that same glow on her own face when she'd looked into the mirror this morning. Wasn't it amazing how much more she was able to see when she wasn't trying to be merely an observer?

The door behind them opened and Angela looked past her expectantly. "Dad! You made it."

Vincent Abbot grinned as he squeezed into

the crowded room. Looking tanned and fit, he dropped his suitcase and greeted his daughters with quick hugs. "Of course I made it. Sorry I cut it so close, but I had some bad luck."

Angela's smile faltered. "*You* had bad luck?"

He gave her a smacking kiss on the cheek. "I would have been here last night, but the baggage handlers defected to the rebels. Then my connecting flight was delayed and the taxi from the airport broke down."

Angela threw up her hands. "It's cursed. It must be."

"What are you talking about?" he asked.

"It's a long story," Lauren said, taking the last boutonniere from the florist's box. She pinned it into place on Vincent's lapel. "We'll tell you about it later."

He caught her hand before she could move away. "And how are you holding up, Lauren?" he asked, lowering his voice.

"Duxbury's in custody. He'll probably have a psychiatric assessment before the trial but—"

"Who's Duxbury? What are you talking about?"

She paused. "You haven't heard the news?"

"I haven't heard anything in days. The communications systems were destroyed by the rebels. What happened?"

"That's another long story. What were *you* talking about?"

"The wedding," he said. "I hope it isn't too rough for you."

Smiling, she squeezed his hand. Her answer was the same one she'd given for years whenever anyone asked about her feelings. But this time, she told the truth. "I'm just fine, Dad."

And she was. For months she had been dreading the painful memories this day would stir up, but now she was no longer afraid. She could handle it, not by hiding from her emotions but by embracing them. She didn't want distance or detachment. It was time to accept herself and her feelings, time to admit she'd been wrong about so many things....

"Oh, my God," Angela murmured. "It's time."

"Yes," Lauren said, helping to assemble everyone into the correct order. "It certainly is."

The music swelled in an exultant crescendo just as Nick squeezed into a vacant spot near the middle of the church. Like the rest of the congregation, he turned his head to watch the bridal party begin their walk up the aisle. He hadn't been to a wedding since his own short, ill-fated attempt at matrimony. He'd been in-

vited to several, but he'd always declined,
knowing his negative attitude would have cast
a pall over what should have been a celebration.

Yet he hadn't even considered missing this
one. He took his hands from his pockets and
buttoned the jacket of his suit coat, then checked
to make sure the knot of his tie was straight.
Damn, he hoped he wasn't making a mistake.
He'd vowed not to push too hard again, to give
Lauren all the time she needed to come to terms
with the idea of having a relationship, but it
wasn't in his nature to sit idly by without making an effort to get what he wanted.

There hadn't been time to settle anything this
morning. They'd been halfway through breakfast when the phone had started ringing. The
first call had been from the station manager at
Channel Ten, an invitation for Lauren to put together a special on her kidnapping ordeal. Despite her problems of the week before, her career was back on track. As a matter of fact, it
was shaping up to be better than ever. Victoria
had decided they needed to put more human aspect into their news program, and she wanted
Lauren to play a larger part.

Next it had been Captain Gilmour, who had
tracked Nick down in order to inform him he
was officially back on the payroll. It was what

Nick had wanted for days, but his first official act had been to ask for the day off. He'd tried to talk to Lauren then, but they'd gone to pick up her car, and she'd had to get ready for the wedding, and he'd had to go downtown and then change into his suit and...

Nick's thoughts whirled to a stop as Lauren stepped into the aisle. She was dressed in green taffeta the color of her eyes. The old-fashioned gown was gloriously feminine, from the snugly fitting bodice to the flaring skirt that rustled against the floor. She'd left her hair loose, her only ornament a spray of tiny white flowers that nestled behind one ear. Nick had seen her in everything from a tailored suit to nothing at all, and he'd always known that she was a beautiful woman, yet today she took his breath away.

It wasn't because of what she was wearing. And it wasn't the shaft of sunlight she walked through as she made her way up the flower-lined aisle. No, her radiance came from within.

As if she sensed his presence, she turned her head, her gaze locking with his. A delicate flush rose in her cheeks, a silent, private shared memory of the night before. Then she smiled, and Nick felt his heart thud hard with a mixture of pride and wonder.

The last remaining doubts about what he was doing here dissolved.

She was *his*.

And she loved him.

The ceremony progressed with a smooth inevitability as Angela and Eddy exchanged their vows. Although Nick tried to concentrate, his attention was fixed on Lauren, and on the words he wanted to say to her. By the time the church echoed with the chords of Mendelssohn's Wedding March, Nick was shifting with impatience, drumming his fingers on the pew in front of him.

Yet even once the wedding was over, Nick didn't get a chance to have Lauren to himself. There were the apparently never-ending photographs to be taken on the church steps, and then the reception at the banquet hall. He only stole a few minutes with Lauren before she left him to join the rest of the wedding party at the head table.

Finally the small band at the other end of the hall began to play a waltz. Nick made his way back to Lauren just as her father led Angela onto the dance floor. Deciding not to risk being separated again, Nick clamped his arm around Lauren's waist and drew her firmly against his side.

She turned her head to welcome him with a smile. "Hi."

"Hi, yourself. I didn't know the wedding was going to be this big."

"Angie has a lot of friends, and Eddy comes from a large family." She sighed, leaning her head against his shoulder. "I can't believe we managed to pull this off without a hitch, considering all the problems beforehand."

"So does this mean you're changing your opinion about weddings?"

She hesitated. "I suppose so. What about you?"

"Yeah. They go on kind of long, though, don't they?"

She laughed. "Oh, Nick. Only you would say something like that."

Nick watched as Angela gave her father a hard hug before she waltzed off in her new husband's arms. Eddy's best man approached Lauren, obviously expecting her to join him for the dance, but Nick glared at him until he changed direction and asked one of the bridesmaids, instead.

Lauren twisted to look up at him. "That was a bit possessive, wasn't it?"

"Yeah. You mind?"

"Actually, I don't. I've been trying to get the chance to be with you for hours."

Nick noticed another man coming toward them. Enfolding Lauren's hand in his, he led her onto the floor. The waltz ended, but neither of them made any attempt to move. One tune blended into the next, and as they moved in time to the music, Nick remembered another dance, when the music had come from his radio, and the dance floor had been his living room. And she had spent the night in his arms.

"Lauren?"

"Mmm?"

God, he loved it when she made that wordless, unthinking sound. He pulled her closer, pressing his cheek to the side of her head. "It was a nice wedding, wasn't it?"

"Yes, it was."

"Angela and Eddy look happy together."

"Yes, they certainly do."

"It makes me think that they might be two of the lucky ones. Not all marriages are doomed to failure."

"Maybe not."

He slid his hand to the small of her back, spreading his fingers over the warm taffeta. "It's impossible to know for sure, though."

"No, there aren't any guarantees."

"But when the stakes are the soul-deep, till-death-do-us-part kind of love, it's worth the gamble, don't you think?"

"Yes, I do."

"And I can't see much point in wasting time with a long engagement, can you?"

"Well, not if two people are willing to work together and make adjustments..."

"Like listening to a different kind of music?"

"Or compromising on little things like canta-loupe."

"Or doughnuts."

"Mmm."

"And as long as they love each other..."

"Oh, yes. They definitely love each other."

"Then I'd say they have a pretty good chance," he finished.

"So Angela and Eddy—"

"I'm not talking about them, Lauren."

She leaned back to look into his face. "Then who are you talking about, Nick?"

Damn, he wasn't good with words. But somehow he had to find a way to say them. "Remember when I told you that I wanted more than one night with you?"

"That's not something a woman can easily forget."

"Well, I do want more than one night. I want

all your nights and all your days." He stopped moving, tightening his grip on Lauren as the other couples brushed past them. "And I know we both said we didn't want promises or commitments, but the love I feel for you is all those things."

"So is mine, Nick," she said, her voice filled with the same certainty that sparkled in her gaze.

He took a deep breath. "So I've been thinking—"

"Lauren!" someone cried. "Come on, you're missing it."

She blinked, turning her head toward the sudden commotion. To her surprise, she realized that the music had stopped and most people had already gathered at the other side of the dance floor.

Estelle nudged her and grinned as she hurried past. "Hurry up, Lauren. Angela's throwing the bouquet."

Through the milling people, Lauren caught a glimpse of Angela's white dress. She glanced back at Nick. "I'm sorry. I have to—"

"Oh, no, you don't," he said. "I've been waiting all day to say what I have to say, and I'm not going to get interrupted again." His jaw hardening with determination, he pulled her across the room with him and led her directly to the front of the crowd.

Eddy had his hands around Angela's waist and had just finished lifting her up to stand on a chair when Nick halted in front of them. Angela grasped her bouquet in both hands and turned her back. "Okay, here goes," she called. "Good luck!"

Before she could toss the bouquet, Nick reached out and took it from her fingers. In the startled silence that followed, his footsteps sounded solid and sure as he strode back to Lauren and placed the flowers in her hands.

"Nick, what—"

"This means you're the next to get married, right?"

She looked from the flowers to his face, her eyes widening in shock. "My God, Nick. I can't believe you did that."

He leaned over and brushed a kiss across her cheek. "It was either this or finding a horse to whisk you away on," he murmured.

"What?"

Angela climbed down from the chair and took Eddy's hand, smiling in satisfaction. "This is perfect. Absolutely perfect."

"What's going on?" her father demanded.

"It's another long story, Dad."

Nick kept his gaze on Lauren. ''You always said you wanted my story, and I intend to make sure you stick around to see how it turns out.''

Her shock was quickly being replaced by a growing sense of happiness. ''Oh, Nick.''

''I don't have a lot of fancy words but...'' He shoved his hand into the pocket of his suit coat and pulled out a small, velvet-covered box. Dropping to one knee in front of her, he flipped open the lid and lifted out a gleaming diamond ring. ''Lauren,'' he said, his voice steady and sure. ''I love you. Will you marry me?''

There was a collective sigh from the people around her, yet Lauren heard nothing but the beating of her heart. Here they were, in front of her family and her friends, and Nick was publicly declaring his feelings...with the kind of courage and commitment they'd be able to build a life on.

It was too fast.

It was too reckless.

It was why they were meant for each other from the moment they met.

She grasped his hand and smiled, giving him an answer as simple as his question. ''Yes.''

*   *   *   *   *   *